"With safeguards now in place, it is all but impossible to kill a million Americans without using nuclear weapons."
— U.S. Biodefense Command internal memo

THEY WERE WRONG...

THE BIODEFENSE TEAM

ALAN THORPE—Biodefense's likable emergency management director. According to one colleague, "He's the sort of guy who could host a Tupperware party for the Hell's Angels."

JAMES SUMMERS—One of the country's leading figures in epidemiology. With a supercomputer, he can predict the course of nearly every disease, one cough at a time, yet—at thirty-four—he looks and acts like a slacker.

STEVE ADAMS—A brilliant and eccentric bacteriologist who keeps exotic reptiles and lives for extreme vacations. He can learn more in an hour about a strain of bacteria with his antique microscope than the whole CDC can find out in a week.

EVA VANORDEN—Arguably the best virologist in the world. A beautiful Dutch woman with a devious mind, she comes up with scenarios so twisted and deadly that the rest of Biodefense is glad she's on their side.

SAM GOLDBERG—A physician who specializes in infectious diseases. A quiet genius with a disconcerting stare, he is famous for making challenging diagnoses.

SLEEPER CELL

JEFFREY ANDERSON, M.D.

BERKLEY BOOKS, NEW YORK

THE BERKLEY PUBLISHING GROUP
Published by the Penguin Group
Penguin Group (USA) Inc.
375 Hudson Street, New York, New York 10014, USA
Penguin Group (Canada), 10 Alcorn Avenue, Toronto, Ontario M4V 3B2, Canada
(a division of Pearson Penguin Canada Inc.)
Penguin Books Ltd., 80 Strand, London WC2R 0RL, England
Penguin Group Ireland, 25 St. Stephen's Green, Dublin 2, Ireland (a division of Penguin Books Ltd.)
Penguin Group (Australia), 250 Camberwell Road, Camberwell, Victoria 3124, Australia
(a division of Pearson Australia Group Pty. Ltd.)
Penguin Books India Pvt. Ltd., 11 Community Centre, Panchsheel Park, New Delhi—110 017, India
Penguin Group (NZ), Cnr. Airborne and Rosedale Roads, Albany, Auckland 1310, New Zealand
(a division of Pearson New Zealand Ltd.)
Penguin Books (South Africa) (Pty.) Ltd., 24 Sturdee Avenue, Rosebank, Johannesburg 2196,
South Africa

Penguin Books Ltd., Registered Offices: 80 Strand, London WC2R 0RL, England

This is a work of fiction. Names, characters, places, and incidents either are the product of the author's imagination or are used fictitiously, and any resemblance to actual persons, living or dead, business establishments, events, or locales is entirely coincidental.

SLEEPER CELL

A Berkley Book / published by arrangement with the author

PRINTING HISTORY
Berkley edition / April 2005

Copyright © 2005 by Jeffrey Anderson, M.D.
Cover design by Rita Frangie.

ISBN: 0-425-19979-7

BERKLEY®
Berkley Books are published by The Berkley Publishing Group,
a division of Penguin Group (USA) Inc.,
375 Hudson Street, New York, New York 10014.
BERKLEY is a registered trademark of Penguin Group (USA) Inc.
The "B" design is a trademark belonging to Penguin Group (USA) Inc.

PRINTED IN THE UNITED STATES OF AMERICA

10   9   8   7   6   5   4   3   2   1

For Keri

Acknowledgments

Writing a science thriller is a phenomenal way of coming to terms with the realization that you don't know anything, and probably never did. When this insight struck, I was most grateful for the following individuals, whose encouragement, wisdom, and discernment made *Sleeper Cell* a reality:

To my wife, Keri, for her patience and enthusiasm in listening to incessant ramblings when she wished it would stop, for her steering the plot and characters in the right direction, and for her love and companionship that make my life beautiful.

To my agent, Kimberly Whalen, who generously gave her wisdom and time to make the novel work, and without whom the story could never have been told.

To my editor, Natalee Rosenstein, for taking a chance on the novel and reminding me it is a thriller and not a textbook.

To my most trusted reader, Karen Dionne, whose imagination and extraordinary writing talent have shaped every page of the novel.

To John Holstein, of Cotse.Net, whose expertise in computer security was invaluable in shaping details of the plot.

To Richard Burdette, U.S. Army Special Forces, whose advice on tactical and strategic details of military operations transformed those elements of the story.

To Hank Baskin, M.D., who checked and rechecked scientific and medical details of the story and gave fantastic early suggestions on core medical issues.

To Max and Mary Anderson, the greatest parents anyone could hope for, who never made me clean my room.

Mistakes that survive to be exposed have always been, and still are, my own, slipping by the watchful eyes of my consultants, probably because I sneaked them back in when no one was looking.

PART I
NANOTHREATS

THE GENEVA PROTOCOL PROHIBITING THE USE
OF BIOLOGICAL AND CHEMICAL WEAPONS

The undersigned Plenipotentiaries, in the name of their respective governments:

Whereas the use in war of asphyxiating, poisonous or other gases, and of all analogous liquids, materials or devices, has been justly condemned by the general opinion of the civilized world; and

Whereas the prohibition of such use has been declared in Treaties to which the majority of Powers of the world are Parties; and

To the end that this prohibition shall be universally accepted as a part of International Law, binding alike the conscience and the practice of nations;

Declare:

That the High Contracting Parties, so far as they are not already Parties to Treaties prohibiting such use, accept this prohibition, agree to extend this prohibition to the use of bacteriological methods of warfare and agree to be bound as between themselves according to the terms of this declaration.

The High Contracting Parties will exert every effort to induce other States to accede to the present Protocol. . . .

Done at Geneva in a single copy, the seventeenth day of June, One Thousand Nine Hundred and Twenty-Five.

ONE

A crisp snap punctuated the sound of Simon's driver ripping the air in its long arc. With one hand in a lazy salute against his visor, he watched the ball propelled over a grove of trees jutting in front of the fairway. The distant splash was a late confirmation of what Simon had already predicted with growing angst as the center of the small lake beyond the trees waited patiently for impact.

His caddie looked reverently toward the lake with stoic, silent eyes, as Simon Westenfeld slowly replaced his driver in his bag. More than a caddie, Winston doubled as Simon's personal trainer and general-purpose sounding board. It was a second career, after Winston's postdoctoral stint in medieval history had failed to land him a tenure-track appointment. He had caddied during college for a local pro shop, but only recently discovered how lucrative the Los

Angeles market was for upscale gurus catering to the rich and eccentric.

Not that Simon was particularly eccentric. He had the composure one might expect from the director of Los Angeles's Emergency Operations Organization. His cast-iron expression of thoughtful patience, however, belied his compulsive competitive streak. In Simon's case, Winston's function was not to keep his client focused, but rather to buffer the stomach acid that came from internalizing the worst nightmares of a city that had its share of them.

"I'm afraid we'll have to retire that driver. It seems to yaw a bit more than your others." Winston's advice was acknowledged with a curt nod.

A shrill bleeping from Simon's belt triggered a reflex that brought a miniature phone to his ear. "Simon."

Simon listened patiently for about fifteen seconds, and commanded, "I want you to check every E.R. on the contact list and find out what the scope of this is. Tell Monica to park herself in the press suite and block any reports until I get there. And call Jack in, please. . . . We'll need to brief senior staff in thirty minutes. Understood?" He snapped the phone back to his belt and began walking briskly toward the cart.

"Thank you, Winston. I'm afraid we'll have to resume another time."

"It's a good thing perfect Saturdays aren't hard to come by here," Winston consoled.

"I'm trying to keep it that way." Simon stretched back with his eyes closed as his caddie rocketed him to the clubhouse.

Appraising the situation, Winston tactfully asked, "Shall I phone Susan?"

"Please, tell her it might take a while." Simon was distracted but polite.

Winston raised an eyebrow and sped his client to his

BMW, lurching to a stop as Simon leaped out and slipped behind the steering wheel. Seventeen minutes later, Simon switched off his siren as he veered into the underground parking of his newly renovated emergency operations headquarters.

As he strode out of his car to the staircase, jumping two steps in a bound, the secured door at the top crashed open and a uniformed guard stood aside as Simon emerged into the Operations Room.

He was greeted by Janet Holbrook, a former attorney who was one of his chief deputies and on this particular Saturday morning the ranking authority at the office. She met him with a worried smile and began her report instantly.

"The report came from public health about a half hour ago. Apparently, it was four patients, all young, no obvious connection, admitted at Harborside Medical four days ago." She paused for a breath. "Symptoms included fever, chills, and a generalized rash. No cause was identified, until two of them died two days ago and the physicians taking care of the other two caught wind of it. They brought in the infectious disease chief from UCLA and she thought of smallpox—sort of an afterthought, I think. Apparently, she had one of the research pathologists from the main campus run some tests and found genetic markers for smallpox virus. The pathologist called public health this morning after he showed up to read out the tests." She looked at Simon for guidance.

"Scope?"

"We called the thirty hospitals on our outbreak-screening protocol, and just talked to the E.R. docs. Of those, seven could remember seeing unusual cases involving fever and a rash similar to the Harborside cases in the last week. None could remember names or dates without checking records."

"So we'll estimate we're dealing with as many as a

hundred index cases, possibly a couple hundred tops." Simon's remark was a statement, not a question. "What does Monica have to say?"

"Not a word from the press. It seems this pathologist and public health are the only ones who know."

"That doc knows to keep his mouth shut?"

"Sam at public health already talked to him about it. He said the doc was a little peeved, but got the idea."

"How sure is that pathologist of the results? Does he know what he's telling us?"

"No B.S. about limited sensitivity or false positives. He told Sam there was no other way the smallpox genetic sequence could end up in his laboratory. Period." The adrenaline was beginning to wear off as Janet's face showed signs of emotional fatigue.

"So you're telling me I am about to make a phone call reporting with a hundred percent certainty a terrorist attack involving hundreds of victims in the middle of Los Angeles that happened weeks ago, and for which we have no clue about the location or perpetrators?"

"So how was your golf game?" Janet smiled awkwardly.

"Arguably more disastrous than our situation here." Simon turned his back to Janet and began walking toward the Situation Room.

He flipped on the lights and began powering up the server that fed each of the terminals around the oblong table in the soundproof room. The headquarters had been the pride of Simon's tenure as director, with the Situation Room undoubtedly its crown jewel. The entire building had been constructed to unprecedented standards of earthquake and fire resistance. Publicizing how the New York emergency management department had been crippled in the 2001 terrorist attack—the office had been located in the World Trade Center—Simon had begun arbitrating for new digs as soon as he was appointed director. The political climate was perfect for securing new funding for a state-of-the-art communications facility.

Simon walked out to the Operations Room and spent the next ten minutes conferring with senior staff, making quick assignments to retrieve protocols from files and review established procedures in their areas of expertise. Throughout this period, Janet tried frantically to brief each of the division heads as they entered the Situation Room. When they had all arrived, Simon ushered himself into the room and sealed the door.

He walked to his position at the table and began restating the facts. "What we have is a doctor from UCLA claiming that four patients admitted last Tuesday to Harborside Medical are infected with smallpox, two of whom have since died. Jack, give me your thoughts."

Jack, the physician consultant for Emergency Operations, cleared his throat. "First of all, let me say that Dr. Pendleton knows what the hell he's talking about. He's spent ten years in emerging viruses at Bethesda, and has enough hot lab experience to know how to isolate a virus without contamination. The genetic sequences he would have tested for are published sequences from the smallpox genome. Here's my first issue. Smallpox is extinct. It's easier to recreate it from scratch than to get at existing samples. They're more tightly guarded than the president. Of course, some people think there are samples in Ukraine that haven't been accounted for. . . ."

Jack continued his musings, knowing full well that as the only physician in the Emergency Operations Organization, he had the stage for as long as he liked. "No, the only answer that makes sense is home-brewed smallpox."

Simon wrinkled his forehead. "Made from scratch? How?"

"The entire sequence for the smallpox virus was published years ago, and any twisted mind with a library card can get at it. With the sequence in hand, you just have to manufacture little bits of the virus at a time, and then string them all together in the right order. You could probably order most of the pieces from a mail-order catalog. Some guys did it back in 2002 with poliovirus just to prove it could be done. Now, smallpox is much tougher than polio, and would take a good brain, but it's doable."

"So we're dealing with a smallpox supply made from scratch." Simon summarized.

"That's right."

"Remind me, Jack. What's incubation for smallpox?"

"Twelve days—let's see—exposure could have been anywhere from sixteen to eighteen days ago."

"Who could do it?"

Jack paused for a moment. "Anyone, really. State-sponsored, some crackpot, a rogue terrorist group."

"What percentage of our population has been vaccinated?"

"Vaccinations never really took hold. I'd say less than ten percent of the medical workforce, less than one percent of the population."

"Monica, anything else out of the ordinary? What's going on in the world?"

His poorly phrased question was understood as intended. Monica was the media relations specialist, whose responsibility it was to follow the international as well as local media outlets like a junkyard dog and control them when emergency powers were deemed necessary. Simon had worked out a compromise with local television news bureaus that enabled her to request a half-hour hold on any story that might compromise public safety until the governor could issue a formal restraining order under newly granted emergency powers.

Monica was biting on the back of her pen. "Not a word. I can't understand it. You might expect some lunatic to claim responsibility or for us to get vague warnings from the feds or something. But I can't think of a time it's been more quiet here."

He looked to Janet. Aside from filling in shifts as operations director, she managed logistical problems for complicated situations.

She responded to his glance. "I haven't put together a full plan, but it seems we have a lot of work to do before we really know the scope of the problem. We've got to get a link shared by these four patients, and work on getting some more names from other hospitals. Without that, we're only Chicken Little—the sky is falling. The attack was weeks ago. I don't know what we're going to accomplish blowing the whistle before we know what we're dealing with."

Simon's face showed resolve. "Here's what we do. I want Janet to coordinate the discovery phase. Jack, get a quarantine on those two patients—quietly. Monica, if anyone breathes a word of this, squash it and I'll go to the governor. By tomorrow morning, I want to have a story I can tell Washington. Any questions?"

There was a knock at the door. Simon glanced at the closed-circuit television on his terminal and frowned at what he saw.

"Pete!" Simon looked angrily at his security chief. "Who are those two outside our door?!"

Pete scrambled to his feet as he walked to the entrance of the Situation Room. He opened the door and stepped outside. A moment later, he reemerged with a man and a woman. "It seems, sir, that these individuals are with the FBI."

She was in her early thirties, holding a soft drink in her hand and wearing a low-cut azure blouse and navy skirt. Her hair was cropped short, around sunken cheeks and European features. Her lack of makeup drew attention to her dark eyes. Her colleague was older, dressed in an ash-colored business suit, with jet-black hair and a long face. His olive complexion and the hint of curl to his hair hinted at Mediterranean ancestry. His weighty bearing seemed more that of a CEO than an officer.

The young woman spoke up. "It seems, Mr. Westenfeld, that you have a problem."

"Who are you?"

"Eva Vanorden, and this is Alan Thorpe," the woman replied. "But that's not important right now. What is important is that you're in way over your head, and you're waiting until tomorrow to make your call."

Simon was growing visibly flustered. "How have you been listening?!"

Vanorden tapped her right ear. "The bureau isn't without its supply of gadgets . . ."

"I need to know what you are doing here and who sent you." Simon's patience was exhausted.

"Why don't you let me," the older man stepped in front of his associate. He continued, addressing Simon. "We are, you might say, consultants. I'm very sorry to have inconvenienced all of you, but this has been a high-level drill also taking place in three other cities across the country today. There is no smallpox, but I compliment you on an outstanding performance. Your speed was exemplary. My associate and I have been quite impressed." He ended with a half-smile as he saw the same silent expression on everyone at the table.

Janet spoke first, confused. "But I talked to Sam . . . All those other cases in different emergency rooms . . ."

Thorpe acknowledged her with a nod. "Any idea how many people in Los Angeles have rashes? As to your other question, Sam Jenkins was very gracious to assist us. That's what I mean about response time, though. We drove straight here from public health, and you folks were all over it. In our simulations, the best we predicted was twelve hours before emergency ops would have a coordinated plan." His complimentary tone wasn't particularly helpful in melting the icy stares of his audience.

Vanorden spoke up again. "There's still an important issue, here. With the evidence you had, you should have called in a report immediately. There's more at stake here than just Los Angeles. You don't have the intelligence data to run your own investigation on something this big." Her partner motioned with one hand to back down.

"I'm going to find out who's in charge of this hoax." Simon narrowed his eyes at the two intruders.

"You know, I think it's time we split," Vanorden whispered as she turned to face the door.

In response, her colleague gave a slight nod and concluded, "Thanks, folks. Again, my apologies."

Making her exit, the younger partner took a sip from her soft drink and walked out the door without looking back.

Simon sank into his chair, the words "Sonofabitch" echoing the sentiment in the room.

TWO

SONIA'S head whipped around as the dented green Pontiac lurched to a halt. The marquee in the parking lot read "WELCOME COMPUTATIONAL BIOLOGISTS."

"You're serious? I can't believe you're taking me on a date to some boring conference! I thought you were taking me somewhere to make out."

Jim pretended to be hurt, then winked as he flipped his ponytail around and opened his car door. "See, I told you it would be a surprise." He smiled and raised one eyebrow. "You said you wanted to see what I did for work all day." The door squeaked as he stepped out.

"I believe my words were: 'One of these days I'm going to prove that all you do at work is play video games.'"

Jim looked back through the open window and waved for her to follow. The driver's-side window was actually missing, and Jim had never taken the time to have it fixed.

Sonia waited a moment to verify that Jim had no intention of walking around to her door before she sighed audibly and climbed out of the cramped car, rushing to catch up with him.

"So what are they going to talk at us about? How to count spores and molds?" She finally smiled, showing her excitement to be included in Jim's professional life. She had spent half of her manicure the last week talking about how it would be easier to get Jim to invite her to dinner with his mother than be allowed to touch his computer.

"Something like that." Jim took her hand as she caught up to him. Other people were filing into the conference center, most dressed neatly but casually. A few wore suits and dresses. Those, Sonia recognized, were salespeople rushing back and forth between exhibits already visible from the bank of open doors ahead.

"I didn't dress for a big meeting, Jim." She hoped Jim would recognize that what she meant was that *he* was not dressed for such an occasion, since she looked terrific and Jim was the one wearing cut-off shorts and a T-shirt.

"We're scientists, not fashion models. You'll fit right in."

"Thanks, I think."

As they walked through the doors to the conference hall, Jim pulled out two nametags with lanyards attached and handed one to his date. They read, "Jim Summers, Ph.D. U.C. Berkeley" and "Sonia Clark, Ph.D. Harvard University."

She fingered hers before flashing it to the uniformed guard outside the convention center. She tucked it into her pocket.

"I can't wear this! I feel like an impostor. I don't think they have doctors of cosmetology." Her voice was hushed.

Jim shrugged. "Printed it myself. Listen, they don't have bouncers here checking your publication record or giving entrance exams. It's just a boring conference, like you said. Besides, I've read papers from a lot of these guys that make me think a good hairstylist is probably more qualified to be here than them." He squeezed her hand.

She slipped the tag from her pocket and put it around her neck, pulling her long dark hair over the strap. "Did you hear they found the missing link?" she asked in an artificially low voice. Her eyes sparkled teasingly as she and Jim passed a pair of scientists talking about something incomprehensible.

"If the title goes to your head, I'm taking it back."

"Hey, I'm just trying to fit in."

"Jim!" A woman's voice called from the next aisle of exhibits as a tall, thin figure ducked from behind the Merck display to join Jim and Sonia. "It's been forever. So good to see you!" She gave Jim a hug. "I spotted you a mile away. Congratulations."

"Thanks," Jim said. He glanced awkwardly at Sonia, then back to the newcomer. "Luann, do you know Sonia Clark?"

Luann's eyes shot to Sonia's nametag. "I'm sorry. Luann Stephens. Nice to meet you."

"My pleasure, of course," said Sonia warily.

"Not at all. Your name sounds familiar; I'm sure I've read some of your papers. What field do you work in?"

Sonia panicked. She stammered for a moment.

"Systems theory," Jim responded for her. "Especially models for multiple-body interactions. Sonia's been a godsend with some backprojection problems I've been struggling with in my neural networks." Jim lingered on the word *backprojection*, obviously enjoying himself immensely.

Sonia smiled and shrugged. "Someone's got to figure out how those bodies fit together." She stepped hard on Jim's foot as they walked.

"Sounds interesting," said Luann. "I'd love to hear more about it."

"We were just heading into the general session," said Jim. "Why don't you join us, and Sonia can fill you in."

"I really don't want to keep you from the exhibits," said Sonia.

"Are you kidding? And miss Jim's talk! That's half the reason most of these people are here." The three had reached the door of the main auditorium.

"Talk?" Sonia asked. She looked inside and saw a large banner displaying the words "SOCIETY FOR COMPUTATIONAL BIOLOGY" suspended over the stage at the front of the auditorium.

"You didn't know? Jim's giving the keynote address."

As they walked inside, a nervous-looking man in a gray business suit caught Jim by the hand. "Dr. Summers, are you trying to give me a heart attack?"

"Sorry. A little held up in traffic."

"Why don't you come up front with me and we'll get started. Your slides are all ready."

Jim gave an apologetic wave to Sonia, and nodded at Luann. "You two have fun."

Sonia's mouth hung open as she watched Jim follow the man out of sight down the aisle. "Come on," Luann whispered, and Sonia followed Luann to a pair of open seats in the crowded assembly hall.

A few moments later the din of the crowd died down as the man who had escorted Jim to the central platform stood at the podium and addressed the crowd.

"Ladies and gentlemen, distinguished guests, I hope you have been enjoying the many excellent exhibits, and am pleased to thank the organizing committee of the Society for Computational Biology's annual meeting for the wonderful job they have done this year." He paused for a round of applause. Sonia hesitatingly joined in the crowd's response.

"Now I am pleased to introduce our distinguished speaker for this evening's conference. Dr. James Summers is a scientist known to many of you, especially here in San Francisco, and who probably needs little introduction." Sonia watched Jim shift in his seat. "Nevertheless, he has such an interesting history I can't resist a few remarks." Scattered chuckles and a sense of anticipation rose from the crowd. Sonia strained to hear.

"Dr. Summers was born in Ames, Iowa, and got off to an early start in science. As a boy of five, he was given a TRS-80 computer and wrote his first computer program. Within a year, he was building simple games for his friends." Sonia gloated at the revelation. The speaker continued, "In his early years, he became infatuated with the programming language LISP and began writing expert systems for language recognition while his peers were playing street football. As his hobby progressed, he learned dozens of computer languages and financed his way through college by developing software for several large corporations.

"He finished college at age twenty, began graduate studies in applied mathematics at Stanford, and completed his dissertation by building a neural network to model disease trends worldwide for malaria." The speaker paused and took a drink of water. Sonia knew that one year of Jim's life had been carefully omitted, a year Jim had spent in the Peace Corps under the mistaken premise that it would be a year of free peyote and interesting scenery. She also knew that the speaker had failed to mention Jim's berth on the U.S. Mathematics Olympiad team in high school, something Jim had taken great pleasure in recounting to her. On the eve of the international competition, he proceeded to hitchhike from the host city of Budapest to Prague, where he enjoyed the hospitality of a crowd of followers who believed he was, in fact, an American rock star. He arrived back just in time to win a gold medal.

"Dr. Summers rapidly earned his reputation as a seminal contributor in the emerging field of mathematical epidemiology. He secured a faculty position at U.C. Berkeley by age twenty-eight, and has had phenomenal output in the three years since. I'm pleased to welcome one of the leading figures in contemporary epidemiology, and this year's Wilkins Foundation Distinguished Researcher, Dr. James Summers." A thunderous roar of applause emanated from the audience.

Jim walked up to the podium without any semblance of decorum, and overhead two large movie screens came to life as he pushed a button on the laptop sitting beside the podium. His black T-shirt covered what Sonia had always considered mostly wimpy pectorals. Blond stubble on his chin was slight today. He had shaved this morning. His hair was pulled back with a single rubber band around the base of a ponytail reaching two inches below his shoulders. His eyes were small, but quick and thoughtful. Sonia thought gratefully that the podium would completely hide his white tube socks. Scanning over the vast audience, Jim began his speech.

"It's good to be here tonight. I appreciate the opportunity to review some recent trends in epidemiology with such a diverse and intelligent group. You know, a friend of mine heard I was coming to the computational biology meeting today and wondered what sort of things one would talk about here. Her thought was that a computational biology meeting is the place one learns to count spores and molds." Sonia slunk into her chair amid the laughter of the crowd. She expected any moment to be asked to stand, and considered standing and waving preemptively.

"Well, twenty years ago that may not have been too far off, since computational biology has really come into its own only since then. What I want to talk about today is an especially exciting field of mathematical biology: massively parallel models of disease."

The title slide over Jim's head faded and a cartoon illustrating three caricatures of healthy, sick, and convalescent individuals appeared. "As most of you know, early attempts to model diseases focused on three groups of people: those who were susceptible to an infection, those who had the disease, and those who had recovered from the disease and became immune."

Another slide showed a block diagram with the letters S, I, R in boxes connected by lines. "To figure out how many people would get sick, several pioneers devised what have come to be called S-I-R models of disease, for susceptible, infected, and recovered populations. The idea is that you can calculate how people move through these three groups." Another slide of three differential equations appeared on the screen.

Sonia began to lose focus on Jim's speech as he began a long, complicated explanation of how the equations in the model were chaotic, mentioning something about unpredictable and using the word *parameters* way too often. She began scheming how she was going to turn the conversation with Luann away from science once the talk was over.

Jim paused midway through his talk, took a long drink of water, and looked out at the audience. Sonia snapped out of her daydream and watched her date. *Some date this turned out to be,* she thought. She couldn't wait to tell her friends at work.

Jim resumed his speech. "And that's why I've completely abandoned the standard model in what I hope is a bold new step for epidemiology." A slide showed a picture of Jim in a ski parka with his arm around a huge bank of computers tangled behind cables and wires.

"Welcome to the next decade of disease modeling. This is a Cray Z1 supercomputer, a massively parallel architecture that allows computing even the last generation of supercomputers couldn't dream about, measured in hundreds of petaflops. For the non–computer junkies in the audience, that means the computer can achieve a million billion computations per second. More important, the computer is engineered to multitask millions of separate computational operations simultaneously.

"Of course, machines like this are hard to come by, and it took some doing for me to bum twenty minutes of processor time from this baby to get the data you're about to see." Jim took a deep breath.

"Imagine, if you will, three hundred million computer programs, independently interacting. You can think of each one as a person, and I've programmed each little person into the computer. They're grouped into cities. They have jobs. They have friends. They ride buses. They fly to visit Grandma in Duluth or to give a seminar in Dallas. They even have virtual preferences on nightclubs and movies they like. I spent nine months programming in every confounded variable I never had the computing power to consider before. Now, when I model a disease, I don't just fuss with some equations. I run the whole epidemic live, one bloody cough at a time. And the results are shocking.

"By programming conditions similar to those that existed in 1918, I have been able to re-create the Spanish flu epidemic, with my predictions of the number of people sick accurate to within twenty percent of the best estimated totals. I have been able to calculate the AIDS epidemic in Africa with accurate predictions of diseased male and female populations over about twenty years."

Jim launched into a presentation filled with graphs and three-dimensional curves, full of elaborately drawn predictions closely matching superimposed real data. He finished his lecture by announcing, "And this is only the beginning. I predict that within a decade we will be able to predict the course of nearly any disease before it ever starts, and stop it cold in its tracks. What I hope we have seen tonight is the beginning of the end of mass epidemics and the beginning of 'managed care,' if you pardon the term, on the global scale." The audience exploded into applause, and Sonia joined the rest of the crowd as they rose to their feet.

When the applause died down, Jim asked for questions from the audience. A burly, bearded man rose in the front. "How stable are your solutions? The bear of this business for twenty years has been chaotic solutions. Have you run them multiple times?"

Jim fingered his ponytail as he answered. "I'd sure like to rerun the simulations and get that data. The processor time is the issue. One of my postdocs is preparing a stability meta-analysis with small experiments rerun millions of times to check that very thing."

The bearded man nodded sagely and sat down. A woman in her mid-fifties stood a bit farther back. "Jim?"

"Yes, Evelyn."

"Thank you. Your data is certainly impressive. Have you thought about implications for bioterrorism? Nobody is really quite sure about what the potential is for a man-made epidemic. Do you think your method could predict things like that?"

Sonia watched his mind racing as he considered the implications. After a time, he responded, "I think that's an excellent idea. Yes, I do think that is possible."

Jim answered a few more questions, mostly obvious

questions from junior researchers seeking to sound clever in front of the large crowd. The moderator again came to the podium and presented Jim with a plaque, and another round of applause ensued.

When the session had ended, Sonia beat a path to the platform with a hasty good-bye to Luann. She arrived just in time to see a new man in a double-breasted gray suit offer his hand to Jim. She stood a short distance away.

"Dr. Summers. A wonderful achievement. I enjoyed your remarks."

"Thanks," Jim said.

"The name's Thorpe. Alan Thorpe. You know, I work for the government, and we could sure use a man with your skills."

"Thanks, but I guess I've had one too many run-ins with the DMV to be excited about a government job."

"Fair enough. You know, I just happen to work for a particular government agency that might be very interested in your talents. What would it take to get you to consider another position? One where you could work independently with a handful of America's best minds in infectious disease?"

Jim looked a bit annoyed. "Well, for starters, how about a twenty-million-dollar supercomputer, a Klingon dartboard, and a pizza oven."

"Done."

"See, thanks anyway—" Jim did a double take. "Did you say done?"

"Well, all but the pizza oven. Fire hazard, you know. But there is a twenty-four-hour Pentagon pizza hotline."

"Pentagon? Who are you really?"

Thorpe put his arm back around Jim's shoulder and walked with him out of Sonia's earshot to an empty alcove of the meeting hall. She followed some distance behind before the two men shook hands, and Jim strode back to where she stood. He looked uncharacteristically dazed.

"Jim, are you all right?" Sonia asked.

He made eye contact. "Sure. Sorry. What did you think?"

Sonia reached over to kiss him on the cheek. "I thought you looked hot."

"That's why I brought you. Nobody else has said that before."

"Good."

THREE

Three years later: April 1

"**LISTEN.** All I'm saying is that before I go tell the rest of the Senate Armed Forces Committee that we've all been bumbling hypochondriacs, I want to meet with these folks." Senator Michael Embry had the walk of a man with a great deal more self-importance than time.

Jacob Levin struggled to keep pace. "I already set everything up. Don't worry. It's just . . . I don't want you to misread their reaction. They're scientists, not politicians, remember."

"So who's in charge?"

"They all are."

"Impossible."

"I guess if you had to pick out someone, it would be Alan Thorpe, but nobody bosses these guys around."

"He's the guy from Seattle?"

"Right. He was their emergency management director."

"I thought you said scientists."

"He's the exception." Levin was speaking in short sentences as he became more winded walking down the long tunnel underneath the Pentagon. Senator Embry sensed his unease and slackened his pace.

"Tell me about him."

"He's the sort of guy who could host a Tupperware party for the Hell's Angels. Everyone likes him. He handles emergencies like he was given the script in advance." Levin chuckled. "After I hired him, he wore a tie for a year until he finally caved in to the others."

"Who else is in the group?"

Jacob Levin fell into a well-rehearsed synopsis, having had the same conversation with at least a dozen government figures equally conscious of their own importance and lack of time. As Undersecretary for Science and Technology in the Department of Homeland Security, Jacob had more than his share of politics.

The Department of Homeland Security, created in 2002 in the largest reorganization of the federal government in half a century, centralized the highly fragmented national biological warfare research effort. In the new department, several existing agencies were combined with entirely new organizations, and despite the central control, redundancy and political infighting were the inevitable outcome.

The new National Bio-Weapons Defense Analysis Center was charged with developing countermeasures against biological terror threats. The Homeland Security Institute was founded to assess threats and suggest targets for research. Numerous university-based centers for biological defense research coordinated private and academic researchers financed by federal grants. Input from the twenty-member Homeland Security Science and Technology Advisory Committee was supposed to advise the Directorate of Science and Technology on priorities for funding. The Office of Science and Technology in the Department of Justice and the Directorate of Information Analysis and Infrastructure Protection were created. All this, combined with ongoing programs at Lawrence Livermore and Sandia National Laboratories, Plum Island Animal Disease Center, Defense Advanced Research Projects Agency, the Office of Public Health Preparedness, and the Centers for Disease Control made for a nightmare of jurisdiction and turf battles.

Several years into the reorganization, the recently appointed undersecretary recognized that the numerous agencies designed for largely similar tasks had the net effect of inviting too many cooks into the biological defense kitchen. So he did the thing any sensible bureaucrat would do. He created a new agency.

The idea was simple. A new division was created under the auspices of the Homeland Security Advanced Research Projects Agency, which itself had been usurped by the recently created National Counterterrorism Center (NCTC). The division, called simply Biodefense, consisted of only four—later to become five—hand-picked individuals, each a celebrated expert in a field such as molecular virology, massively parallel computing, or emergency management. Although the group technically fell under the auspices of the NCTC administration, Levin had managed to assure that they enjoyed an unprecedented level of autonomy within the NCTC, reporting directly to the secretary of homeland security.

It had not been easy. Levin knew that any agency operating under layers of bureaucracy within the NCTC would be reduced to just one more committee to join in interagency feuding. He began by negotiations with the Department of Defense to form a "collaboration" for a small joint project. He knew all of the vernacular, and used to his advantage the fact that the entire defense department was consumed by talk of "joint operations" and "joint task forces." By promising shared research and capabilities, he successfully negotiated to house the organization within the Pentagon. Removing their physical proximity from NCTC headquarters had been they key hurdle to Biodefense's special status.

Levin summarized for Senator Embry. "Well, there's Steve Adams. He's their bacteriologist. Keeps exotic reptiles and takes time off each year to go catamaran racing. They say he can learn more in an hour about a strain of bacteria with his antique microscope than the whole CDC can find out in a week."

Senator Embry nodded, used to receiving briefings in the hallways as he walked with advisors between meetings.

"Jim Summers is their epidemiologist. He's still a kid, at thirty-four, but no slouch." Levin frowned at the thought. "Actually, he kind of looks like a slouch. Long hair, shaves once a week whether he needs it or not. He's their computer expert—runs simulations and models outbreaks. It was sort of an afterthought on my part to put a computer guy in, but he's been critical."

"Who else?"

"Eva Vanorden is even younger. She's Dutch, I think. Probably the best virologist in the world. Trained at Hopkins in molecular virology with a postdoc at Cold Spring Harbor. By the time she was twenty-eight, she was a principal collaborator on the influenza vaccine. It was her group that identified the epitope now used in the SARS vaccine. She knows her genetics cold, and has an imagination that makes Moriarty seem like an altar boy. Be glad she's on our side."

Levin continued his summary. "Sam Goldberg is their physician. Specialist in infectious diseases. He organized a clinic in Namibia while he was still in medical school and studied tropical diseases. He gravitated to NIH pretty early in his career, and started one of the first molecular immunology labs before he became chief of medicine there. His referral clinic is pretty famous for making weird diagnoses."

Levin took a few steps before continuing. "There's something about him. It's like he stares right through you. When I was checking him out at NIH, the two things everyone could agree on were that he was a genius, and that he had eyes that could read your mind."

They passed a uniformed guard, who saluted the senator crisply as they passed. The senator nodded in response.

"And you hold their leash?" Embry asked as they neared the elevator.

"Not for a second. I picked them; I pay them; I leave them alone. Truth is, I'm a bureaucrat these days. These guys can think circles around me, and I don't try to fight it. They set their own agenda. That's the whole idea. I gave them only one directive: Play wargames, and win them. If a bioterrorist attacks, this group will function as the principal advisory command structure to the president." They stepped into the elevator.

"How much do you pay them?" The mention of money focused Embry's attention like a hungry Rottweiler.

"You don't want to know, sir."

"I suppose not. I admit I'm skeptical that your little group is that much better informed than the thousands of people we have working on the same issues in defense, energy, and intelligence labs."

"Then it's good for you to meet them. These people are the best America has, Senator. What you're about to see is the biological equivalent of the Manhattan Project, only on the defensive side. I believe these five individuals know more about planning, implementing, and defending against a bioterror attack than the rest of the world combined." The elevator door opened and they made their way to a guarded entrance around the corner.

The senator flashed his badge at the officer, who saluted and opened the door. Levin took a deep breath.

FOUR

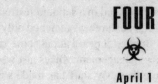

April 1

JACOB Levin and Senator Embry stepped inside the Pentagon office to find the members of Biodefense strewn out across couches in what looked like an upscale lounge. Jim Summers stood at the far end of the room throwing darts at a target. The wall was studded with his less accurate attempts. Alan Thorpe was the first to stand. As Thorpe strode over to shake the senator's hand, the other three casually straightened up. Sam Goldberg glanced at his watch.

"Welcome to Biodefense, Senator," Thorpe greeted their guest.

The senator nodded amicably. "So this is the group who decided the fears of the Senate Armed Forces Committee were nothing more than smoke and mirrors," he remarked testily.

"We'll talk about that, sir. Why don't you make yourself comfortable." Alan Thorpe motioned toward two chairs next to the others. "Dr. Levin, always a pleasure." When their heads were turned, he waved at Summers, who reluctantly moved to join them.

The senator sat rigidly in his three-piece suit, surveying the members of the team now seated in a semicircle around him on a ring of couches. His posture was matched only by Thorpe's. Embry began, "But first, I heard about some kind of stunt in a few emergency management offices last week. And it's not the first time either. My staff has made some phone calls. Apparently, these 'drills' have been going on for a few years. This has been you people, I understand?" His look was stern and unforgiving.

Steve Adams looked uneasily at the senator, fidgeting in his seat. Alan Thorpe nodded gravely.

At that point, Embry broke into a broad grin. "Took a lot of balls, I'd say."

"Thank you." Eva Vanorden spoke up promptly. "It was my idea." She clasped her hands behind her neck and leaned back. Following the senator's eyes, she subconsciously pulled up on her uncomfortably sheer blouse.

Alan Thorpe glanced at Jacob Levin, and addressed Senator Embry. "You want to talk about our memo?"

"I sure do. But let me cut to the chase. There's one sentence where I want to know point blank what you mean. Let me quote." He pulled a paper from his jacket pocket. " 'With safeguards now in place, it is all but impossible for a terrorist to kill a million Americans without using nuclear weapons.' " He looked at the group. "You have a very unconventional point of view. Everyone in government is scared shitless that we're vulnerable at any time to a devastating attack by some cloud of spores. Now you kids come along and say it can't happen? What gives?"

Steve Adams cleared his throat. His broad shoulders and deep-set eyes commanded attention when he spoke. "We certainly did not say it can't happen. We simply pointed out that fears of catastrophic damage were exaggerated."

"And that's what I need you to explain to me."

Thorpe answered the senator. "It's complex. These are conclusions from nearly three years of our work. We tried to summarize as best we could in the memo, but I think Jim would be the best one to fill you in on our thinking." He looked hopefully at Summers.

Jim uncrossed his legs and gave a sheepish grin. "It's pretty obvious, once you really think about it." He looked at the senator as though nothing more need be said. The senator's face didn't flinch, and Summers continued.

"It's like this. The civilized world is deceived on two counts. First, most people have no idea how easy it is to make some designer germ that could be used as a bioweapon. But second, and more important, people also have no concept how difficult it is to design and deliver a bioweapon of mass destruction. It's all about epidemiology."

The senator looked receptively but suspiciously back at Jim.

Summers continued. "Here's the basic principle. Germs have evolved over billions of years to survive. They're very good at what they do . . . for a reason. They're not too greedy. There's a basic compromise that every germ faces: Do you try to reproduce like rabbits in a bathhouse, or try to keep your victim alive and healthy enough to spread to his friends? It turns out the most successful germs are the most benign ones. The problem with all of these philo-sophical 'supergerms' is that they kill too fast."

"I don't follow you," the senator admitted.

"Suppose you engineer some kind of supergerm that kills its victims. When you run the simulations, just about anything that would excite a terrorist is too strong. Any virus that will kill its hosts is basically committing suicide, dying with its hosts. Such a bug may cause a small epidemic, but will burn through its victims before you get large numbers of casualties."

"So what if they settle for a slightly less potent killer, or one with a long incubation period?" Embry looked unsatisfied.

"These make lousy bioweapons. They can't be effectively administered in one attack. You have to expose victims gradually over a long period of time with multiple epicenters to really take hold. People these days look at diseases like Ebola or Marburg and think that it's real easy to start a big epidemic with something like that. Truth is, it's nearly impossible. It's hard to explain without a lot of mathematics. It's just what the simulations predict."

"Listen, son. I'm sure your computer works just fine, but let's suppose you punch in the wrong number somewhere down the line. We let down our defense, and guess whose groin ends up as football when the next version of the bubonic plague comes around?"

"With all respect, sir, this isn't the fourteenth century we're living in." Summers glared at the senator.

"Tell him about the simulations, Jim," Alan said.

"What do you know about epidemiology, Senator?"

Senator Embry raised one eyebrow to answer.

Jim took a deep sigh, and stood up. "In my computer is a scale model of the entire American population. When I run a simulation, hundreds of millions of people are going about their business, interacting with each other, and the disease is spread from one person to the next until the disease burns out or runs its course."

"Like a computer virus?" Embry asked.

"No. Like a real virus. That's the point. The simulations have become lifelike enough that what we have is a dry run for every scary epidemic we can come up with. Anything that seems remotely likely to be used as a terrorist weapon doesn't have the ability to cause mass casualties."

"Impressive. I had no idea. Am I in your computer?"

"You died in the first Ebola outbreak a few years back," Summers answered with a grin.

"What about Ebola?" The senator appeared anxious about seeming uninformed, but couldn't resist asking the question.

Eva answered. "People don't realize how difficult it is to transmit Ebola. You can get some initial exposures if you freeze-dry it, but it's hard to get the kindling to catch fire into an epidemic."

"Even if mass exposure were attempted?"

Alan Thorpe stepped in. "That's a whole different can of worms. Mass exposure is fiendishly difficult. People in the media talk about crop dusters full of viruses as though it's the easiest thing in the world to manufacture a metric ton of potent biologically active material. Some of us have been thinking about this for five years, Senator, and it just can't be done without an astronomical price tag, top-notch scientists, and custom-designed facilities. We don't even think we could do it."

"I'm glad to hear that," the senator said.

Jim Summers resumed his lecture. "Even more comical are the bugs that most of the public are scared of. Do you know how many more people in the last decade have died of lightning strikes than of anthrax?"

"Don't get me started, Jim," Steve Adams broke in. "He's right, Senator. Anthrax has to be one of the most impotent bioweapons ever attempted. It's not contagious, sunlight and wind kill it, and we have two dozen antibiotics that treat it. Sure, anyone can knock off a few Americans now and then, but you're not going to get Armageddon. At least not with anything like anthrax."

"Maybe you all think this is just a game, but knocking off a few Americans now and then has consequences: economic tailspins, political unrest . . ."

Alan Thorpe cut off Embry's incipient speech. "Of course it does. The truth is that there are many bioweapons that we can't defend against any more than we can against conventional explosives. But that's our point. There's nothing magical about bioweapons. They aren't going to trigger any kind of mass outbreak that can't be stopped. The consequences of a bioterror attack could be disastrous economically and politically, but we would recover. What we worry about is whether it's possible to start an infection with casualties so massive it could bring this country to its knees. At that point, we're talking a million or tens of millions of casualties. It turns out that to kill a lot of people, you have to directly expose a lot of people, same as with conventional explosives. And our calculations show that in every case we can dream up, it is cheaper and more effective to use conventional explosives to do a comparable amount of damage. The only true weapon of mass destruction is a nuclear weapon, Senator. Period."

"I think I see what you're saying, but it's a pretty big leap of faith."

Thorpe continued. "We haven't even talked about dozens of other scenarios: poisoning water supplies, destroying the ozone layer, mass asbestos exposure, viruses that infect crops and raise immune responses to cause an epidemic of multiple sclerosis, bugs that make their host infertile, horrors you've probably never imagined. We've studied them; they're too difficult to execute and have lower yield than conventional explosives in today's world and our current state of defense readiness."

"So what's the worst thing you've come up with?"

Eva giggled. "You'll laugh."

"Try me."

"Our worst nightmare so far is a fully vancomycin-resistant staph. It will come on its own sooner or later, but we project that more deaths would come from hospitalized elderly people and diabetics by creating a multidrug-resistant staph than anything else we can imagine."

"You're telling me that the brightest minds in bioterrorism are most afraid of some terrorists circulating a bug that's designed to slowly attack America's nursing home residents? I can live with that—it doesn't sound like the terrorists we know."

Senator Embry stood, followed by Dr. Levin. "Keep me informed," he said to no one in particular as he walked out of the lounge.

When the door closed, Steve Adams looked at the rest of the group. "He doesn't have a clue what to be afraid of."

Sam Goldberg shook his head.

FIVE

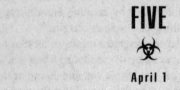

April 1

A blinking light flashed on the small flat-panel display on the dashboard. A moment later the sound of the car's internal modem was heard faintly over the noise of the interstate. A feminine voice sounded from the dashboard, "Mr. Al Rasheed, my right front blinker is no longer functioning. I have arranged to have a replacement installed this evening at home. Is that satisfactory?"

"That is fine," Ahmed responded to his forest green Jaguar XK convertible. The blinking light disappeared. "I spend more on that service contract than I did on the car," he muttered to himself under his breath as he slid onto the off-ramp nearest his Santa Monica home. The GPS-link road map on the display updated itself in real time as he snaked toward the villa he had lived in for the last twenty years.

The expense was not particularly disconcerting, however, as money had never been a constraint for Ahmed Al

Rasheed. Knowing from his birth that his inheritance was all but inexhaustible, Ahmed had moved to the United States for college more out of boredom than any sense of personal ambition. He had continued in school for the same reason, until he finished his doctorate in microbiology, only to find he was no less bored. The last ten years he had worked sporadically as a consultant for a number of higher-end pharmaceutical supply houses. In the interim he had married and had two children. None of these events had quieted the sense of ennui that consumed him while he waited.

He drove by the mosque he had attended for so many years, and the bile crept up his throat. He stoically swallowed to keep from spitting the word *cowards* as he drove by the community he had invested so much time in creating.

As he pulled into the beachfront gate that surrounded his estate, the doorman nodded respectfully. Ahmed knew the doorman would admit the repairman later that evening to change his right turn light. He knew the doorman, or one of his associates, would similarly keep watch over the estate while he slept. And he knew the doorman would not pick up his mail, since that was the one job that Ahmed had kept jealously for himself.

He walked out of the car and retrieved his mail, leaving the car for the doorman to dispose of. Thumbing through the junk mail of the day, he found a padded, letter-size manila envelope, and his casual walk toward the door stopped as his eyes reread the return address. Trembling, he tore off the opening strip on the package and peered into the envelope. He withdrew a single half-sheet of paper and read the message carefully several times. Looking up, he waved to the doorman and proceeded to enter his house. As he walked, he opened further the padded wrapper and dropped a single vial into his pocket.

He greeted his wife in his usual fashion and acknowledged his children with a tear in his eye. She was a good wife, and she knew her place. He didn't expect her to understand the importance of his work, or his role in the grand scheme of things. It was enough that she was a good mother and a devout Muslim. His children were appropriately reserved, home schooled to avoid the destructive influence of a Godless society.

He excused himself and slipped away, unlocking the sacred room on the second floor that his family had never entered. He would work tonight. His discipline had once again sustained him through the long years of waiting as it had once before. Closing and locking the door behind him, he withdrew a rug from beside the doorway, and fell to his knees with his prayer already falling from his grateful lips.

SIX

April 4

THE five members of Biodefense met in the central lounge for their weekly brainstorming session. After several years of working together, they had established a routine that accommodated their differing schedules, with Jim agreeing to come in before noon one day a week. The day they met together, discussions often lasted for several hours. They all looked forward to the group sessions. Steve, in particular, enjoyed the company of the others, especially since so much of their work the rest of the week tended to be done independently, given the high level of specialization of the team. After a busy academic career that had increasingly weighed him down with administration, teaching, and national meetings, the intellectual challenge and interaction of the group in Biodefense was the perfect escape for someone with Steve's sense of adventure.

Steve had never been a typical scientist. Early in his

career, he constantly challenged core dogma. The safest course for a young scientist was to ally himself with a big name in his field and extend whatever doctrine his mentor had developed. It was risky to go it alone, and riskier still to alienate big names in the field. Steve did both, and thrived. His first major project out of graduate school was to challenge the standard bacterial classification, proposing instead a scheme based on DNA similarities. The proposal was received like a cold shower at first, but after many years a variation based on ribosomal RNA was ultimately accepted.

Fortunately, Steve's gentle manner and humble personality managed to preserve friendships even with the very scientists he opposed, and his career had been a solid, steady rise to preeminence in first cellular, then molecular biology. His reputation made him a natural choice for the Biodefense bacteriologist, and Jacob Levin had told him he had been chosen in no small part as well for his ability to get along with other scientists.

He had been a facilitator as well at Biodefense, and it was ultimately Steve's behind-the-scenes negotiating that had made the weekly brainstorming run so smoothly. The meetings would start whenever Jim showed up, with a review of grant proposals for extramural research projects. Although nobody enjoyed the tedious process, they all admitted it was important to have a qualified group choosing where the nation's counterterrorism funds were spent. The knowledge of who was working on what projects at what institutions was also exceptionally useful if they ever needed quick access to materials or information concerning a particular threat. After years of grant review, the team knew by heart every major research project concerning bioterrorism throughout the country, their preliminary results, and the people involved.

Once a month, the group would plan a drill or training

exercise at a local public health office or emergency operations center. It was a welcome break from the routine, and gave them vital information about the nation's bioterrorism preparedness.

The rest of the meeting was spent imagining new types of bioterror attacks, exploring how they could be carried out, and discussing solutions to the threats generated in the weeks before. Addressing these imaginary threats required high-level gamesmanship and occupied most of Steve's time between the weekly meetings. The intellectual challenge of keeping up with the rest of the group in analyzing threats was extraordinary, more satisfying than any other work he had ever done.

On joining the group, Steve had first enjoyed the challenge of coming up with creative, nefarious schemes to dissect. For several reasons, he now preferred the job of analyzing casualties and planning defenses in the war games. It was getting much more difficult to devise new attacks, given how much ground they had already covered. The standard agents like smallpox, anthrax, and Ebola were such completely worn-out territory that he could spew the routine defense plans in his sleep.

Plus, he couldn't hope to match Eva's criminal genius at generating new ideas. None of them could. Steve had realized he was utterly outclassed over a year ago when Eva came up with a plot to plant a virus in obstetrics clinics across the country with genetic markers that targeted the placenta, producing a toxin that would cause a massive rise in levels of birth defects. By the time Jim had worked out the parameters needed to detect such an attack from computerized public health data, she had already created an equally well-thought-out strategy using radioactive hormones absorbed through the skin off toilet seats in obstetricians' offices. Keeping up with Eva was like that.

Today, the team had ordered out for lunch, as was their custom, and had just finished discussing one of Sam's ideas from the prior week, a virus that was disseminated in street heroin, producing aflatoxin, a potent toxin that produced fatal liver cancer years after exposure. His claim had been that this technique would allow the virus to spread rapidly. Not only did the population allow intravenous infection, but their needle sharing and sexual carelessness encouraged quick spread. The idea was also novel in that detection would be slow, given the high rates of hepatitis and liver cancer already seen in drug addicts. The long latency of the virus would allow it to spread from the abusing population to the general public just as AIDS had, with much lower possibility of a cure.

Although Sam and Eva invented the most new territory for discussion, Jim provided the most conceptual guidance about what sort of attacks to envision. His computer simulations had imposed strict constraints on what types of diseases could cause the most damage, and consequently where the team spent the most effort. Ever since Jim had worked out how narrow a window a disease had to break out into a pandemic, the rest of the group used his analysis to hone their search for the special combination of factors that made an attack potentially catastrophic.

Alan's contribution was most valuable in evaluating psychological, economic, and political consequences of a potential threat. His training in managing various types of disasters suggested implications the others often failed to consider. And it was hard to imagine a more engaging discussion facilitator than Alan.

"So where do we go next, Jim?" Eva asked.

"We've got to work more on delayed attacks. That's where the money is."

"What do you mean?" Steve asked.

"Don't you notice we keep running into a common theme? Instant gratification doesn't work. If a terrorist tries to kill a lot of people quickly, the disease never gets off the ground. I know this is old material from our memo, but I can't emphasize it enough. Deadly, front-loaded attacks burn out. A germ that kills that fast is committing suicide."

"So what's the strategy then?" Alan asked. "How do we evolve our threats into something that's still deadly, but takes its time?"

"I think we need to focus more along the lines of Sam's last idea. That was really powerful. Something that takes a few years to kill. Diseases that maim or impose a huge cost to health care. Those are the sort of things that could really take off. Remember when we were playing with asbestos a while back? Maybe we should look at that a bit more. High psychological impact."

Steve frowned. "Yeah, but with asbestos you're talking thirty years before you get your first cancers. No terrorist is that patient."

Eva's face contorted into the evil grin familiar to Steve. *"Wat leuk!"* she exclaimed in Dutch. "What about Goodpasture's disease?"

Sam cocked his head. "Interesting. What've you got in mind?"

"What's Goodpasture's disease?" Alan asked.

"It's a disease of the lungs and kidneys. Pretty rare. Nobody's real sure quite why it happens, but it's caused by an autoimmune mechanism. A host starts making antibodies against his own kidneys and lungs, and within a week of symptoms he can have complete renal failure and end up on dialysis. What would it do to this country to put a million more people on dialysis?" Sam had become skilled at providing brief synopses of medical issues in their brainstorming sessions.

"That's nasty," Jim said.

"Eva did it again. Sounds like we've got a week's work in front of us. Any obvious reasons it couldn't work?" Steve asked. *Quick today,* he thought. Usually it took longer to germinate a viable project.

"How would you spread it?" Jim asked. "Antibodies aren't easy to make. Difficult folding mechanism. Pretty specialized protein. Eats up a lot of energy. Probably need half a dozen genes to do it. Might not be feasible for anyone but a top lab."

"True," Eva admitted, "unless it was a virus, maybe something that attacks white blood cells?"

"How about a modified HIV?" Alan suggested.

"Maybe," Eva said tentatively. "Hard to spread. HIV is pretty impotent. Wouldn't be my first choice. Maybe something more like human T-cell lymphoma virus . . ."

"The more benign the better. We don't want to hurt the patient with collateral symptoms. It would also slow down detection."

"Sounds reasonable enough to take seriously," Sam said. "How do we beat it? Should we shoot for solutions by next week?"

Alan looked at Steve. "I, er, Steve and I were planning a little vacation this week. He got this adventure bug into my daughter and we're going to try a little whitewater. Why don't we make it two weeks, if we come back, that is."

Steve winked at Alan. He was pleased to finally get some of the group to try something more unconventional. He was convinced that the experience of being thrown off your guard was invaluable preparation for a real emergency. "Keep telling you, Alan. Piece of cake. Glad to finally get one of you to try something a little daring."

Jim tightened his ponytail. "Good for you, Alan. You could use a little loosening up."

"You want to come?"

"Thanks, but I prefer a cabana on the beach to getting smashed on the rocks."

"All right, so let's flesh this out as much as we can today, and we'll present solutions in two weeks." Alan steered the team back on topic.

SEVEN

April 6

"TRIAGE." The overhead speaker announced another patient's arrival into the Ronald Reagan UCLA Medical Center Emergency Department. A few moments later, Daru Shah watched indifferently while a triage nurse squeezed into the tangle of bodies surrounding the flow board and jotted the words "BARKER—frgn bd" in green on the slot for room 31. "Foreign body," Daru translated to herself, filling in the vowels that were left out in mock adherence to new confidentiality laws that forbade public display of patient diagnoses.

One week into her emergency medicine rotation, Daru was still surprised that anything ever got done in the E.R. It had taken her most of the week to realize that the perpetual motion, shouting, and squalor that teemed through the halls was nothing more than a spinning top, whirling out of control but going nowhere in particular. Not the aggressive type by nature, she had taken to watching the other doctors and nurses, all of whom spent most of the day trying to look busy. Even in the multitraumas that came through, where dozens of people converged on a flailing or asphyxiating patient, Daru's cynical eyes increasingly saw ten guys standing around a hole drinking coffee while one guy ran the jackhammer.

A gurney squeaked by, and Daru whiffed the bourbon that the occupant wore like perfume. "Put me down for three-forty!" she shouted out.

"Three-forty for Shah," one of the nurses replied. A standing game in the E.R. was to guess the blood alcohol level of the drunks who rolled in on a daily basis. It had been a universally undesired outcome of a city ordinance that whenever a report of a "man down" was called into 911, the paramedics had to either rouse them or bring them to an E.R. This meant that whenever some citizen called in a report of a wino passed out on a park bench, the paramedics had to respond. When they got little more than a grunt from their patient, they wheeled him in. Every hospital in the city was convinced they got more than their share of these non-paying patients, who took a bed only to gradually sober up and stumble out.

Daru looked up at the board, painfully aware several times an hour that as a third-year medical student she needed a strong evaluation more than she needed her peace of mind or self-respect or sleep. Pacing with purpose and transferring papers to and from clipboards, she avoided at all costs being caught sitting. To this end, she had settled into an ambitious pace of seeing four patients an hour during her twelve-hour shift. She might as well see a more interesting patient than be stuck with another alcoholic.

"I'll take thirty-one, Steve." Daru's offer was acknowledged by the charge nurse only by his turning around and writing *DS* in the box next to room 31. She stopped for a drink of ice water on her way to the room. The fact that the patient's name was written in green meant the triage nurse considered the case nonurgent. More urgent cases were written in orange or red. Nonurgent suited Daru fine.

As she walked into the room she waved to the guard. In her week on the service, she had been surprised by how many of the patients were prisoners, tagging along with their handcuffs, bright orange shirts, and uniformed guards. She, personally, had seen seven this week. Four had complained of scrotal pain, looking for a trip out of prison for the inevitable scrotal ultrasound and the stories they could tell on their return.

As she looked toward the patient, her training took over. Most of her work was done in the first ten seconds of observing a patient. The rest was done over the five minutes she used to take a history. At that point, she ordered a battery of tests and lazily waited for results to come back before she could "dispo" her patient, either by admitting him, discharging him with a few sage words of advice, or referring him elsewhere.

What she saw sparked her curiosity. The prisoner was bucking on the table, one arm handcuffed to the metal side rail. His face contorted with each wince of pain. An incoherent stream of vocalization came from beneath his food-covered beard as if from an evangelical prophet speaking in tongues. His hands were as gnarled as his hair, with a faded tattoo jerking with his arm against the cadence of his speech.

"Mr. Barker?" She tried not to sound tentative. "Mr. Barker?!" He turned his yellow eyes toward Daru, as his movement subsided and his speech slowed. "I'm Dr. Shah. Nice to meet you," she prevaricated twice. "What is the trouble?" Her question hung in the room for either her patient or his guard to answer.

"Swallowed a toothbrush, maybe something more," the guard said passively.

Barker flashed his eyes at Daru. "Do you know what it's like to have your intestines ripped out from inside you?" he shouted, emphasizing the word *ripped*. A look of insane pleasure beamed from his face.

Great, Daru thought. *Another JPN'er.* It was standard lingo to refer to the sizable minority of mentally imbalanced patients coming through the E.R. as Just Plain Nuts. She shifted roles, assuming the more matriarchal tone she used with her psychiatric patients. "What did you swallow, Mr. Barker?"

Her patient contorted his mouth as though he were chewing tobacco, and wrinkled his nose. "Toothbrush, a razor blade, and a sock!" he shouted with inexplicable pride. "Do you think they'll see the sock on the CT scan?" He clearly couldn't contain his enthusiasm long enough to bait his doctor as he had fantasized.

"How long ago did you swallow them?" she continued in the same tone of voice she would use to run down a list of questions on an insurance physical.

"Mebbe two hours. I warned 'em!" The look on his face was grave and unrepentant.

Daru's curiosity got the better of her. "Why did you swallow things like that, Mr. Barker?"

The guard put his hand over his mouth to keep from laughing. Totally unaware that his guard was amused, Barker took the question at face value as though he hadn't expected to be asked. "There's about twenty of us swallowers up at the state hospital. Gets in your blood." He leaned his face into Daru's. "Do ye know what it feels like to have your insides ripped out?" He tossed his head back, as though he were about to lose consciousness, and then flashed his eyes back to Daru. "My friend, Zeek. Once he got a whole

bath towel down. Betcha could find that on yer CT scan."
He spoke the letters *CT* with contempt.

"I'll be back after the X-rays, Mr. Barker." Daru turned
to leave.

"Doc," he beckoned.

She turned around, pleased by the title.

"Are you going to show the X-rays to me?"

"We'll see," she announced, turning to leave again.

"There's more!" Barker called after her. She turned
back to face her patient.

"Didn't they tell you? I've also got a pencil up my penis
and a paperback in my ass. I gotta pee, doc!" He began
rocking again on the gurney.

Daru cocked her head to one side in disbelief. She
walked over to stand next to the patient and began pressing
on his belly. The tense, distended lower abdomen confirmed
her patient's story. Unnerved, she nearly dashed out of the
room.

Still in the doorway, she called out to the crowd of people scurrying around the nurses' station. "Steve, make
thirty-one red. Dr. Andrews, can I staff a patient soon?"

Robert Andrews turned around with a concerned, tired
look, hanging up the telephone receiver he had been holding. "What's up?" he asked.

Daru's pulse quickened as she approached. "I've got an
acute urethral obstruction. I think we better put in a supra-
pubic catheter right away!" *Don't blow it!* she thought.
This was her chance to make an impression on her attending physician.

"Whoa. Slow down, Daru. How about we start over in
standard form?"

His critique took the wind out of her sails instantly, but
she regrouped. "Forty-three-year-old prisoner with a com-
plaint of swallowing foreign body." Andrews nodded,

though his mind appeared elsewhere. Daru continued. "He states about two hours ago, he swallowed a sock, a razor blade, and a toothbrush."

Andrews cut her off. "No jewelry?"

"Huh?"

"He didn't swallow any jewelry this time? This is Barker, I'm assuming."

"Yes, I didn't realize you knew him."

"Comes in a couple times a month. I'll show you the films we have on him sometime if you remind me. Anything else?"

"Apparently he has a pencil in his urethra, and his belly is as tense as a drum. He also says he has a paperback up his rectum."

Andrews smiled disarmingly. "That's a new one. He's getting more ambitious." His tone softened. "I really wish he wouldn't do this, you know. The pencil is old news, though. Usually we can fish it out. Go see what you can do, and I'll come see him in a while and see if we still need to put a needle in his bladder. Go ahead and order the CT."

Daru nodded eagerly.

As Andrews turned to leave, he commented, "And Daru? Why don't you have Steve leave him as green."

Daru swallowed the lump in her throat. Overreacting to a patient's urgency was a sign of losing one's cool, and was the cardinal sin for a medical student in her E.R. rotation. She cursed under her breath as she turned around.

A few minutes later, she stripped off her gloves and dropped a very soiled copy of *Wuthering Heights* in the trash can next to the pencil and the cellophane wrappers from her sterile instruments. "They'll call for you when they're ready at the scanner," she said spitefully as she left the room.

"Thanks, doc. Do you think we'll see the sock?" Barker called after her.

Why am I paying forty thousand dollars a year for this?
Daru thought as she walked, defeated, back to the nurses'
station. Not excited about facing Dr. Andrews again, she saw
a new patient on the board and called to one of the nurses
to sign her up for room 17. Another green. She could handle this. Maybe she could save some face.

The nurse nodded. "She looks a little pasty, but her vi-
tals are OK," she responded to Daru.

"Triage," the loudspeaker intoned.

Daru heard an uptick in the commotion as she made her
way to her next room. Someone was rolling the crash cart
into one of the trauma rooms. *Funny.* She hadn't heard anyone announcing a trauma coming. She shrugged and continued walking.

She entered her next room to find a well-dressed woman
in her forties sitting in the chair by the wall, holding her
head in her palms. In an adjacent chair, a man Daru guessed
was her husband sat with one hand on his wife's knee.
Daru's discouragement vanished as her professional side
took control.

"Mrs. Rowland?" she announced her presence.

The woman looked up, pale with bloodshot eyes. "Yes."

"What brings you in today?"

"I don't know what's wrong with me." She dabbed
faintly at her mascara with a tissue.

Her husband answered for her. "She was fine last night,
except for a little diarrhea. It seemed like last night she
started feeling strange. Didn't sleep all night. Fever,
chills . . . This morning she started passing clots. She looks
pale, don't you think?"

"Blood clots?" Daru asked. She was interested in
gynecology.

The woman nodded.

"Vaginal bleeding? Are you menstruating?"

"I had my period last week. I'm not sure where the blood is coming from."

"We'll need to do a pelvic exam," Daru thought aloud. She began to organize her thinking. This case would need a full history. "What was the very first symptom you noticed?" Daru pulled out her pen and began writing on her clipboard.

"I'm feeling kind of funny . . ." The woman began to sway in her chair.

"Do you need to lie down?" Before Daru finished the question, her patient fell face forward, smacking her head on the tiled floor as she crumpled to the ground. Daru crouched to her knees, turning the woman over and looking into her eyes. She quickly took her pulse.

Her husband began to panic. "What's going on?!" He moved to cradle his wife's head.

"Your wife has just fainted. Let me go get some help to get her on her bed." As Daru stood, she saw the dark stain on the woman's pants where blood had soaked through her clothing. Daru ran out of the room.

Don't panic, she repeated to herself.

She panicked. "I need lift help and a crash cart in seventeen!" she shouted toward the nurses' station. Two nurses left a gurney they were wheeling and rushed over. Another bolted for the red cart in the hallway. Dr. Andrews strained his neck and began walking toward the door.

Twice in one night, she thought. *I'm dead.*

She returned to the room as the first two nurses converged on her fallen patient. Dr. Andrews arrived a moment later. One of the nurses reached for the woman's arm and called out, "I don't have a pulse."

The other sprang into action. "Backboard, now!" she yelled. She took the husband's arm and began tugging him out of the room. "I need you to wait outside for a minute, please."

"That's my wife! What's going on?"

"Please wait outside." The nurse nearly pushed him out the door as a crowd of four other people entered the room. Someone slid a flat blue board underneath the woman on the floor.

"Shah, what's the story?" Dr. Andrews knelt with his stethoscope already poised over the woman's chest.

"Forty-seven years old. No symptoms before yesterday. Complained of diarrhea, then had some vaginal or rectal bleeding this morning. She was a bit pale and just passed out. It looks like she's soaked through."

Before Daru had finished her update, one of the E.R. residents had bounced into the room, already holding the defibrillator paddles from the crash cart. "Stand back. Assessing rhythm." He placed the paddles onto the woman's chest and all eyes turned to the portable monitor, where a sawtooth waveform filled the screen.

"We have V tach," Andrews assumed control. "Charge to one-twenty."

Daru's head began to spin as the drama unfolded. She had been in dozens of codes, but never one quite like this before. She felt dizzy and stepped out of the room, with the sound of beeping alarms and shouted commands rushing over her shoulders. She sat down.

"I need an amp of epi. Who's going to intubate? I need access!"

Daru looked through glassy eyes at the patient's shocked husband, then turned her gaze back into the room, where she saw a pool of blood oozing across the floor from the woman's midsection.

"Let's have some amiodarone. Stop chest compressions for the injection."

Daru knew she should stand up. She knew she was putting the last nail in her evaluation's coffin. But all she could think about was the woman's pale expression and the stain on her clothes.

"No! Squeeze the bag! I want those fluids in wide open!"

Daru walked over to the patient's husband and put her arm on his shoulder, as he began to sob openly.

A few moments later, the tired voice of Dr. Andrews pronounced. "Calling the code at eleven-twenty-five." The room became quiet.

"That's the fourth one tonight, Rob."

"What's going on?"

"I need a crash cart in twenty-three!" A voice sounded from across the hall.

"Triage."

EIGHT

April 8

DARU rubbed her eyes. It had been a long shift, and it was only half over. *What difference did it make now?* There was no point in kissing up to anyone today, not after her performance the last two days, she thought harshly. After losing her composure and making so many embarrassing mistakes, she figured her evaluation was a lost cause. She might as well take it easy now.

"You gonna take off?" asked Carol. Her friend and fellow student sounded jealous.

Daru nodded. "I've got a nasty case of the runs. And my head's pounding." She wiped her nose on her sleeve. "This place is a total germ factory."

Carol nodded. "I think I had three separate colds during my pediatrics rotation."

Daru watched as the charge nurse cornered Dr.

Andrews. She walked up to the E.R. doc and interrupted, "Dr. Andrews?"

The charge nurse paced over to the water cooler as Daru got Dr. Andrews' attention. Carol had followed Daru, and stood a safe distance away watching.

"Oh, hi, Daru. Something up?"

"Well, nothing much. I guess I was just wondering if . . ." She stalled, unsure how to ask if she could go home.

"Hey, there's a great case of psoriasis in room seven. You should take a look."

"I'll do that." She lingered on the phrase, hinting that there was more on her mind.

The charge nurse walked back from the water cooler, looking impatient. Maybe she would broach the subject of going home a little later.

"ROB, can I talk to you in the conference room?" Lisa Holland's voice sounded urgent, resolved.

"Sure, let me just finish a few scripts." He scribbled his signature twice as he spoke, then followed Lisa's brisk walk around the corner into an empty conference room amid curious glances from the nurses' station.

Lisa backed against the conference table and stared Dr. Andrews into closing the door behind him.

"Rob, that's fourteen cases in two days. When was the last time you saw anything that looked like this?"

"Come on, Lisa. We get a dozen cases of rectal bleeding in here every week."

"I mean it. Tell me the last time you had someone bleed out like this."

Robert Andrews tapped his knuckles on the conference table. "No. I don't know. Can't we talk about this in the pit?"

Lisa's sarcastic expression answered for her.

Andrews sighed. "You know the business. One week it's strokes, the next it's meningitis. Weird cases always seem to cluster."

"Not like this."

"Lisa, how long have you been a nurse here?"

"Twenty years."

"I'm sure it'll blow over and we'll be talking about a rash of ectopics or gastric cancer."

Lisa paused for a moment. "Maybe. But I'm charging tonight, and I don't want fourteen more on my shift. I don't get excited very easy, but I'm scared. And it's not just me. Look around. People are worried. They're talking."

Andrews nodded dispassionately.

"What do you think's causing it?"

"Not sure," Andrews admitted. "Could be a ruptured blood vessel. A bad shigella outbreak. There's a huge differential."

"But have you ever seen anything like it before?"

"I know what you're getting at, Lisa. Fourteen gastrointestinal bleeds and fourteen deaths. Healthy people. Less than twenty-four hours of symptoms." He raised his voice just enough over his normal monotone to show emotion. "I don't understand why I'm losing patients, but that's what this job means—keeping your cool when you don't know what the hell to do. We're doing everything we can."

"That's just the point. What if this is something new? We have outbreak protocols. I think it's time to think about calling in public health."

"We have protocols for mass casualties. We don't have protocols for throwing our hands up in the air and saying something funny is going on. Our resources are stretching just fine, and I don't see any reason to shake our staff's confidence any further by acting like we need someone to come in and save us. We're a level one trauma center, and one of the best. And I'll decide when we need to call in the Mounties. I need you to do your job."

"I always do my job." She turned around sharply, yanked open the door and nearly stumbled over the resident bounding toward the door.

"Rob!" he gasped. "You need to see this now." The resident strode toward the open break room, where nearly the entire emergency room staff had clustered.

"Triage."

Andrews peered overhead at the lone television set mounted from the ceiling. A red bar with the byline BREAK-ING NEWS: PENTAGON HACKED stretched across the screen. The lone reporter on the screen was stalling to fill time.

". . . Once again, we have no confirmation that the reference to Los Angeles is anything more than an elaborate hoax. We have so far no comment from Pentagon spokespeople. In a short period of time we expect to have commentary from computer security expert. . . ."

"What is she talking about?" asked Andrews impatiently.

A short woman in flowered scrubs turned around. "Someone hacked into the Pentagon's Web site. They left some kind of threat. The Pentagon hasn't said what the threat is yet."

". . . We will have an update from Los Angeles shortly. Again, as of yet there is no confirmation that this is anything more than a hoax . . ."

"Why did she say Los Angeles?"

Andrews backed out of the room, lost in thought as he wandered toward the flow board.

"Dr. Andrews." The insistence in Carol's voice drew attention to her ashen face as she pointed toward a chair by one of the computer terminals where her friend was sitting. "It's Daru. She's sick."

"Daru?" Andrews walked around the table to where she sat. The pallor was only partially hidden by the perspiration on her forehead.

She looked dazed. Her voice was soft, uncharacteristically slow. "I'm all right. I just need to sit down for a minute."

Gently, he spoke to her. "Daru, it's been a rough couple days for all of us. I really don't want you to feel discouraged. This is not typical, and you'll bounce right back. Why don't you take the rest of the day off?"

Daru nodded weakly. As she stood, a thin trail of blood trickled down her pant leg onto the white marble floor. Her frightened eyes met Andrews's.

"Wait right there, Daru. Carol, why don't you keep an eye on her for a minute."

Andrews turned briskly away. "Lisa," he announced into his walkie-talkie.

"What do you need, Rob?" Lisa's curt voice emerged from the break room.

"Lisa, Daru's not well. Can you type and cross her now for eight units of blood, right after you put in two large-bore IVs?"

Lisa's surprise lasted only a second before she turned toward the supply room. "I'll put her in twenty-one." She referred to one of the three negative air-pressure rooms used for infectious isolation.

"Full gown and gloves precautions. Please enforce that on anyone who fits the bill tonight. I'm going to give public health a call. It might be a long night."

Andrews walked toward his office after taking a quick detour to wash his hands.

"Dr. Andrews!" a voice called from the front desk. "There's a phone call for you. Caller ID says they're calling from Washington, D.C.!"

NINE

April 8

JIM Summers sauntered down the corridor toward the Biodefense office, passing dozens of staff officials wearing shirts and ties. Ahead of him in the corridor, he saw dozens more walking purposefully through the halls, cutting in and out of offices along the way. *Why are they all walking so fast?* It was only eleven-thirty.

Of course, for most of the ties, the day is half over by then. Jim referred to the nameless Pentagon staff by their dress code. Jim was not one of the ties. Although he occasionally ran into a few people who dressed down a bit, no one else took it to an art form the way Jim did. His "Welcome to Hell" T-shirt from Hell City in the Cayman Islands was in a class by itself today.

He got a few uneasy looks by passersby, and thought the crowd could use a little lightening up. He whistled a few bars from the "Colonel Bogey March" from *The Bridge over the River Kwai* and savored the collective awkwardness of the corridor's occupants. He ducked into the mail room around the corner from the Biodefense office to check his box.

"Morning, Moneypenny," Jim greeted the secretary in the room. Ever since he had started to work at the Pentagon, he fancied himself a spy of sorts and never tired of the joke.

The secretary sighed as she looked at her watch. "I do hope you'll get some sleep one of these days, Jim. You can't keep up this schedule."

Jim supposed he was the only one in the whole Pentagon who rarely made it to work before noon. He had never quite made the switch from his academic schedule. He still considered late evening his most productive hours.

He passed one of the mail clerks on the way to his box. "Howdy, ma'am."

She was in her midtwenties, and hot. Jim rarely lost the opportunity to get to know her type. He'd asked her out once before, and she had gracefully declined. Jim was getting up the courage to ask her again.

"Hey, Jim."

"What's new these days?" Jim hoped for a conversation.

"Lot of commotion in the computer wing. No idea what's going on."

"They installing a new patch or something?"

She shrugged. "Don't ask me. I just work here. See you later."

"Yeah, that would be great," Jim commented to her back.

Jim retrieved his mail, then walked into the lounge in the Biodefense office. He leaned back on one of the couches and sifted through the handful of envelopes. With his other hand he reached toward the telephone on the end table and pushed one of the speed-dial buttons.

"Computer Support."

"Hey, Tom. How are things?"

"Oh, Jim. It's nuts down here. People are leaning on us, hard. I've never seen so much finger pointing and shouting."

"Why?"

"You didn't hear? Network was hacked."

"I'll be right over." Jim hung up the phone, dropped his mail on the end table, and jumped to his feet. Since Jim relied so heavily on his supercomputer, he had made friends with most of the technical support group. Actually, Jim considered himself one of the techies, and often had visits from the information technology staff wanting to sound off on some security problem with him. Jim only knew he had an in with the network crowd, though, when he got his first invitation to attend a Star Trek convention with "the guys."

A minute later, Jim opened the door to the network administration office. Sure enough, inside was a who's who of the Pentagon information technology staff. Two of them were having a spirited discussion.

"But we weren't hacked. Our system is totally secure."

"Tell that to the secretary of defense."

"He called you himself?"

"Mad as a hornet."

"Did you tell him it wasn't us?"

"Tried to."

Jim walked up to the pair amid several other onlookers. "What's going on, guys?"

"The media is having a field day saying our network was hacked."

"Was it?" Jim asked.

"Hell, no. Some doofus infiltrated a bunch of name servers across the country. He changed the domain lookup for our Web site to some hack page with a message."

Jim thought through the jargon. "I see. So when people try to connect to the Pentagon's Web site, they get redirected somewhere else?"

"Exactly, classic DNS hijacking, only this guy made it real transparent. That's why everyone thinks we were cracked. It's completely bogus. All the security breaches happened somewhere else, not here."

"Just to show he could do it? What'd he redirect people to, a porn site or something?"

"No, the site that comes up just shows some sort of a cryptic message. Just a rant. Doesn't mean anything."

"Can I take a look?" Jim asked.

Someone in the group handed Jim a sheet of paper. "This is what our Web site showed up as."

Jim read the message carefully, then read it again.

The epidemic in Los Angeles
is Allah's warning of the coming plague.
He will unleash the nanodeath on the infidels.
His nanomachines cannot be stopped until they have
destroyed every American man, woman, and child.
The jihad is at the doors of New York and Chicago and
will spread to every faithless village unless
America leaves Israel to its place in Greater Palestine.

"Why didn't anyone tell me about this?" Jim demanded.

"What, it's just some psychotic mumbo-jumbo."

"Yeah, maybe. But this reads to me like a bioterror threat."

"You serious? You think it's real?"

"Is anyone looking into it?"

A few of the group shrugged. No one answered.

"I need this." Jim folded the paper and headed immediately for the door. *What do these guys get paid for? How could they sit on such an obvious threat?* Jim slammed the door to the office as he walked back to the lounge.

On entering Biodefense headquarters, he called out, "Eva! Sam! Get out here!"

His colleagues emerged from the back offices. "What's the matter, Jim?" Eva asked.

"Look at this." He handed the paper to Eva. Sam read the message over her shoulder.

"Where did this come from?" asked Sam.

"It's a hacked message. Just showed up on the Pentagon Web site."

"Is it confirmed?" Eva followed up.

"I don't have any idea. I don't think anyone even knows about this. I ran into it by pure chance."

"We better get on the phones," Sam suggested. "Let's start with Los Angeles emergency rooms, see if anything turns up."

"Where are Alan and Steve?"

Eva looked to the schedule on the desk. Their two colleagues were on vacation, she knew, but Alan was neurotic enough to leave an itinerary of their trip behind in case of emergency. "Looks like they're going to be on the river this morning."

"Lousy timing."

Eva suggested a plan. "Let's get started. Jim, why don't you see if Alan has his cell phone on? Sam, you check the hospitals. I'll check in with Los Angeles public health and emergency ops people. It just so happens I've met them once before." Eva walked toward the nearest phone. Looking back over her shoulder, she said, "Maybe we finally get some action, eh? Good work, Jim."

"I'll start with UCLA," Sam agreed. "If something big is going on, one of the big E.R.'s might have noticed something by now."

TEN

April 8

"LEFT reverse! We can't take this one head on!" Steve Adams shouted his command over the sound of crashing water. The champagne foam of the river beneath bubbled only five meters ahead where the rapids coursed over a submerged rock. The sun baked the side of Steve's blue raft, reflecting off the gold inscription on the boat's pontoon: *Wandering South.*

Alan Thorpe thrust his paddle backward as the current nearly jerked it from his hand. His wife, Anita, and his daughter, Emily, were already vigorously stabbing the water in front of him. Emily shouted, "Pull your weight, Dad, or we'll leave you in the river!"

Alan formed a retort, but lacked the breath to reply. The raft gained speed until it folded nearly in half before sliding around the rock through a chute on one side. The raft then spun around completely as it coasted into calmer water.

Emily shook the water out of her hair while Alan's white knuckles slowly relaxed on his paddle grip. The raft coasted into an opening in the sheer cliffs that had lined the river, and the water eased into a gentle roll along the newly exposed shore.

Alan felt uncomfortably dependent on the others in his first real whitewater run. It was about the only aspect of his life that Alan could remember when he had not been the leader, officially or otherwise. This included Biodefense, despite the fact that Alan Thorpe was the only nondoctor on the team. Having completed an MBA at Stanford, his first job was with Boeing, where he had rapidly risen to senior executive. Subsequently, he had served as a chief political advisor to the governor of Washington, and later as director of emergency operations in Seattle, where his tenure had been a template for emergency ops centers throughout the country.

Part of his success, Alan knew, was his fanatical insistence on leaving nothing to chance. In high school, his first act as student body president had been to lobby for doubling the number of fire and earthquake drills the school ran. As a reward for his well-known aversion to risk, his graduating class had voted him "most likely to stuff his money in his mattress."

It might be expected that a man who had his own private bomb shelter in his basement would produce a daughter voted "most likely to lose her shirt" by her high school class. Emily had been the sole reason Thorpe's blood pressure was twenty points higher than normal. Nevertheless, he doted on her, and followed her social life as a journalism student at UCLA like a private detective. At least that's what Emily kept telling him it felt like. Since they had arrived at the North Fork of the American River, Alan had reminded his daughter more than once that Steve was a full generation her senior.

The whitewater trip had been Steve Adams's idea, and as soon as Emily had gotten wind of the possibility, she hadn't let her parents rest until they agreed to take her on one of Steve's adventure vacations. Adams's exotic hobbies were well known to all of the members of Biodefense, and included poisonous reptiles, catamaran racing, and dangerous bacteria. Steve had tried for years to lure the others on some of his more unconventional vacations, but this was the first time any of them had agreed.

"Looks like that's the last of it," Steve said calmly as he put his paddle across his lap, content to enjoy the pristine wilderness they were now drifting through. That same morning, the river had raced through a canyon with two-thousand-foot cliffs and difficult rapids known as the Giant Gap. They had spent their first night on the shore in the Tahoe National Forest, and after shooting the Gap, had planned on some fishing in some of the calmer waters.

Steve had promised relaxation, something Alan had badly needed. But now that Alan was here, he wondered exactly what "relaxation" meant to Steve. He had once visited Steve's Washington, D.C., home. Although it appeared on the outside like just another house in a lawn-mowing, barbecuing, suburban neighborhood, the impression faded quickly once Alan went inside. Part laboratory, part Indian snake-charming pit, the home smelled of the reptilian pets Alan noticed had the roam of the house. Steve's "rare germ collection" was enough to make even Alan question what sort of enthusiast he worked with. Alan had wondered at the time what Steve must have been like at the neighborhood block party. Most likely, any neighbors who had been inside Steve's home would have passed on the homemade sushi he was fond of making.

But Steve was affable enough. As complimentary as he was perceptive, he rarely joined in the teasing that sailed back and forth between Jim and Eva. He was softspoken, thoughtful, and gentle. And he was thorough. His meticulous attention to detail was unmatched by anyone on the team, and the notes he brought to the team's brainstorming meetings were more like legal documents than the sketch pads the others would bring. Alan often thought it odd that such a careful academician would so freely abandon common sense on his frequent adventure vacations.

Alan and Anita welcomed the change in scenery, hoping to catch their breath. Emily, a bit disappointed, stretched her legs over the side of the *Wandering South* and dangled her feet in the water. Her position seemed coincidentally to flash less of her swimsuit and more of everything else toward Steve than the other members of the crew. She glanced at him periodically for effect.

Alan exchanged a weary look with Anita, but then cocked his ears when a distant mechanical clicking descended from the sky. Adams muttered to the others, "Some people always take the easy way in." A helicopter descended toward the beach ahead of them, keeping its distance from the cliffs rising up beyond the beach.

Emily put her elbows on her knees and looked up. She turned her head toward Steve and asked, "What on earth are they looking for? There's a road just a few miles up . . ."

A loudspeaker on the helicopter echoed its intention as it hovered over the shore.

"Mr. Thorpe, please beach your raft."

"Now look, Steve. I agreed to the rapids, and I did it. I didn't agree to some kind of wild helicopter game. I need a rest, for heaven's sake."

Steve shrugged innocently. "I didn't arrange this." Anita shot him a questioning look. "Honest!" Emily swung her paddle into the water and helped guide the raft toward the shore underneath the deafening chop of the blades.

The travelers disembarked and looked up toward the helicopter. The insignia *U.S.A.F.* splashed across the military green of the fuselage. The door swung open and a rope ladder tumbled down. The close-shaved head of a soldier emerged from the helicopter and he shouted out, "Dr. Adams, Mr. Thorpe. Please step inside." After a pause, he added, "All of you."

Thorpe yelled back uneasily at the figure in the helicopter. "Who the hell are you and how did you find us?" He received only a beckoning wave as an answer.

Thorpe grabbed the rope ladder and hoisted himself up, motioning for the others to stay put. As he ascended the ladder, the soldier reached out and grabbed his arm to help him inside. "What's the meaning of this?" he demanded.

"There's been an attack." The soldier said as he reached out to wave up the others, and Thorpe nodded for them to follow.

"What kind of attack?" Thorpe shouted above the roar of the rotors.

The soldier turned without speaking and crawled toward the front seat, pulling out a single sheet of folded paper from a folder. He handed the paper to Thorpe.

Alan scanned through the text on the paper.

Adams climbed into the chopper. "What's this about?" he asked.

Thorpe ignored the question. He handed Adams the sheet of paper, and asked the pilot, "Where are you taking us?"

"To the Pentagon—direct flight, sir."

Thorpe shouted back, "No! There's no time. We're going to Montana."

"I'm sorry, sir. My orders are from the secretary of homeland security, relayed personally."

"Then get me the secretary now, so I can tell him to call me in Montana!" Alan turned toward Emily and Anita.

"Come on, buckle up. Let's hope this part of the trip will be a lot less bumpy!"

"Where are we going?" Emily asked.

"There's an outbreak. I'm going to Montana. Once we get there, you're taking the first flight back home to D.C."

Emily gave a disappointed look. "Why can't we stay with you? This is supposed to be our vacation!"

"It's only vacation until you get deathly ill. I want you as far away from the disease as you can get."

Anita's unsettled look pierced Alan's sense of control, conveying effectively the worry she would feel until they were back together. Alan felt his gut sink long before the helicopter took off.

ELEVEN

April 8

JIM Summers yanked his cell phone from its holster as he watched the roof come into focus through the helicopter window. He jabbed at the buttons with his stubby fingers. The breathtaking vista of mountainous green folds of evergreens coursed by networks of rivers was utterly lost as Jim fixated on finding the right phone number.

"Have you got the link?" There was a short pause.

"Listen, Mike. I know the Pentagon has this thing with security, but I don't care if you link me through the damn telephone. All I have to do is send commands. I . . ." Another long pause. "But there is nothing on that computer that anyone can decipher without a computer twice as big as mine, and there's no such thing!" Summers drummed his fingers on his seat belt harness. "Let me put it this way. Unless I can pull that computer's strings from Montana, I may as well be in Antarctica. OK. You said they had a satellite link. Find a way to secure it." He snapped the phone shut.

"What's the matter? Did we interrupt your chess game with your computer?" Eva Vanorden winked at him from the next seat over.

Jim smiled. "Gotta be tough with them, Eva. They're cut from the same cloth as every other government employee. Giving me a bunch of B.S. about how I can't run my Pentagon workstation remotely from a nonsecure site. How am I supposed to fight a war without access to the battle plans?"

"MacArthur never knew how easy he had it." Eva shook her head sympathetically.

The pilot stood and motioned for his passengers to unfasten their straps and disembark.

Jim had been peeved for the last few hours, and was just starting to loosen up. He could handle an emergency. He just didn't like to hear about it from one of the mail room employees, however pretty she was. Even that hadn't been too bad. What bugged him was that he had finally gotten to the punchline ahead of Alan, only to discover that Alan was still a step ahead of him.

Once Jim had discovered the message, he and Eva and Sam had spent the next two hours trying to phone emergency rooms in Los Angeles to confirm that the threat was a hoax. They got an earful that something was happening that may well be the real thing. By the time he started to piece together a rash of unusual deaths in Los Angeles, he got a call from Levin telling him that Thorpe wanted the whole team relocated to Hamilton, Montana.

Summers had no idea how Thorpe found out about the situation faster than he did, and had even less idea what would possess his colleague to suggest such a rash move. *Why not just cut ourselves off from every useful bit of infrastructure we have and set up camp in the local YMCA?*

Such thoughts had been running through his mind, with various backwater locations substituted as the punchline, while he had been struggling to arrange access to his computer from whatever swamp in Montana Thorpe had picked as his destination. Soon Thorpe was going to hear in plain terms what a stupid decision this whole relocation had been when the team should be getting to work.

Sam Goldberg was the first off the helicopter. A guide was waiting for their arrival, and led them inside to an elevator. Jim and Eva followed them inside, through a series of corridors, to a large bank of offices. Before they had even turned the corner, Jim heard Thorpe's voice issuing commands.

"Right. We're going to need to clear out everyone except a secretary and the lab operations manager. Just temporary, I'm sure. And the conference room has got to be secure. Nobody goes near it without top-secret security clearance. That's just the way it has to be." Thorpe acknowledged Goldberg, Summers, and Vanorden with a grateful expression.

"Good to see you," he greeted them.

"Hey, Alan, why the camping trip? It's been some job to find something out here that can talk to a real computer."

"Tell you what, Jim. I think everything will be clearer in a minute. I've got a video conference set up inside. Steve's just setting up the equipment." Thorpe pointed to a conference room annexed to the offices. He looked at Eva. "How was your flight?" he asked.

"Exciting. I didn't realize how beautiful it was up here. *Gezellig!*" Jim was used to Eva's scattered Dutch exclamations.

Jim looked out the window and noticed for the first time

that the mountains were a lot more picturesque than he had realized. The stress of the last few hours was wearing off, and Jim was anxious to get to work. His mind was already running through the possibilities for how he and his computer could figure out the scope of the problem they faced.

Thorpe nodded. "I hope we get a chance to see some of it before too long."

Goldberg shook Thorpe's hand. "Good idea to come here, Alan. They say this place is the best in the business."

Summers frowned. "Why does everyone act like we just showed up in Shangri-La?" He followed the others into the conference room.

Steve Adams waved to the others. Next to him, a woman in her midforties crawled under a lectern plugging cables into a bank of electronic equipment. She shook herself off and walked toward the new arrivals, extending her hand. "Susan Patrick," she said.

Summers nodded as Thorpe introduced him as well. "Susan," Alan continued, "is research operations director of the Rocky Mountain Laboratory. She has a top-secret clearance, and I've invited her to be a part of our discussion. We are setting up shop here by her gracious invitation, and as laboratory director, we're going to need her cooperation."

"I think we're set, Alan," said Adams, who adjusted a pair of cameras on the wall by the lectern, and then joined the others in seats along an oblong table facing a mosaic of flat-panel monitors against the far wall. The monitors flickered to life, coalescing as an image of a woman came into sharp focus. Subtle motion evidenced that the image was a live video feed.

Alan began by looking toward the woman on the screen. "Thank you for your patience. We now have our entire Biodefense team assembled, as well as Susan Patrick, who is director of the laboratory here." He turned his attention to the Biodefense team. "We're connected to the Pentagon, where I'm sure you'll recognize Sandra Ewington, national security advisor." Thorpe looked back to the cameras. I understand you have some questions for us, Ms. Ewington."

Seamlessly, Ewington took over. "Thank you for assembling so quickly. I had hoped to meet with you in person, but this is indeed a close substitute. A new priority has emerged in our national defense. As you know, earlier this morning a number of computers that serve as part of the backbone of the Internet were hacked, redirecting visitors to the Pentagon's main Web site to another location. The new site, we have discovered, links to a server in Indonesia that displays the text you are by now familiar with." Alan made a motion for her to pause, and handed out copies of the message on the Web site to the Biodefense members. Jim fingered the document as he reread the message.

Ewington resumed her briefing. "Our assets in place in Indonesia have seized the server. The owner is a small businessman who used the Internet for advertising his textiles business. He seems to be genuinely uninformed about the message on his computer, and has no record of association with unsavory groups in the area. My colleagues have assured me that we have people working on the breach of the Internet servers as well.

"The message in question makes reference to a plague directed at the city of Los Angeles. I'm getting conflicting reports from Health and Human Services, the CDC, and local public health officials in Los Angeles, all of whom are looking into it. I'm getting the sense that this means they all keep calling each other asking the same questions. I was hoping you might have some more definitive information."

Jim watched Eva's impatient expression. They had presented this problem over and over to seemingly deaf ears.

Despite intense national attention on bioterror defense, the chain of command was still redundant and competitive. At least five totally separate chains of command were in operation, each one eager to assume center stage and likely to investigate independently in an emergency. Local public health officials were likely to do their own research before reporting an outbreak. The health and human services department was likely to do the same. Once the CDC was informed, a separate investigation was begun. Local response liaisons for bioterrorism in the defense and homeland security departments had only informal contacts with other public health agencies. Intelligence agencies, including both FBI and CIA, had their own totally separate counterterrorism command structures. Every time Alan had brought this up to Biodefense's congressional oversight committee, the response was something like, "Which group would you cut? Besides, the more people looking into it, the better."

Sam responded first to the NSA director's question. "On discovery of the security breach, we made inquiries to public health officials and emergency rooms in Los Angeles to assess the seriousness of the threat. We discovered that several hospitals have contacted the public health department over the last twenty-four hours with news of a series of unusual deaths from sudden, unexpected gastrointestinal bleeding. Most of the reports were just notifications of planned autopsies. Estimated combined casualties have been greater than fifty. Because the presentation, gastrointestinal bleeding, is not uncommon, it is only within the last few hours since we started making phone calls, and particularly since news of the Pentagon Web threat hit, that anyone suspected this was part of a larger pattern.

"Of particular concern, UCLA Medical Center has reported that now three health care workers serving on consecutive days have shown similar symptoms to early victims, and one of them has died. In none of these cases were doctors able to identify a clear cause of death, and the spread to health care workers suggests an infectious cause."

Sandra Ewington frowned. "So there is something going on?"

Jim looked to Sam. He nodded. "Very likely."

The national security advisor continued. "Another question. Does anyone report anything similar in the other cities mentioned in the message: New York or Chicago?"

Eva shook her head. "I made some calls, but found nothing similar in either place."

Jim looked at Alan. "I have a question. If this sounds like the real thing, what are we doing in Montana?"

Sam looked sideways at Jim with surprise. "What, you don't know?" he asked. More diplomatically, Sam continued, "Sorry, no reason you should know. The Rocky Mountain Laboratory is the newest, best-equipped facility in the world for biosafety level four operations. It seems, Jim, we're dealing with a possible deadly pathogen that strikes quickly and is highly infectious. This laboratory, and one in San Antonio, are the only labs remotely equipped to study such a disease west of Atlanta."

"Oh."

Ewington asked nobody in particular, "I'm not yet clear on the phrasing of the message. *Nanomachines* and *nanodeath* are odd words to use. How do you interpret these?"

Jim cleared his throat. "We were talking about that on the flight over. My impression is that such a reference can only mean the threat of a nanotechnological weapon."

Ewington gave a puzzled look. "I don't know what that means."

Thorpe looked at Jim. "Have we even talked about a nanotechnological weapon? What the hell is that?"

Jim shook his head and answered. "Nobody believes it's

possible. The idea is that you design a microscopic machine that can reproduce itself. Such a machine is essentially an artificial virus. But nobody has any idea how to manufacture such a machine, what properties it would have, or what impact it would have if it contacted living organisms."

Ewington resumed speaking. "That is reason for concern, Dr. Summers. Perhaps somebody knows after all. If so, we are dealing with a fourth type of weapon of mass destruction. We're pretty familiar with the usual chemical, biological, and nuclear weapons. If this disease is the manifestation of a new type of weapon, it's one we know nothing about, and it's time we found out. Please keep me advised as soon as you have any new information. If this is real, the nation is counting on you to find a way to stop it."

The screen went blank, and the members of Biodefense looked at each other solemnly.

Eva spoke first. "How is that even possible, Jim? If someone were developing such an advanced weapon, shouldn't we have intelligence on it years beforehand? I guess I don't know what the raw materials or precursors would be, but something that high-tech needs supplies, and how is some crackpot terrorist going to develop this without us knowing? It smells fishy to me."

Thorpe massaged his temples in his hands. "Right, Eva. I don't think it is possible. But there are dozens of dead people who don't care what I think. What if it's true? We've always talked about how the main reason our worst nightmares aren't here is because nobody has the gall to study them. Maybe it's easier than it sounds. You name the field, and there's no shortage of disaffected scientists to be seduced."

"It's bogus, Alan. Just a cover story, nothing more," Eva said. "We need to get to work, and the first thing is to get some samples."

Goldberg agreed. "And I can't do anything here. I have to get to L.A. where I can see the patients, talk to the docs there. We'll beat this thing, quick."

"Good to have some real work for a change, no?" Jim's enthusiasm seemed to resonate with Eva and Steve. Alan and Sam seemed more reserved.

Alan looked at Jim. "Wish I could help you get set up here." He then looked to Adams and Vanorden. "The lab's yours, kids. I hope I'm overreacting, but I have to get back to Washington. Things are going to happen quickly, and my job is to advise the president."

Jim heard a waver in Alan's voice. *He's scared,* Jim thought.

Steve gave Alan a reassuring look. "You taking the girls back?"

Alan nodded.

Alan cleared his throat and rubbed the corner of his eye. "Try to figure it out before I get there. *Please.*"

PART II
NANOGAMES

People tell me about miniaturization, and how far it has progressed today. They tell me about electric motors that are the size of the nail on your small finger. And there is a device on the market, they tell me, by which you can write the Lord's Prayer on the head of a pin. But that's nothing; that's the most primitive, halting step in the direction I intend to discuss. It is a staggeringly small world that is below. In the year 2000, when they look back at this age, they will wonder why it was not until the year 1960 that anybody began seriously to move in this direction.

—Richard Feynman, at a speech to the American Physical Society on December 29, 1959.

My budget supports a major new national nanotechnology initiative worth $500 million . . . Just imagine, materials with ten times the strength of steel and only a fraction of the weight; shrinking all the information at the Library of Congress into a device the size of a sugar cube; detecting cancerous tumors that are only a few cells in size. Some of these research goals will take twenty or more years to achieve. But that is why—precisely why—there is such a critical role for the federal government.

—President William J. Clinton, at a speech to the California Institute of Technology on January 21, 2000.

I think it is no exaggeration to say we are on the cusp of the further perfection of extreme evil, an evil whose possibility spreads well beyond that which weapons of mass destruction bequeathed to the nation-states, on to a surprising and terrible empowerment of extreme individuals.

—Bill Joy, cofounder of Sun Microsystems, discussing genetics, nanotechnology, and robotics. *Wired*, April 2000.

TWELVE

April 8

"YOU'RE the healthiest-looking patient we've ever had."

Goldberg felt like smacking the pilot after he made the comment for the third time during the flight. The closest transport he could get to fly him to Los Angeles was a LifeFlight helicopter stationed in Billings. It amazed him how much bureaucracy could live in the upper levels of an organization that handled nothing except unpredictable life-or-death emergencies. After half an hour of wrangling over a flight plan, permissions, and staff, the chopper was dispatched to Hamilton, Montana.

He was irritated about the delay, and irritated that he had had to wait while two useless crew members were rounded up—"It's policy: we always fly with a full medical crew." He probably wouldn't have been as irritated, however, if his thoughts hadn't been continually interrupted by the curious pilot's quest to pry information out of him throughout the flight. He ignored him again. It hadn't helped that Sam had made two cryptic phone calls on his cell phone as soon as he stepped on board the chopper. Can't blame the pilot for being curious.

Sam plucked another hair from his beard. *It'll probably be something obvious,* he consoled himself for the hundredth time as the helicopter circled over the ocean from the setting sun back toward the sprawling city. *It always is.* All he needed to do was see a few cases, find out what the doctors had missed, and reason it out. Doctors always thought of themselves as scientists. Goldberg had long since recognized that nothing could be further from the truth. The only profession that medicine genuinely had much in common with was auto repair. *We're just a bunch of cocky mechanics.* Take a history. Run diagnostics. Everything had an algorithm. There was nothing genuinely new in medicine—new diseases were just wrinkles on old processes.

What bothered him was that he couldn't yet see it. *Lousy data,* he thought for the two-hundredth time. Why couldn't anyone be trusted to relay something as simple as a few symptoms correctly? *The patients had massive gastrointestinal bleeding—probably,* he added. *Bled out almost on presentation. Short incubation period. Maybe a day. Has to be infectious, spread by mouth. No other way.* He subconsciously seemed to think that running through the logic again would change the conclusion. It didn't. There was no conclusion. He couldn't think of any virus or bacterium that he knew that fit the data. *Lousy data,* he thought again.

The helicopter descended, and the red cross on top of the helipad at the Ronald Reagan UCLA Medical Center sharpened into focus. The chopper touched down uneventfully. Nobody was there to meet him. *A bad sign.* He closed his eyes while the pilot ran through his postflight procedures, and finally pushed open the door with one last look askance at his mysterious passenger. Sam stepped out.

He looked around. The helipad was totally deserted. He walked toward the single large elevator on the roof. Once inside, he pushed the button for the ground floor, marked ER in bright red letters. The door opened after a slow descent. Goldberg was assaulted by a faint smell.

It was a lemony smell, sickeningly sweet, that evoked a visceral response to a trained nose. It was the smell of Lysol, in industrial doses that could only mean a coverup. A half-second later Goldberg whiffed the undercurrent, a nearly imperceptible odor of bloody stool. As he stepped from the elevator into the loading bay of the E.R., the smell unwillingly triggered half-memories from site visits to VA hospitals and long-forgotten days on inpatient wards, when the inimitable smell of bloody diarrhea trailed through hallways like sinews of an invisible web. The elevator door closed.

Sam's ears adjusted to the noise coming at him from every corner. Walking into the E.R. was like emerging into a busy corner of a morbid version of Disneyland. People crisscrossed gracefully, walking briskly to scattered destinations while others slouched on benches or against walls. It was anyone's guess whether the scene depicted utter chaos or an intricate machine.

The patients were the ones without scrubs. The thought oriented Sam as he subconsciously enumerated hospital staff and their charges. There had to be more than a hundred patients. They lined the hallways, sitting in chairs or simply on the floor. Every room appeared full or overfilled. He walked past the first room along the block of corridors circling the nurses' station.

Outside the room, a young Hispanic child sat on her

mother's lap. *Probably three years old,* Goldberg thought. Her huge dark eyes looked up at Goldberg, frightened. Her mother held her about the waist tightly, bouncing the girl on her lap nervously. The girl was pale, uncomfortable, but alert. On the girl's wrist was a plastic tag indicating she was a patient.

Sam looked into the room. An elderly woman lay on a bed, half clothed, half covered by blankets. A nurse was adjusting one of many wires on her chest, glancing at the monitor displaying the patient's vital signs. A fold-up barrier stood in the middle of the room, warning of a recently mopped floor.

Sam felt pangs of remorse. He looked enviably to the staff scurrying about with stethoscopes around their neck, immersed in caring for the horde of sick, frightened patients. He wished he could put on his stethoscope and join them, carrying out a clearly defined job. He looked down. He was dressed in a sport shirt and slacks. He must look like a tourist, coming to see the carnage firsthand.

His insecurities mounted as he walked across the tiled floor. Instantly regretting his job, his responsibility, his charge, he sensed a danger around him that nobody else really understood. He began breathing more quickly, his chest tightening as his skin began to crawl. *What can I say to them? I'm not even trained in critical care.* And he was frightened in a way he had never experienced.

He'd had sick patients depending on him before. That was different. He knew his territory, knew how to examine a patient, how to review a colleague's report for weaknesses, missed diagnoses. But now someone had appointed him to a position known about by only a few hundred people in the world. He was in charge, and he was the only one who knew he was in charge.

A country of hundreds of millions of people thought that

they were protected from strange, horrible new diseases. They thought, if they thought about it at all, that their taxes had been spent for years on legions of trained scientists with contingency plans and antidotes. All they got here was one over-the-hill administrator five years removed from clinical practice wandering aimlessly across an emergency room contaminated with something no one could identify.

A nurse put a hand out to stop him. "You lost?" he asked.

"Who's your staff?"

Not used to being ordered by visitors, the nurse pointed. "You'll have to wait outside. We'll get to everyone."

"I'm Dr. Goldberg, from the National Counterterrorism Center. I'm here to speak to whoever's in charge."

The nurse straightened up and apologized. "Take your pick. Every E.R. doc and nurse we have is on around the clock rotating shifts now. There are eight docs here now."

"Is there a Dr. Andrews here?"

The nurse nodded. "That's him, over there." The nurse pushed the dispenser on a bottle of sterilizing alcohol hand gel clipped to his shirt, and rubbed his hands together as he walked away.

Goldberg strode over to the man indicated. He held out his hand. He felt his pulse in his throat. "Robert Andrews?"

Andrews turned around. "Yes?"

"Hi. I'm Sam Goldberg." Andrews's eyes were bloodshot. They stared blankly at Goldberg. A blue surgical mask hung loosely around his neck beside his stethoscope. Several pairs of latex gloves folded out of his shirt pocket. "Anyone tell you I was coming?" Sam added.

Recognition slowly crept into Andrews's face. "Thank God you're here. This place is insane. Come in here where we can talk." Andrews led Goldberg toward the conference room on the near corridor. He closed the door.

"Sorry to meet like this. Can you fill me in?" Sam opened.

Sam watched as gears churned while Andrews's sleepy brain processed the question.

"All right. Welcome to hell." Andrews looked back expectantly, then continued. "Sorry. This place gets to you, and this is way beyond anything we've seen before. I don't need to tell you we thought we'd seen everything." Goldberg nodded for him to continue, reaching up to finger his beard as Andrews spoke.

"First patient I can remember was almost three days ago. One of my students saw her first. Midforties, with mild flu-like symptoms for less than twenty-four hours. Diarrhea, muscle aches, fever, chills. The night before she presented, she started having some bloody discharge. Wasn't sure if it was vaginal bleeding or bloody diarrhea. In the morning on the day she came in, she had passed a few clots. By the time I saw her, she had arrested on the floor. Pale, toxic, dehydrated. Probably down at least five liters of fluid. Her entire pants were stained with blood. Almost as if a valve had turned on and the blood came out."

Goldberg refocused him, welcome to have the comfort of a traditional case presentation to grasp hold of. "Past medical history?"

"C-section. That's it. Family history of diabetes. No medications. No allergies. No sick contacts. No travel. Worked as a paralegal in a corporate law office."

Goldberg thought for a moment. "Regular periods?"

Andrews nodded. "Last period one week ago."

"So where did she bleed out from? I'm assuming you did an autopsy."

"Path is still working on it. They've never seen anything like it. Until now. We've had dozens of cases almost identical. I've been hounding them for preliminary results. They say she had hematomas in both the uterus and the bowel."

"Colon?"

"Right. Nothing in the small bowel. The colon was diffusely ulcerated. Uterus was the same way. This wasn't a bleed from an AVM or an ulcer—it was something eating the colon and uterus out from inside. And something else—though path is still investigating it."

"Tell me."

"Oral ulcers. Fresh. Whatever was eating her colon is in her mouth as well."

"Any of the other cases through path yet?"

"That's the problem. We've given the morgue more work in two days than they usually get in a month. Slow progress, but so far all the cases look about the same. Something is ulcerating right through mucosal surfaces in the GI tract as well as the genital tract in women. It happens within a day or two, and it invariably creates massive bleeding."

"Painful?"

Andrews shook his head. "Not at first. Kind of vague abdominal pain, no more than you'd expect from a case of gastro. Poorly localized. Usually nontender until the bleeding really starts, or until the bowel perforates. But if the patient survives for a day or two after the symptoms start, the pain can be excruciating. Probably from ischemic or ruptured bowel. We've already had one case of perforation with free air in the belly. We're pretty sure the bowel wall got eaten clear through. Pain is like you might expect with appendicitis, only at forty locations in the colon rather than one."

Goldberg turned his head. "What have you tried?" He plucked another hair from his chin.

"Just trying to keep them alive is hard enough. At first we thought it was just the usual GI bleed. Once one of our students got sick, last night, we started thinking about infection.

Two more nurses got sick about the same time. One is already dead. Then I hear about this weird note on the news, claiming some kind of terrorist threat. I don't know what to think. I'm sure hoping you have answers."

Goldberg ignored the comment. "You tried antibiotics?"

Andrews shrugged. "Too soon to really tell if it's helping. We started dripping in imipenem on a few patients. Thought we'd just kill every bug in sight. We'll see. Like I said, it's hard enough to keep on top of blood loss in these patients. They get shocky real easy. The GI guys scoped a few patients and said all they could see was blood. Nothing they could do. They're frustrated too. The surgeons are talking about surgically removing the large bowel on these patients, or embolizing the blood supply to it, but we're finding that the same bleeding from the mouth and esophagus starts a few hours later. We can't resect everything."

"What's the incubation time?"

"Maybe a day, two days at most."

"Do you have a quarantine?"

"Just gown and gloves. Some of us are wearing masks."

Goldberg winced. "We don't have much time. How are you handling the volume?"

"We're not. Every ICU bed is full. So are our floor beds. You can see the E.R. is crammed way past anything safe. Someone's looking into it—thinking about starting a mass casualty protocol. Look, the staff is scared to death. More than a dozen are refusing to work. Quit on the spot. I just hope we've seen the worst of it."

Goldberg stood at full height. His voice held a slight tremor. "I don't think we've even seen the beginning of it. If you didn't have another case, you could expect every person in Los Angeles with a sniffle or diarrhea to show up at your door. And there are going to be a lot more cases. You need a more aggressive approach: dismissing noncritical patients, mass triage on the first floor, using every office and closet as a patient room, strict hot zones for quarantine, and biofilter masks for everyone inside the hospital. How soon can I brief the senior staff?"

"I'll have everyone paged in twenty minutes."

"Make it ten. We've got another thirty hospitals to get to that are even less prepared."

"We?"

"Pay attention. You'll be doing the briefings in north Los Angeles tonight. All night."

Andrews's face tightened as Goldberg began to walk toward the exit. "Where are you going?" he asked nervously.

"I'm expecting someone. See you in ten minutes. And one more thing."

Andrews looked expectantly.

"Choose one patient, someone stable enough for life-flight to go to my colleagues at the Rocky Mountain Laboratory. They need samples, need to see a case. Let's send one of your intensivists with the patient. The facility has everything they'll need, but we'll need a good doctor out there to care for the patient. The helicopter is on the pad waiting."

THIRTEEN

April 8

GOLDBERG looked at his watch and cursed. He felt like pacing, like throwing up, like starting out at a jog and running until the hospital was a bad memory and he was safe. But he just stood passively, incapacitated by silent panic that he neither expressed nor confronted. He knew he would not be safe, no matter where he ran. He ran his fingers over his beard and plucked out a hair, only to look at it and discard it onto the asphalt.

It was like Windhoek. He remembered his first week there, arriving in a truck with a few crates of equipment and drugs in the capital of Namibia. Two years into medical school, he took off a summer to study infectious diseases in Africa. Arranging in advance for a small hut to use in the outskirts of Windhoek, he had planned to spend his first week observing at the hospital, talking to doctors there and setting up his research clinic.

As the truck pulled up, a throng of thousands of people nearly assaulted him, some prying at the crates in his truck, others looking emaciated and sickly sitting on the ground around the hut. He saw people with massively swollen legs, some with fungating masses on their faces, others with bright yellow tired eyes looking at him desperately. The visceral sense of fear when he realized for the first time he could not diagnose one in ten of these people's ailments with his paltry skills and equipment, let alone treat them, came flooding back now with a sense of déjà vu.

Finally. Sam watched a car pull up to the ambulance bay outside the loading dock of the E.R. A single man in his late fifties wearing a cardigan and slacks walked toward the hospital carrying a suitcase under one arm.

"Jack Harmer. L.A. Emergency Operations." He introduced himself. "Do you know where I could find . . ."

Sam cut him off. "I'm Goldberg. You got the supplies okay?"

Jack nodded.

Sam turned around and walked into the hospital, leaving Jack to follow him. As they reemerged into the E.R., a woman in pastel scrubs leaned over from a bedside in the trauma room to shout out, "Dr. Andrews said they were ready in the conference room." Goldberg nodded and kept walking toward the nurses' station.

Rounding the corner he stopped and turned toward Jack. "Look, Jack, there's no way I can get to enough hospitals tonight. I'll need you to run the show at a few."

He turned around before Jack even acknowledged the comment and opened the door to the conference room. Inside were about fifteen physicians, some sitting, some leaning against walls in groups of two or three. A few stopped talking as Goldberg entered. He walked toward a lectern at the front of the room, then thought better of it and sat on the edge of one of the long banquet tables.

Sam did not wait for the scattered conversations to die down before he started speaking. "I'm sorry I don't have time to get to know everyone and do this properly. I'm Sam Goldberg, working as part of an advance team on counter-bioterrorism." The room had suddenly become as quiet as the background noise from the E.R. would permit.

"This is it?"

Andrews looked apologetically. "It's tough to get everyone notified so quickly. More are probably on their way . . ."

"Who's chief of staff?"

"I'm Dr. Varno." A man from the back of the room stood.

Goldberg held up a hand. "You'll have to make sure everyone gets the information quickly." He sat up straight, one leg folded under and the other leg dangling off the table. "Most of you know a little of what's been going on, I assume. Sorry to bring more bad news. Let me tell you what I know.

"The last three days have seen an unusual number of cases of fatal GI bleeds in several areas of Los Angeles. You can discuss the case presentations and clinical details at length after I go. I'm here to tell you that we have received credible information that these cases may be an act of bioterrorism."

Several hands were raised among the physicians, which Goldberg ignored. "The threat is unusual in several ways. First, the diseases we're seeing do not fit any conventional pattern of disease or poisoning. The causative agent seems to cause diffuse ulceration in the colon and female GU tract, yet seems to have an unbelievably rapid incubation and disease course. The closest analogy I can get is a souped-up shigella outbreak more virulent and rapid than anything any of us have seen. You folks were kind enough to confirm that whatever is going on is probably infectious, as three of your staff have already acquired the disease. Thus far, everyone treated with the disease is still sick or dead.

"Here's what doesn't fit. An infectious diarrhea like shigella doesn't involve the oral mucosa or female GU tract. The symptoms also don't quite match, and cultures show none of these organisms. There's another hitch. The primary claim of responsibility came on a high-tech infiltration to the Pentagon's Web site. In taking responsibility, the perpetrators claimed that the agent was a nanotechnological device, an artificial virus. They refer to it as the 'nanodeath.'"

A murmur spread across the group. Goldberg continued, "I don't know how to fight this any better than you. I don't know what an artificial virus means, what it's capable of, except to say that since we have the opportunity to make history as the first victims, I suggest we don't underestimate the disease by assuming it will follow conventional rules about spread or containment.

"Here's what I want to see happen. I know these measures will seem dramatic to those of you who haven't been working with this disease yet, but I have no choice. Any issues of cost control are to come second—I have personal assurances that any cost overruns will be reimbursed as part of federal disaster relief.

"First, I want strict hot and cold zones enforced, with armed security guards. The entire first floor is to be a triage station only. The E.R. is hot. The main entrance to the hospital is hot. I want someone to mark a path on the floor in red tape connecting the two. You will expand triage from the E.R. into first-floor clinics for more space. I suggest you use one station for GI patients and the other for everyone else. Anyone not expected to die in the next week should be turned away. They're safer at home.

"On the floors upstairs, GI patient rooms are separated and hot. Every closet, every office, every room is to be cannibalized to expand capacity, if needed. I want you to be prepared to operate at five times your maximal capacity. Again, I want red tape with guards on each floor to remind staff of hot and cold zones.

"Visitors to cold areas must pass through decontamination. No one coming into the hospital—no one—is to cross into a cold zone without alcohol decontamination of hands and arms. Everyone working in a hot zone is to wear gloves, biofilter TB mask, and a dispenser with alcohol gel clipped to clothing that they must use between touching every patient.

"Triage is to happen quickly and efficiently. We do not run labs on everyone who comes in. We do not take samples. Everyone with clinical history of GI bleed or severe diarrhea is to be admitted. Because I want hot zones kept to an absolute minimum of patient rooms and first-floor triage, anyone with symptoms is to be transported in biocontainment. Jack Harmer, my associate from Los Angeles Emergency Ops, is to explain what that means."

Goldberg rested from his monologue, recited with precision and certainty, mesmerizing the horrified listeners. Jack Harmer stood up and unzipped his suitcase, pulling out a pile of plastic.

Harmer began speaking. "These are plastic pods, developed by the Department of Defense to contain breathable biofilters. They are in essence Ziploc bags for human beings." He pulled one off of the pile and shook it out to full dimension. "The procedure is simple. Whenever a decision is made to admit a patient from triage, they are placed in the bag, zipped in and locked, with sedation if necessary, and transported on a gurney to a patient room. Once inside a hot room, they are unzipped and instructed not to leave their patient room under any circumstances, similar to a locked TB ward. Pods are to be sterilized before reuse."

Goldberg nodded and resumed speaking. "For rooms without restrooms, patient gowns and masks will be required for transport to and from patient available restrooms, which are considered hot."

A woman from the back of the room interrupted. "I'm sorry; we can't do that. This flagrantly violates patient rights to refuse treatment. You want to run a sixties-style asylum. Not to mention we would terrify patients and families. People will be claustrophobic. It's unacceptable ethically."

Goldberg shot an icy look at her. "I'm sorry to bring this all so abruptly. The ethics debates have already been held, and I am informing you of the decisions. As a representative of the U.S. government, I am telling you that this hospital now falls under the jurisdiction of the U.S. military and is considered a war zone. I accept responsibility for the ethical consequences of these acts, and refer you to the secretaries of homeland security and health and human services for corroboration. You will enforce the guidelines, or you will be relieved, forcefully if necessary, from your responsibilities."

The woman nodded silently.

Goldberg swallowed. "One final note. I do not know if this is indeed an artificial virus. I do not know how it spreads. I don't know how it replicates. I do not know whether autoclaving or bleach will kill it. I don't know how or if we can treat it. I do know you will need to put your ancillary staff on a rotating schedule to handle the volume. This is not a time for vacations, for days off, for usual business practices. How you enforce that is your domain. I suggest that you inform personnel who will be working in the hot zone of the uncertainties that I have mentioned, with the caveat that we have every reason to believe that usual barrier protections are likely to be effective against this disease, as with any other. Your courage, hard work, and hopefully your successful diagnosis and treatment will have the assistance of the prayers and pleas of hundreds of millions of Americans before this is done."

Goldberg stood up and began walking toward the door. "Any questions?" His hand was on the doorknob. No one spoke.

"Good, because unfortunately, I doubt I have either answers or time." Goldberg swallowed hard. "If problems arise, contacts will be routed through the L.A. Emergency Operations office until the CDC can establish a presence here. Can someone show me to pathology?" A physician stood to join him, and Goldberg walked out the door with a nod to his guide. Harmer followed them out, leaving the suitcase of plastic pods behind.

AMIR Khalil watched the orange anemone fish duck in and out of the coral rock. Two red sea cucumbers waved as if a breeze were floating through the waters in the glass tank. The peaceful journey of the fish did nothing to temper the anxiety of its spectator. Amir looked again over his shoulder, now a half hour into his vigil. It was a half hour he had prepared for most of his life.

His job was as but one on a team of players whose size he did not know in a game with rules he only dimly perceived. Yet he knew his job was important. Supremely important, he sensed, as the years of waiting, contacts, assignments had never been handled with such urgency.

A hand touched his shoulder. "If only they could be set free." A man appeared aside Khalil, speaking softly, wistfully to his fellow observer.

Amir's pulse quickened at the sound. He studied the

features of a man he had never before met, but about whom much of his life revolved. Nearly as tall as Khalil, with angular clean-shaven face, the man's striking composure humbled Amir. He was dressed in olive drab scrubs, with coarse black hair visible only around his ears under his blue surgical cap. A nametag bore his photograph with the words "Vadim Mahmoud, Surgical Pathology."

After several long seconds Amir answered as instructed. "Without protection, how could they live?" Khalil studied the man's face, memorizing his every feature.

The man thrust an envelope from the pocket of his scrubs into Amir's hand.

Amir began to tremble as he looked down at the letter. When he looked up, he saw only the back of his colleague, and the figure of Ahmed Al Rasheed turned a corner out of the UCLA hospital lobby.

FOURTEEN

April 8

IT was Eva's seventh trip to the bathroom since arriving in Montana. Between those seven trips, she had visited the lab commissary twice, arranged for Susan Patrick to provide a hot lab orientation, and downed about a gallon of Diet Coke. Whenever her work became tense enough, her 20-ounce desk mug was replaced with a 128-ounce guzzler that rarely left her hand. At such times, her caffeine habit worked her smallish bladder about as hard as it did her brain. On the few occasions she had thought about it, she had decided her trips to the restroom were probably just one more way of keeping her awake longer.

And her brain didn't stop working when her bladder did. It never stopped, except for the four hours each night when she crashed into sleep. Friends, and especially boyfriends, had been forced to adjust quickly to her style of conversation, in which she would start a sentence, and before reaching the end of it, switch to another topic. To Eva, by the time the point was made halfway through a sentence, she had long been processing two or three other ideas. This game of conversational speed chess worked the same way in reverse. She seemed never to listen to the last few words of a sentence, after anticipating them and processing them before they were spoken. Her friends often recognized this and didn't bother finishing their sentences. On one occasion, the habit had been so annoying that her date dropped her off early from a party.

This had often been a source of quiet frustration between her and Steve Adams. Steve, a methodical and careful thinker, felt a special pleasure in the complete articulation of an idea, and Eva found herself wanting to speed him along with hand gestures whenever they talked. He seemed to respond by speaking, if anything, more slowly, deliberately choosing the words that Eva had already more or less decided were going to come. She found herself occasionally mouthing the last part of an idea with Steve, which didn't seem to bother him in the least, since he was usually quite satisfied in having gotten his point across. Steve never seemed to be irritated by her mannerisms. Or at least he never showed it. He was the sort of older brother that a girl was always grateful for but secretly envious of. Jim was the other brother, the kind who put spiders in your purse before a big date.

Although Eva knew her contribution to the team was valued, she lacked Steve's self-assurance and Jim's complete unflappability. As the youngest member of the team, though not by much, she often felt herself trying to compensate by enthusiasm. Her energy had always been a sort of defense for her. In graduate school, when she was also the youngest scientist around, she had made a point of keeping longer hours and a more intense workload than anyone else in the department. The more nervous she got, the faster she worked. One of her most important discoveries in graduate school, a novel immune factor that sensed one of influenza's viral coat proteins, had come only hours before her qualifying exam.

With a fresh problem, Eva's baseline hypomania was accentuated. Whether her energy came from the caffeine or the thrill of the chase was unclear, but she was a supreme game player and had never felt more focused than now, with perhaps the greatest game of her life. Her youth and her luminary career had rarely given her time to reflect on the human consequences of her work. To Eva, her trip to Hamilton had been all about strategy, tactics, and victory in a mind duel between herself and some unknown opponent. As she went about preliminary orientation in the lab, her thoughts were organizing themselves subconsciously, two or three ideas at a time. Now, walking back to the conference room to plan with Steve, she had pretty well identified her opening moves.

"Ready to talk, guys? We have a few minutes before the tour." She spoke before waiting until she had actually opened the door completely. As she stepped inside, she sighed, threw her hands up, and looked at Jim. "How can you eat?"

Jim had set up a microcosm of his Pentagon office. In a corner of the conference room, a table served as a makeshift desk for his computer. A snarl of wires crisscrossed behind the table without any attempt at order. A pair of cables meandered across the middle of the room to the lectern, where the ethernet hub and multimedia control outlets were housed. On his table, a cardboard box overflowed with Doritos next to a metal mixing bowl filled with a piquant salsa that Eva could smell from across the room.

Without looking up from his keyboard, Jim responded,

"Brain food. You should know; you've been drinking like a wino in Watts ever since we got here."

Eva gave him a look that said *humph* and commented further, "I see you brought your pinups with you." She pointed to four poster-sized printouts taped to the wall behind the computer. Each showed complicated tables of syntax and memory architecture that Jim used as frequent references while programming.

"We all have our vices. Maybe if I had your memory, I could leave these girls home."

Eva walked to the main conference table, where Steve sat writing in a notebook.

Sitting across the table from him, she stared Steve down until he looked up. "What did you learn about the lab?" Steve asked.

Eva watched Jim walk around the conference table and sit next to Steve. She knew Jim would violently deny it, since he was a brother to her in every sense but the biological, but she noticed he sat opposite her more often on days her blouse was somewhat more revealing.

"Definitely has adequate hot lab space. Good techs if we need them. I think we could be up and running as soon as we have samples to analyze. The whole basement is full of sequencers we can monopolize if necessary," she answered.

Steve put his pen down on his notebook after processing her answer. "That's the real question, isn't it? Is this thing going to be biologic? If it's not, I don't even know where to begin. Jim, what do you know about nanotechnology?"

"Fair amount, I guess. Sort of comes with the territory in high-end computing. Old college roommate's a nano jock at Caltech. I'll give him a ring today and see what I can learn." He stood up and went to retrieve his chips and salsa.

Eva looked at Steve. "If it is nano, don't you think it's going to be bionano?"

"You mean based on a bacterium or virus or something?" Jim walked back toward the table.

"It makes the most sense. It would be so much more complicated to create something so devastating from scratch." Eva sipped from her drink.

"Who's working on artificial life forms these days?" Steve asked Eva.

"Surprisingly few people. The problem is too difficult to give to a graduate student, so most academics are loath to take it up. The most high-profile group would be Craig Venter and Blake Hamilton."

Eva knew that Steve was also personally acquainted with the pair. The Nobel laureates had formed a joint venture back in 2002 for constructing an artificial life form. They were attempting to strip down the most simple of bacteria to the genes absolutely necessary for life.

"That's a thought. Maybe this 'nanobug' is really just a modified, targeted bacterium. But how would a terrorist group get the skill set to reprogram an artificial life form? Venter's experiment is proof of how tough it can be, and that's just in a laboratory setting, not in the cold cruel world."

Eva waited patiently for Steve to finish his analysis. "Maybe not; if you don't have a conscience, it might surprise you how quickly you get something that could thrive. The whole idea is to make something dangerous. Plus, a stripped-down bug could . . ." Her mouth skipped ahead to catch up with her brain. "It doesn't have any of the membrane proteins that would trigger an immune system. As a weapon, it could slip through the body undetected. And our antibiotics would be totally ineffective since these bugs lack most of the complicated proteins that the drugs target."

Steve tapped his finger on the table. "Eva, what about a prion? Wouldn't that be the ultimate nanomachine?"

"What's a prion?" Jim asked.

"It's a single protein that causes disease. Mad cow disease, Creutzfeldt-Jakob disease, and a few other nasty diseases are all caused by prions. They . . ."

Eva interrupted Steve's comment. "You're right, Steve. I didn't even think about that. There's a huge untapped realm of disease if you had reasonably sophisticated protein technology. Nobody in the West is stupid enough to create new prions, but if your goal is to cause trouble . . ."

"I *still* don't understand what a prion is."

Eva took over. "Protein zombies."

"What?" Jim and Steve asked simultaneously.

"A zombie. The legend is that zombies walk around spooky places at night and touch human beings, making them into zombies too. A prion is a single molecule—a protein only a few millionths the size of viruses. It has the same sequence of amino acids as a normal protein. The problem is that it's folded wrong. And when it comes in contact with normal proteins of the same type, it causes them to misfold too. That causes disease. In the case of mad cow disease, it destroys your brain."

"And these prions are infectious?"

"Very much so, only most of the known prion diseases tend to affect the brain. There aren't any known prion diseases of the GI tract."

"How would you detect such a disease?" Jim asked. He dipped a chip in his salsa and ate it.

"It's almost impossible," Eva answered back, trying to ignore Jim's open-mouth chewing. "When you sequence them, they show up just like regular proteins. They don't grow in culture. Unless you know what you're looking for, they're completely invisible."

"Sounds like a perfect bioweapon. How do you develop a new prion?" Jim asked.

"I don't know . . . randomly mutating heat-shock

proteins? Unless someone had solved the protein-folding problem . . ." Eva paused to consider the implications of her idea. "Then who knows what they could come with up. I'm losing focus. We need to talk about strategy. We could go on all day with possibilities."

"I assume you already have a plan," Steve raised one eyebrow at her.

"First we need a live patient or two for samples. Sam should almost be to Los Angeles by now, and we'll have him send someone back. Hopefully they've had the standard cultures growing on these patients for a couple days already. We'll check those first. If that doesn't turn anything up, we need to start looking for viruses, toxins, and maybe we should think seriously about developing an animal model."

Steve shook his head. "We don't have time to develop an animal model. I agree with your other first steps, but there's just no time to waste. I don't have a good feeling about this situation. Something about it really bothers me."

Eva shrugged. Steve's comment worried her more than she let on. He had a knack for sensing problems. When Steve was worried about something, he was usually right.

Jim looked anxiously at Eva. "I'm sure you two know what you're doing, but I am assuming you have a plan for keeping this thing contained."

Eva responded, "Of course all work at first will be done in the hot lab. We can't risk losing containment until we know what we're dealing with. That means patients will be treated in the medical decontamination ward." While she spoke, the door opened and Susan Patrick walked into the conference room. Eva beckoned to Susan, who slid into a chair at the table.

Jim pressed her further. "We're also assuming we know more or less what this thing could be. What if we're wrong, and it really is something totally new? What's to say a nanomachine couldn't eat through plastic or steel, for that matter, as well as it could through the colon?" He dipped another chip in his salsa.

Steve turned his head toward Jim. "That's the business, Jim. When you work in a hot lab, you never know who's coming to dinner."

Jim left the chip in the salsa.

Susan looked at the group. "On that thought, let's talk about safety."

Eva nodded. "Susan's going to get us off the ground in the hot lab. Coming, Jim?"

"Sounds like a good idea to know where the walls are in your own fort."

Susan stood, and led the group out of the conference room to a set of elevators. She handed out packets to the other three scientists while they were waiting for the elevator. The first page, Eva saw, was a floor plan for the hot lab, and she studied the design while Susan spoke.

"There is an elevator key for each of you to level six, where the hot labs are located. I know this is probably all review for you, so stop me if I bore you."

"Hey, I'm just the guy who runs the computers. You better start at square one." Jim paged through the packet of information.

"Very well. Biosafety level four was established to provide a safe place to study the most deadly and exotic of diseases. Just about everything we work with here is so dangerous that what you can get under your fingernail can kill you. There are half a dozen level four labs in this country, and anyone who's spent time in one isn't crazy about there being any more than that. They're dangerous places. Every step you take in this lab should be deliberate; the microorganisms that live here are only here because they can take advantage of any lack of focus."

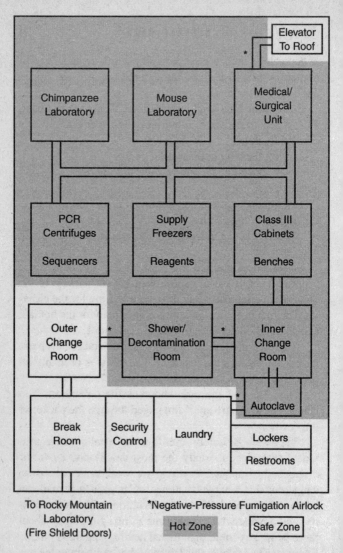

Elevator
To Roof

Chimpanzee
Laboratory

Mouse
Laboratory

Medical/
Surgical
Unit

PCR
Centrifuges

Sequencers

Supply
Freezers

Reagents

Class III
Cabinets

Benches

Outer
Change
Room

Shower/
Decontamination
Room

Inner
Change
Room

Autoclave

Break
Room

Security
Control

Laundry

Lockers

Restrooms

To Rocky Mountain
Laboratory
(Fire Shield Doors)

*Negative-Pressure Fumigation Airlock

Hot Zone

Safe Zone

Rocky Mountain Laboratory
Biosafety Level 4 Facility

The elevator door opened, and the group stepped inside. Eva gasped. The back wall of the elevator was glass. Beyond the wall was a breathtaking glass-and-chrome sculpture of a DNA molecule, spiraling down six stories along a central opening above a fountain in the atrium on the first floor of the laboratory. Light reflected off each of the glass facets like a DNA diamond running between the two glass elevators on opposite sides of the giant atrium. Glass-and-steel scaffolding surrounded the walls of the atrium like the gridwork of a crystal palace.

Susan took out her key and snapped it into the lock on the control panel. A feminine voice sounded from the ceiling, "Authorized Biosafety level four, Susan Patrick." The elevator lurched upward.

"If you look at your maps, there are only two ways in or out of the lab—this one and an elevator to the roof for emergency use only. There are no windows. The entire lab is encased with state-of-the-art fire and earthquake shielding. The keys you have use electronic encryption and for all practical purposes cannot be duplicated. The elevators and hot lab are monitored around the clock by our security team." The elevator doors opened to reveal a double set of steel doors, labeled prominently with biohazard symbols. Eva glanced up to see a video camera above the door.

"Your keys will open the sealed doors. Once inside, the first room you encounter we call the break room. There is a secretary here monitoring all entrance and work going on in the lab during business hours. All after-hours work in the lab must have my personal approval." She inserted her key and the steel doors slid open silently.

Eva walked into a sparsely furnished room. An empty desk sat in the corner. A refrigerator, microwave, two bland couches, and a table with chairs were the only other objects in the room. The walls were white, and two other doors exited to the right and directly ahead.

Susan took a few steps forward and turned to face the group. "Behind me is the entrance to the outer change room. One person at a time is permitted to enter. There you are to strip down completely. You will find jumpsuits and helmets to change into. The process is voice automated, and you will be guided through the procedure. Suits contain breathable oxygen for four hours of work."

Eva looked to Jim, expecting a quip about the procedure. She suspected it would be lost on their straightlaced guide, but knew he couldn't resist all the same.

Jim didn't let her down. "So whose job is it to watch the cameras in that room?"

"There are no cameras in the changing and shower rooms." Susan otherwise ignored the question. "Once you are suited up, you may pass through the negative-pressure airlock to the shower room, and from there through the second airlock into the inner change room. Airlock doors are sequenced so only one may be open at a time. When you leave the inner change room, the change and shower rooms are sealed and chemically fumigated to kill any microbes remaining in the rooms.

"When leaving the lab, you must strip down again completely, and put jumpsuits and helmets in the autoclave for sterilization. You will then pass into the chemical shower rooms, and back to the outer change room where you may again dress. Any questions?"

With one look at Jim, Eva knew he had already considered the implications of what would happen if one's clothes had been removed from the change room in the interim.

Jim asked, "So all the, er, work in here is done commando?"

Susan looked tired of Jim's questions. "The jumpsuits are comfortable. The lab is not."

Steve changed the subject, "What do you study here?"

"Q fever, some of the encephalitis viruses, and Marburg. All specimens are kept in a locked safe in the cabinet room."

"What about ventilation?" Eva wondered out loud.

"Every room is connected via a HEPA filter to a ventilation system that is fumigated continuously and is separate from the rest of the lab. All laboratory waste is autoclaved before we dispose of it. Work surfaces are decontaminated every morning."

"How do you keep security? Some of the stuff you keep here could be pretty valuable to the wrong people," Steve asked.

Susan led the group into the security control room. "These controls here open the airlock to the roof elevator. When we're not in the lab, we seal them off so no one can get in. Be sure to deactivate them if you ever go to the roof or you could get stuck there. It's embarrassed more than a few of my staff."

"We need to get started in the lab," Eva pressed.

"Soon. Everyone allowed into the lab must have baseline serum drawn and stored on site so we can verify if exposure has occurred in case of a suit breach. If you'll come downstairs with me, we can draw some blood right now."

Steve looked to Jim. "You coming in?"

Jim checked his watch. "All this talk about dressing and undressing has made me a little anxious. I think I'd better get back to my programming. I think I'd just as soon leave this little place to you two."

"Suit yourself," Eva said.

"That seems to be the idea." Jim turned back toward the elevator.

FIFTEEN

April 8

ALAN Thorpe emptied his pockets for the second time as he passed through another security station, this time on entrance to the West Wing of the White House. Holding still while the guard passed a wand over his body and limbs, Thorpe watched the guard finger his palmtop and cell phone, verifying that they were functional just as the last set of guards had done.

He had just spoken with Goldberg and Adams, his conversations disappointingly brief. He had hoped the contact would calm his frayed nerves, although now he felt all the more tense for knowing that they were no closer to an answer than when he had left Hamilton. It was not his first trip to the White House, by any means, nor his first meeting with the president. That alone would not be unnerving.

Yet the meeting immediately ahead represented years of work in preparing, and involved those much more pivotal than the president. After working as a chief advisor to the governor of Washington, Thorpe knew firsthand the circles of power brokers that surrounded politicians of influence. One of his priorities at Biodefense had been careful study of the current administration's power structure. His immediate political superior, Jacob Levin, was seen as a low-level administrator in major power circles. Alan knew that in a real emergency the best course would be to bypass the chain of command and work with the real power brokers in Washington. Slowly, delicately, Thorpe had unraveled the web of advisors to the few individuals that had not only the president's ear, but the president's mouth as well.

From a list of eleven "top advisors," individuals with no official title because they needed none and preferred relative anonymity, Thorpe had eventually whittled the list to two. Zachary Collins and Amanda Burgoyne represented, as closely as Alan could tell, the core of power in Washington. Their influence did not extend to every issue reaching the president, but certainly they had a voice on every issue they cared about. Monumentally ambitious, and entrenched in power, these two in particular chose their battles as strategically as they did their advice. Thorpe had known for at least two years that if Biodefense ever became involved in a real confrontation, these were the people he needed to reach. So he made sure the relevant underlings knew how to reach him and when they should.

Thorpe had once held just such a job as these two, though at the state level where an order of magnitude separated his experience from that of his audience. Nevertheless, he knew that in the meeting just ahead, good advice would be sought avidly, pointed questions fired rapidly by those who had no time for incompetence and no tolerance for bluffing. If Thorpe was to be involved in making decisions, he would

make his case immediately, or he would be ignored there-
after.

So far, so good. His carefully placed seeds had sprouted.
Before he had even arrived at Hamilton, he had received a
phone call from Amanda Burgoyne's secretary asking when
he could meet to discuss the situation. Thorpe had set up a
meeting for late evening, and requested that contacts from
the FBI and the homeland security department be present.
He was about to see if he had been taken seriously.

"Right in here, Mr. Thorpe, sir." The guard/escort opened
an office door and stood at attention as Alan went inside.
The large office was exquisitely functional. Along one wall
was a set of desks housing two computers, two fax machines, and teleconferencing cameras and displays. On the
other side of the room was a mobile table that looked like
an old-fashioned video game. Thorpe knew from hearsay
that this was a high-resolution map display, with encrypted,
up-to-the-minute access to satellite maps of any part of the
world, as well as programmed digital street maps of every
major city in the world. The maps in the more sensitive areas of the White House and Pentagon could pinpoint the
location to a square meter of every six-person team and
their humvee in the entire U.S. military around the world
in real time.

In the center of the room was a conference table designed
to seat twelve, with secure telephones at every seat affixed
into the table. Seated at the table were six individuals, all
but two of whom Thorpe recognized. Amanda Burgoyne
and Zack Collins sat together. Next to Zack was Sandra Ewington, national security advisor. On the opposite side of the
table, their backs to Alan, were homeland security secretary Javier Rojas and a stocky man with glasses Thorpe did
not know. Next to him was a smaller, gaunt man chewing
on a pencil eraser.

"Alan Thorpe?" Zack Collins asked from the table.

"Yes, sir."

"Grab some dinner if you want and come join us. We're just getting started."

Alan looked behind him to see a table by the door filled with foil boxes containing catered Thai noodles and satays. The display reminded him of similar meetings he had attended in Seattle, only with cheap pizza and a much plainer office. The differences were a striking reminder that he was in the big leagues now. As if he needed any more reminders. He passed on the dinner, as hungry as he was, and took an adjacent seat at the table. A quick round of introductions revealed that the two unknown individuals were Oscar Morris, deputy director of the FBI, and Paul Vallos, senior analyst of Information Analysis and Infrastructure Protection, the intelligence wing of the homeland security department.

"The question of the hour, Mr. Thorpe, is who is responsible for what we believe is a bioterror attack. Mr. Vallos was enlightening us." Zack was a master facilitator, deftly guiding discussion with each refocusing comment.

Vallos stammered, visibly unaccustomed to high-stakes politics. "I . . . I was . . . As I was saying, our NET Guard has now more information on the Pentagon hacking. The exploit was traced to a computer in Jakarta, Indonesia, sent out to about thirty core name servers in the United States." Vallos became more comfortable as he dove into details he could spew off in his sleep. Thorpe recognized why Vallos had been invited. Though he was likely political deadweight, he was the intelligent, nerdy, quick-speaking, fast-thinking type who could assimilate such a rapidly advancing puzzle with so many disparate pieces.

Vallos continued. "He's dirty. Dirty as hell. We jumped all over the Internet service provider that owns the computer in Indonesia, and found that the IP address was in use by a shop owner in Jakarta at the time. We broke him in less than an hour, like a whimpering puppy. He's not giving us names yet, but we don't think he knows any. Someone supposedly came in, spent a week with his computer, and left last week. Came back three days ago to finish the job. Near as we can figure, there are thirty major UNIX-based core name servers in the United States that are lagging behind in installing security patches. These thirty servers were hacked into with a self-mutating worm to exploit a known security hole. Presumably the other root DNS servers were attempted as well, but they couldn't get in. Pretty simple stuff. Any time someone opened the Pentagon Web site through one of these lookup servers, they were redirected to the computer in Indonesia displaying the threat."

Sandra Ewington interrupted. "So it is a foreign threat. We should get CIA over here."

Vallos raised a skeptical eyebrow. "CIA is for busting drug lords and starting wars. If you want information, we can handle it. Don't send a man to do a geek's job."

Amanda Burgoyne looked at Oscar Morris. "What does FBI think?"

Morris shrugged. "This is news to us. Indonesia is an interesting wrinkle. Biggest Muslim population in the world. We know they've got huge cells operating there. Government can barely keep from collapsing each year, let alone silence their loose cannons."

Javier Rojas leaned back on his chair. In a simple loud voice that reminded Alan of the secretary's roots in a poor Hispanic ghetto, he interrupted. "You're telling me we have to hit Indonesia?"

"Naw. Hardly worth the effort." Zack refocused the group. "There are a lot of other groups I'd much rather take out. The real target is Syria. They've gotten away with murder for way too long with their sham of cooperation. We can always link them in. People will buy that. This is exactly what the president needs, don't you think, Mandy?"

Amanda frowned. "I don't know, Zack. Syria is powerful. We're not talking about knocking off Iraq or Afghanistan here. Besides, we send troops to the Middle East and you know damn well Israel will use it as an excuse to pummel the Palestinians for good measure. Russia will ice off whatever Chechen widow survived the last raid. I'm not sure our PR can take it. Every glossy-eyed eight-year-old in the Middle East will be pulling out his AK-47 to go join the holy war. They hate us enough already."

Alan swallowed hard. It was a calculated risk, but he needed to earn respect quickly, and this was his chance. He looked directly at Amanda. "We don't believe it was a foreign group."

The six other members at the table stared at him in surprise.

Alan continued on while he had the momentum. "I don't think it's likely, anyway. I work with the best bioterror minds around and the one thing they agree on is that this isn't your run-of-the-mill plague. It's innovative, clever. Too clever. It may be a whole new type of weapon. There's only one possibility in my mind. It's Western."

Sandra Ewington asked, "You're saying Americans are behind this?"

"Most likely. You have a coordinated attack with a computer expert, a skilled bioweapons expert, and enough foot soldiers to deliver the bug in the most imaginative campaign I've ever seen. This is a highly organized, highly intelligent enemy. The only thing that makes sense is a sleeper cell in the United States."

"Sleeper cell?" Amanda asked.

"It shouldn't be too surprising." Alan pounced on the chance to expound. "What's the next step for a network that planted pilots in flight school years before a planned attack? You infiltrate America's best R&D labs, the ones that have no security. It wouldn't surprise me a bit if our attacker has been a full professor of microbiology for years. Forty percent of the Ph.D.s we grant are to foreign nationals. I'm betting this is the fruit of a crop of foreign grad students planted years ago, working happily on perfecting their attack right under our noses." Alan watched the group react to his suggestion.

Oscar Morris was first to speak. "There's no shortage of suspicious grad students. We've been tracking them ever since September 11."

Vallos pressed him. "You got any people on it now?"

"I checked in with our human intelligence folks and they're going to query our assets. So far, I haven't heard of anything going down, but I'll find out. We have a few people in place covering American universities."

Rojas cracked his knuckles. "You know, Thorpe. I bet you're right, but I don't know how to tell the president this is coming from within our own borders. That's very bad PR."

Zack jumped in immediately. "You don't. Let me handle it. I'm not sure you should hear this next part, secretary."

"All right, I'm in the bathroom." The secretary sighed, implying this wasn't the first time he had been excused for a "bathroom break" in a discussion.

Zack continued. "If the attack is coming from America, that's not a viable political option for the president. Someone has to take the blame, and fall. We have to absolutely pulverize them, publicly. So I don't give a damn who did this. There're plenty of people that wanted to, and we're going to pick the most annoying bunch of them and destroy them. Is that clear?"

Amanda said nothing.

"Good to see you back from your restroom break, Mr. Secretary."

The secretary spoke up. "I'd like to have more time to discuss this, but the president has called a meeting of the Homeland Security Council. Thorpe, I'd like you there to outline for the president what steps we're taking to solve this most disturbing situation. You have ten minutes."

Thorpe nodded, knowing it would not be wise to ask, "What steps?" His gamble had paid off. Whether right or wrong, he was now in the door. He stood and walked toward the back table, asking, "Satays still warm?"

SIXTEEN

April 8

ALAN followed the group through the West Wing to the Cabinet Room. Although he had never set foot in the room, he felt as though he knew it by heart. It was the natural meeting place for the Homeland Security Council. Alan knew that everything he had worked for on Biodefense would be tested right here. Either he would get the nod to lead the U.S. response, or Biodefense would end up just one more redundant committee in a government that had more than enough of them.

The stress of his turn on stage was heightened by the increasing sense of gravity among the group as they walked past the guards standing watch at the Cabinet Room. His most vexing question, though, was not what he would say or whether he would stumble. He was too consummate a politician to worry about anything other than the key issue facing him first. Where was he to sit? He knew enough of

Washington to realize that such decisions made all the difference in hidden messages of arrogance, competence, and respect.

Amanda Burgoyne put her arm on his shoulder and whispered, "Sit with me, Thorpe." He gratefully acknowledged her offer, all the while realizing she was simply looking out for her own status in sitting next to a key participant.

As they entered the Cabinet Room, Thorpe saw the huge, oval mahogany table that had filled the room since 1970. Stately chairs were seated around the table. Alan knew that each chair was home to a particular cabinet member. Most of the secretaries were so possessive of their seats that when their term of service was over, they purchased their chairs to take with them. About fifteen individuals were already in the room.

Alan glanced at the table. On the east side, one chair in the center was taller than the others, and overlooked the Rose Garden. That would be President Sutherland's chair. On the president's right, the secretary of state was already seated. To the left of the tall, vacant chair, the secretary of defense was thumbing through some documents. Across the table was Vice President Atkins. Next to him were the attorney general and secretary of the treasury.

Amanda led Alan to a row of chairs along the west wall, behind the attorney general with a direct line of sight to the president's chair. Several senior staff members were milling around the room, watching suspiciously as Alan took the seat next to Amanda. Secretary Rojas took his seat near the edge of the table. Despite his prominent position in the Homeland Security Council, tradition prevailed, and he sat at the periphery since cabinet heads were "prioritized" by the date of their departments' establishment. The chairs for cabinet members not part of the Homeland Security Council would remain vacant.

On the walls around the room, Alan observed the artwork. Each president remodeled the room on taking office, and President Sutherland had made a bold statement in the move. Years earlier, during a stretch of Republican control, grave portraits of Lincoln and Jefferson were displayed prominently. Now, the new administration had turned the room from a stiff photo gallery into a museum, most of the pieces on loan from institutions in New York, Washington, and Chicago. Mostly American painters were featured, showing domestic scenes of ordinary American life and representative milestones in American painting. The only former presidents eyeing the room from the wall were depicted in a portrait of Woodrow Wilson and *The Prayer at Valley Forge,* depicting George Washington kneeling in a forest.

Alan turned his head toward Amanda and whispered, "Zack serious about attacking Syria?"

Amanda nodded without looking back. "Vice President and Sec Defense will eat it up. Don't try to stop it. You'll lose."

"That's exactly what they want—the United States striking blindly, uniting the entire Muslim world against us. We all lose."

Alan knew that the vice president held inordinate sway over military policy, since his addition to the ticket had primarily served to balance President Sutherland. A veteran of the Vietnam War, the VP was known for his hardline stance toward foreign policy. Zack was a personal recruit of the VP. Alan took Amanda's advice seriously, recognizing that she was already plotting several steps ahead on how to redirect the others toward a more circumscribed strategic response. He sensed in her an ally, someone more interested in finding the real perpetrators and minimizing victims than in a high-profile military response.

Amanda visibly stiffened, and Thorpe looked as President Sutherland strode toward the chair at the center. Tall and thin, the president seemed to Thorpe alternately graceful and gangly. As a political strategist, Alan had watched with admiration the young two-term representative from California ascend to the presidency. Like the rest of the country, Alan realized just after the fact that the campaign was nearly perfect, and that the candidate had managed to tap a niche that was obvious only in retrospect.

During the campaign season, a Democratic party in retreat was looking for another spokesperson. A war-weary, security-conscious public yearned for the days when thoughts of the unthinkable weren't continually broadcast as inevitabilities prophesied by various heads of intelligence. President Sutherland's message focused on domestic priorities, social security reform, and efficient government. Promising economic stimulus in the form of innovation grants that would replace American business at the top of the world, Sutherland campaigned as a technocrat, a new breed of business-friendly, technology-savvy Democrats that swept the political center out from under the unwary Republican establishment. His opponent had all but folded as Sutherland carved out support from big business, identifying the Republicans with religious-right extremism.

Alan also recognized that the success of the campaign was not particularly the message, but the messenger. As everyone in politics had continually asserted, America was ready for a fresh face. Anthony Sutherland was relatively young at forty-seven, articulate, not particularly attractive, and humble, a combination that seized the imagination of the public. The result, when combined with a fixture of the Senate Armed Forces Committee as running mate, was a comfortable victory.

Alan was convinced the architect of the campaign was

Amanda Burgoyne. A personal friend to the president and his wife since Amanda and Sutherland attended business school together at Stanford, Amanda had shaped Sutherland's public image, coaching him to the right combination of self-assurance and compassion. Alan suspected that the president's reliance on her went far deeper than most of the president's senior staff appreciated.

Several other cabinet members and their attendant staff scurried nonchalantly to find their seats as the president sat down to convene the council. He came directly to the point, adjusting his wire-rim glasses as he spoke.

"Folks, we have one purpose here today. We need to address a threat that I perceive as a direct terrorist attack on U.S. soil using weapons of mass destruction." The formality in his tone was unusual, even for President Sutherland. A chill ran down Alan's spine at the remark.

"I want to hear from State, Intelligence, Defense, and Homeland. I need answers, or at least parameters for a constructive response. We don't have time for vain speculation or extended debate. Johnson?"

Alan noticed how collected the president was considering the circumstances. Though Alan knew Sutherland would understand that his secretary of state, Thomas Johnson, had relatively little to contribute, he respected his role as a popular public figure and gave him air time whenever possible. A smart political move, Alan suspected, toward someone the president had had a very difficult time recruiting and keeping in harmony with his foreign policy agenda.

Johnson ably recapped global hot spots and suspects for the attack, adding generous disclaimers about lack of any concrete developments from any of his embassies to suggest a definite perpetrator. As he spoke, Alan watched the members at the table, feeling their reaction and mood. He was particularly interested when Defense Secretary Feinberg made eye contact with Zack Collins. Alan watched Zack return his gaze with a nod. Zack looked next across the table toward the attorney general, a longtime political colleague of Feinberg's, who in turn exchanged looks with National Intelligence Director Richard Stern.

Alan was intrigued by Richard Stern. The National Intelligence Directorate was an offshoot of the 9/11 commission report, a political card shuffle that everyone supported but no one wanted. Surfacing in the heat of the 2004 Bush/Kerry presidential campaign, the report became an instant bestseller, and its prized intelligence recommendation was the creation of the NID. Previously, the CIA director had had authority to coordinate all fifteen U.S. intelligence agencies, and was given the title director of central intelligence. What had become all too clear over the years, however, was that since the CIA director had no budgetary control over anything but the CIA, he had little real power to coordinate with other agencies or force them to provide updated information. The infighting between CIA, DOD, and FBI was legendary; hence the commission's recommendation of creating an intelligence czar who could coordinate all U.S. intelligence and serve as principal advisor to the president.

It looked good on paper, but as just about everyone had predicted, it had only added another cog in the intelligence bureaucracy machine, and more cogs meant more turf battles. The National Intelligence Director was quickly shut out of any useful budgetary control, and the CIA director, stripped of his ceremonial powers as director of central intelligence, had been none too eager to make the NID into anything but a glorified analyst. Alan knew that Stern was smart, and looking for ways to expand the authority of the NID, and that meant looking for allies. If not CIA, maybe Justice or Defense?

When the secretary of state finished his briefing, President Sutherland thanked him and looked across the table, acknowledging Director Stern.

"Mr. President, we are working to get human intelligence resources in place. I should have information soon. In discussion with Justice, we've decided to have the bureau take the initial lead in the investigation, since most of our concrete leads are domestic." Stern sat down.

The attorney general stood, as though on cue. "I've asked Oscar Morris, deputy director of the FBI, to review our leads so far."

Oscar Morris buttoned his sport coat and stood. "Mr. President, our sources are building a case that this despicable attack is directly funded if not masterminded by hardline elements in the nation of Syria." Alan looked at Amanda in shock. Her face was unreadable, calculating.

Morris continued, exchanging glances with Zack. "The first piece of the puzzle fell into place when we discovered that the computer used to broadcast the threat was located in Jakarta, owned by a small Indonesian businessman. As you know, since the 9/11 commission report, the FBI has forged cooperative counterterrorism operations with the CIA and homeland security. I'm pleased that these reforms, and some quick work from the FBI computer security division, have in this case enabled rapid breakthroughs from our overseas colleagues.

"Within hours, this Indonesian businessman found it expedient to share with us the names of individuals he had overheard from the programmers who left the message on his computer. Most of them we've never heard of. One, Al Anwar, is a known figure, on our most-wanted list for ten years. He freelances, was based in Pakistan for a time. We have solid evidence that he has been one of Syria's highest-ranking operations officers for more than three years now."

Alan watched as anger crept over the face of Javier Rojas. The homeland security chief seemed on the verge of springing to his feet as Morris took credit for discoveries of Rojas's own intelligence office, embellishing as he went. Alan recognized that Rojas would understand that the setting would not allow for a dispute over credit, not now, but he sympathized with Rojas's indignation.

Alan leaned over to Amanda and whispered, "That's bogus, isn't it?"

She nodded.

"Who's going to call them on it?"

"Nobody, Alan. We need to be thinking ahead. We can't win taking them head on."

The president looked directly at Alan. He interrupted, "Somebody have a question?"

"No, Mr. President," Amanda answered. Alan felt a pang of conscience, wondering how he could phrase his remarks to redirect the council without getting trampled under the war hawks.

Morris resumed his account. "The threat occurred long before anyone knew the attack had taken place. It implies foreknowledge and culpability."

"That's all you've got? A name spoken by a shop owner not directly involved?" President Sutherland questioned.

"Direct links are hard to come by so quickly in this business. With all respect, we've acted on less before. We have enough evidence to consider action against Syria, and our recommendation is that military action would be justified at this time." Morris sat down.

"We now have two nations in the region, Iran and Pakistan, with nuclear capability. We know Iran and Syria have chemical weapons. We can't go knocking off countries there at will anymore." Sutherland looked flustered. "I thought Syria was playing ball with us lately."

Defense Secretary Feinberg shook his head. "It will never come to nukes. We're talking about a handful of warheads, and we know where every one is. We could take out any nuclear capabilities in minutes if anyone else joined the fight."

Secretary of State Johnson spoke next. "Syria, along with Pakistan and Iran, has been the untouchable center of the terrorist backbone for decades. Hamas, Hezbollah, most of the big groups—if you trace their funding back far enough, you travel through Damascus every time. They just seem to have a way of distancing themselves politically, all the while funneling money to guys like Al Anwar. They put up a friendly front, but make no mistake that this is a dictatorship that uses us at will. And they've been growing bolder and more overtly hostile to the West every year. Take out Syrian and Pakistani backers, and you've dealt a much bigger blow to the fundamentalists than anything we ever did in Iraq or Afghanistan."

The stodgy defense secretary, looking as though he badly needed a cigarette, stood for his remarks. "Mr. President, I don't need to remind this group that an act of war has been committed against the United States. We don't know the extent of the damages this attack will bring, but dozens of American citizens have already died. We have to respond. Our people will demand nothing less than rooting out the terrorists responsible and destroying them."

The secretary stopped speaking, reached down, and pulled up a folder with some notes inside. The gesture seemed overly dramatic to Alan. "I don't know about a full-scale invasion of Damascus at this point, but something needs to be done. If they can't control their loose cannons, we will."

A din of whispering echoed through the chamber. "An invasion?" the president asked in surprise.

"With appropriate air cover and tactical support. We start with a quick bombing campaign, take out their chemical missiles and main garrisons of troops. We could have control of the capital within a couple weeks. Anyone who thought the Iraq invasion was fast will be blown away. All of the plans have been sitting in my drawer for years. This is an unprecedented attack, and deserves our hitting them hard, hitting fast. If we wait for the UN to discuss it like we did Iraq, they'll string us along for years until Europe completely loses their appetite to help us. We've been down this road before."

The president leaned back in his chair. "I don't know, Jacob. I'm not prepared to invade at this point. What do you think, Amanda?"

Amanda answered quickly, dispassionately, "We'll have some time without losing significant tactical advantage. They won't be expecting anything aggressive that fast. The logistics alone will take weeks at the least. In the meantime, we need some kind of public outrage before we even consider an invasion or the media will eat us alive. I suggest we focus on the victims, our response targeted to minimize damage. Then, if new data bears out what FBI says, we can act."

Vice President Atkins shrugged. "A few days can make a lot of difference. I think Defense makes a good point."

"Zack?" the president asked.

"It needs to be done anyway. This is an excellent opportunity. The people will support an aggressive strike. They're sick of terrorism, sick of hearing about it. You won't have to worry about America dragging their feet. Hell, the media will appreciate the story so much they'll keep it balanced no matter what we do."

President Sutherland's face displayed the weight of his decision. "I need military options." He looked pointedly at Feinberg, "More than one. In the meantime, Amanda's right. We need to help our people. Javier, where do we stand?"

Rojas gestured to Thorpe. "Alan Thorpe is the project leader for Biodefense, Mr. President. It is our premier response team for biological terrorism. He is prepared to update you."

"Very well. Mr. Thorpe, good to have you on board."

Alan stood to his full height. "Thank you, Mr. President. My team is on site in Los Angeles, and staffing one of the finest biosafety labs in the country, in Hamilton, Montana. We have an efficient group of America's best scientists already examining patients and working to identify the weapon used in the attack. We will work around the clock until we find the organism, and a cure."

"That's good to know, Mr. Thorpe. Your efficiency will be appreciated, and rewarded." Alan sensed that he meant he would also be answerable for failure.

"As of yet, we know very little about this disease. There is a possibility that it represents an entirely new kind of weapon, one with which we have no experience. It may be an artificial organism, a nanotechnological device. We know it is infectious, it strikes quickly, and is lethal. I have a few recommendations at this time, and expect to have more soon."

Several of the members in the room pulled out pens to take notes. "First, I think we have to prepare for the possibility that this could be a significant outbreak. I have our top epidemiologist making projections for possible casualties." Alan thought as he spoke, *our only epidemiologist*. "This means that we need a contingency plan for a total quarantine of Los Angeles, enforced by the National Guard, that could be implemented at short notice if the disease spreads more quickly than we can contain."

"That's impossible," Zack spoke out.

"I don't think so," countered Thorpe, "and I agree with you that the people will support aggressive moves in this regard, even with some loss of personal liberty. From what I've seen, people on the scene are frightened. Maybe that can be an asset."

The president looked down the table to his secretary of health and human services, the only female member of his cabinet. "Why don't you work with Transportation on that, and have a plan ready by tomorrow."

Thorpe continued on without waiting for further comment. "Second, we need a central authority to direct medical efforts. It could be chaos if we leave each individual hospital to its own devices."

President Sutherland answered immediately, "Your team up to the job, Mr. Thorpe?"

Thorpe nodded once, trying not to show his excitement at getting the approval to lead the response. He continued with a final point, choosing his wording carefully. "Third, I recommend that intelligence resources be open to the possibility of cells within the United States that may be in league with whatever terrorist organizations are responsible for planning the attack."

Secretary Feinberg looked uneasily at Thorpe, "This just a hunch, or do you have information we don't?"

Thorpe responded, "The nature of the agent is most peculiar, one that you can't buy off the shelf. In what little we have seen so far, it suggests a highly developed R&D effort, perhaps involving technology developed in the West. That's all I know." Thorpe sat down.

President Sutherland solicited any remaining comments from the group. With none forthcoming, he took a deep breath. "Please set our terror threat level to red. Hold Defcon where it is for now. We will reconvene tomorrow." He paused and looked around the room. Alan realized this was the first time the homeland security warning level had been set to red, meaning under attack, since it had been created in 2001. "Thank you, everyone. You all know how important this is. I appreciate your efforts more than you know." As he stood to leave, the remaining Homeland Security Council stood with him, nobody speaking until he had left the chamber.

Alan looked to Amanda, seeing the strain on her face and recognizing at once how emotionally spent she felt. She spoke in a low voice, offering half a smile. "Well done. Keep in touch. We're going to have to move quickly on this if we want to keep this beast in its cage." Scratching his forehead with his fingers, he wondered how soon he would regret the new authority he had been given.

SEVENTEEN

April 8

AMIR Khalil drove into the underground parking for his condominium. Quickly exiting his car, he walked toward the elevator, pressing the button for his floor. He watched the orange numbers above the elevators descend until one of them reached his level. The envelope felt heavy in his pocket. The slight pressure it made against his thigh dominated his senses. Reaching in, he lightly fingered the envelope again, feeling the cylindrical contour inside the envelope with anticipation. Most of his life had been spent earning the respect to participate in such an event.

The elevator door opened with a muffled tone, and he rode silently, stopping once to let on another tenant. Arriving at the eleventh floor, he walked with forced composure to his home. Outside the door, above the bell, was an inscription in Arabic. It was a poem, written in the twelfth century, speaking of the justice of Allah and the destiny of mankind.

Khalil turned the key to the lock. His anticipation heightened with the familiar scent of curry as he opened the door. The room was sparsely but comfortably furnished. He removed his shoes on entering. He had been having dinner, alone as always, when the call came. It was a voice he had heard only twice before in two years, but a voice that he recognized no less readily. Amir remembered the first time Ahmed Al Rasheed had called him at home.

For two years before that he had lived a nomadic existence, traveling from mosque to mosque around the country. He was becoming something of a legend. Wherever he went, whispered stories often preceded him of the one who knew the mullahs. Some wondered if he had been given a commission; others suspected he was a fraud. Yet whenever he had visited a new mosque, he came with a message.

He spoke of doctrinal purity, of the curse that awaited the followers of Allah who knew nothing of the Qur'an. He taught all who would listen, chastising those of weaker faith for their impurities. The people of Allah must be united, must be pure, must be true children of Abraham if they were to regain power and dominion on the earth.

He rarely stayed long enough to make more than passing contacts, but after two years, he found that he could remember dozens of acquaintances in more than a dozen cities. He had often hinted that the faith of the faithful must be tested, even unto death. Occasionally, a lifted eyebrow or a reverent nod acknowledged that someone took his message more seriously than perfunctory rhetoric. The one thing nobody disputed was that his example of religious orthodoxy was beyond reproach, though admittedly no one knew him well enough to be certain of this.

The change had come just two years ago. After extending his influence throughout the Islamic community in the United States, he was staying in Los Angeles, and heard rumors of a prominent Muslim who no longer attended the mosque. Ahmed Al Rasheed had taught many similar ideas to Khalil years before, some said. Perhaps Khalil might help him restore his faith. Amir made inquiries, without avail, until his phone rang, and the caller introduced himself as Al Rasheed.

The call had been mutually complimentary. Al Rasheed stated he had heard of a follower of Allah who showed unusual dedication. Khalil quoted to Al Rasheed passages from the Qur'an, known so well by heart. They spoke of the plight of Palestine, the tyranny of the West against their fellow brothers, the shared belief that someday America would belong to the faithful. It concluded with a proposition. Al Rasheed stated that there were those who believed such changes were at hand.

Khalil had listened carefully, and offered his gratitude to those who would not cower from their beliefs in the face of intimidation, and Al Rasheed suggested that Khalil might have a place among those whose names would forever stand as leaders toward the day when Islam covered the globe. Khalil was counseled to remain in Los Angeles, for this was to be the center of the change.

One month later, Khalil had received another phone call. Al Rasheed had contacted the brethren, and Khalil was found worthy to join them. A period of time must elapse before he would gain full standing as a founder, and he must first prove his loyalty. His first assignment had been to retrieve two brothers who had been stranded in Mexico, brothers who had forgotten their passports.

Khalil had gone at once, had escorted his brothers across the border, and had enjoyed stimulating conversation about the state of faithlessness among American Muslims. He had received no further assignment until tonight. An important package was to be delivered, and he was to be the messenger. Could he please meet Al Rasheed in person at the UCLA Medical Center lobby?

Now he had the package in hand, and his curiosity tugged on him like an addiction. He switched the light on at his bureau, and he pulled out the envelope. On the outside was an address and a phone number. He dialed the number.

An unknown voice answered in Arabic. "Yes."

Khalil responded in his own fluent Arabic. "I am instructed to call, and I have been given a package which belongs to you. When may I meet you?"

A slight hesitation was heard at the other end of the line. "Where are you?"

"Los Angeles."

"Do you have my address?"

"Yes."

"Please meet me at nine tomorrow morning there. The contents are undisturbed?"

"Praise be to Allah."

"Praise be to Allah." The receiver clicked.

He immediately retrieved his phone book and dialed another number. After a short pause, he asked, "I need to purchase the next available ticket to Chicago from Los Angeles. Yes, eleven P.M. would be perfect. No, coach is fine."

With the telephone receiver to his ear, Khalil took out his key and opened the drawer to the bureau. Inside was a digital keypad, on which he typed seven digits. A metallic snap was the reply, and Amir opened the disguised metal safe paneled into the side of the bureau. He withdrew a box and placed it on the bureau.

"Khalil, Amir Khalil. That's K-H-A-L-I-L. Yes, A-M-I-R. MasterCard, please." He recited the number from memory.

Khalil grabbed the envelope in one hand and reached toward the light on the desk with the other hand. He unscrewed the light bulb and replaced it with a larger bulb found in the bureau. He flipped the switch on the lamp, and a brilliant light illuminated the entire room.

"Thank you very much." He hung up the phone.

Grabbing the envelope now in both hands, he held it up to the halogen bulb and scrutinized it carefully from all sides. The powerful bulb transilluminated the envelope and he saw the outline of a single tube inside. From inside the box on the desk, he withdrew a sponge and a canister and dabbed the sponge with the bottle of solvent. He pulled out a pair of latex gloves from the box. He rubbed the sponge along one edge of the sealed envelope. Carefully, he slid open one corner of the envelope enough to tip it on its side and drop out the vial from inside onto his palm.

The vial was tightly capped, and contained graduated markings showing the meniscus of the clear fluid inside reaching to exactly the five-milliliter mark. Amir looked inside the box, and retrieved a microflask in a rack of tubes, a micropipette with a yellow tip, and a mask. He placed the mask over his face, then deftly unscrewed the cap on the vial. With his other hand, he lowered the tip of the pipette into the solution and drew up five hundred microliters, which he proceeded to place in the microflask. He capped the flask, placed it in the rack, and replaced the cap on the vial as well.

Next he retrieved a container of bleach from the box and placed the pipette tip in the bleach, screwing the bottle shut tightly and agitating the container gently. He placed the flask back inside the envelope and took out a tube of adhesive to reseal the envelope, placing it on the side. He replaced all of his instruments, except for the tiny microflask, which he placed in a Ziploc bag and slid into his pocket. Finally, he rubbed his hands vigorously with alcohol gel and moved straight for the kitchen sink, turning the water on with his elbow and touching nothing en route. He stripped off his gloves into the garbage and washed his hands carefully and methodically.

Only then did he replace the envelope into his pocket and sit back down at the desk, now cleared of everything except the box of supplies. He dialed a number at FBI headquarters. "Could I have a secure line, please, to the director of operations?" He gave his ID number. A moment later he was connected through.

"Hi, this is Amir Khalil in Los Angeles. I need to arrange an immediate dropoff of a hot package."

"MILITARY action would be justified? What the hell?" Defense Secretary Feinberg slammed the door of the White House conference room, sweat drooling from his temples. He glowered at the attorney general.

"It's not what you're thinking," Zack Collins held out his hand to the two cabinet members, motioning them to sit.

"Damn bleeding hell it ain't!" Feinberg slumped into his chair and thumped his fist on the table. "Your candy-ass little analyst just walked in and told the president it's time to go invade Syria!"

The attorney general shifted in his chair, looking at Collins, then back to Feinberg. "Look, Jacob. I thought we'd discussed . . ."

"We discussed getting off our fat asses and doing something, not playing Don Quixote with a turban gunning down the Syrians."

Zack interrupted, "Nobody's going to invade Syria. It was my idea, and a calculated risk in the briefing."

Feinberg wiped his forehead with his beefy, hairy arm. He answered slowly, calmly, "Then maybe you'd better just explain how some punk political analyst just managed to make me look like a total moron by telling the president we needed to go bitch-slap Damascus. My nuts are the ones that get served as fried raisins for suggestions like that, boy."

"Thanks for backing us up. Here's the point. We've had a major terrorist attack on our own soil. There has to be a reprisal. You know the drill as well as I do. Nobody wants to do shit about it. It's all talk until the bastards have crawled down their little caves and all we can do is bust a few drinking fountains here and there. These things take time. I was a staffer when 9/11 broke. The way those guys talked, you thought you were staring at ten old men with a half a Viagra between them. It took months to actually get something off the ground, and it was too late."

"So how in Sam Hill is spooking them with talk about Syria going to help?"

Zack stared directly at Feinberg. "We prepare them for the worst. Then when we suggest something more limited, they swing at it. Trust me on this one. I know Sutherland. He's a pansy. You talk up how you're going to go bang Iran or Syria, and he'll love you when you give him a chance to do something smaller scale. But he'll do it."

Feinberg nodded. "All right. So what then?"

Collins smiled. "Whatever you want."

"How about flying a plane from Israel to Russia and tossing nukes out the window until the whole Middle East is fried?"

Collins's smile vanished.

"OK. Here's what I want. Let's use this to behead a few of the really ugly terror groups. We might even give a couple of them a real kick in the balls. Something that would keep them out of play for a while. We get a few of the players and bleed 'em for whatever they know."

The attorney general nodded agreement. "It's got potential. Seems like we could get away with that no problem. I know Stern will play ball with intelligence. He's pissed off enough at CIA to pass on whatever we tell him. And if we tell him who did it, that's who gets whacked."

Feinberg grunted. "I don't know. Even a decent small-scale op takes time to plan. My experience is that anytime something big goes down, these guys are in hiding as soon as they can crawl off their mistresses. We don't have time."

Collins shook his head. "That's exactly why I'm preparing the president for something big, something fast. Why not go this week? It's a perfect explanation. Nobody knows what the hell to do about this attack. The only way to fight it is to capture the guys who made it and persuade them to tell us how to stop it."

The attorney general flinched. "There could be fifteen people who did this."

Collins nodded vigorously. "Let's get all fifteen."

Feinberg buried his head in his hands. "What are you talking about? Launching fifteen major operations in a week? Who do you think I am? Moses? With unlimited funds and a president with titanium nuts I could launch two or three in a month. You don't just go walk into a terror clearinghouse and tip over the tables. There's strategic objectives, then operational plans, then tactical. You have to control airfields, secure airspace, coddle Europe along, set up refueling stations, train the troops, move thousands of tons of steel choppers and humvees. You have to arrange supply lines, a launch base, coordinate dozens of commanders and their plans and egos. Am I making myself clear?"

"So what can we do in a few days?"

"Nothing."

"Gotta be something."

"Well, what do we have in theater? We've got a carrier group in the Mediterranean and another keeping an eye on Taiwan. They could probably steam to the Middle East and

Indonesia in a day or so. We've still got a pretty good presence in Iraq, but not much in the way of air support. A few Chinooks. Afghanistan is a little beefed up for a joint special forces exercise. We're doing Cobra Platinum there this year and we have assets moving in. But we're talking scraps. What are we going to do, drop a few bombs? We need infantry for the stuff you're talking about."

"Or special ops forces."

"Run the whole mission with SOF? I take it back. You really do have a wiener, kid."

"Sure, you can't take out these groups, but what about a massive snatch-and-run? Just using Tier 1 special ops. Take a few godfathers out of each organization and see what information you can get. That might even have a chance of helping us fight this current attack. Something this big won't be totally silent. One of these guys will know about it."

"I'd still need weeks."

"Casualties are mounting quickly. If it takes weeks, then so be it. But why not just move now? Get people in place, draw up plans . . ."

Feinberg shrugged. "You're right. Why the hell not. We just might be glad we had them there, and if nothing else, we can put some special ops on recon and intelligence."

Collins sat back in his chair, "Not bad for a candy-ass analyst, eh?"

Feinberg grunted.

EIGHTEEN

April 8

EVA'S breathing accelerated. She listened to every metallic breath, frightened by her own heartbeat—her own presence. The itch on her nose again teased her. The light fog inside her helmet blurred her vision. *How much oxygen was left?* She looked at the clock. Still three hours. Would she consume more by breathing faster? No, she reasoned again.

Eva had worked in a level four facility before, but that was different. Then she had worked in a cabinet lab, not a suit lab. Government regulations specified that biosafety level four materials must be handled either in specialized class three cabinets or in a spacesuit lab. Rocky Mountain Laboratory had both capabilities, a growing trend in biohazardous microbiology. It was her first time in a spacesuit.

She stretched her gloved fingers, wondering what it would take to perforate the double latex lining stretching over the sleeve of her jumpsuit. The suit maintained positive air pressure, so even in case of a breach she shouldn't be exposed to airborne pathogens. Of course, a needle stick would go right through the gloves into her skin.

She looked around the room again. There were six beds, spaced about ten feet apart along the far wall. Accordion-shaped dividers were bunched against the wall between each bed. The wall was littered with air valves, plugs, and assorted monitors and machines between the beds. It reminded Eva uncomfortably of her hospital stay several years ago for appendicitis.

A voice in her head startled her. "You okay?" It was Steve.

"A little spooked, I guess," she answered into the microphone on her suit.

"The helicopter just landed. I'll send them down the back way and you can meet them inside."

"What about the doc?"

"I'll take him around to suit up once the materials are inside."

"OK."

Eva wished for her Diet Coke, wished for a bathroom, wished she could at least scratch her nose. She wondered who would know if she went in the suit. *Certainly don't need it that bad,* she reasoned.

Now that she had only minutes to go, her thoughts shifted to what she would say. What could one possibly say to someone who was dying, for whom you could probably do nothing?

This thought was what made Eva particularly uncomfortable, and overshadowed the more primal needs of security and a bathroom. In the laboratory, life and death was removed from her by the glacial pace of research. Studying a disease was something that took years, decades. Six months would pass here or there while a paper was being reviewed, or during which she just didn't have time to make the last few graphs for the manuscript. Individuals were never the concern.

Now the clock began to tick by minutes and seconds instead of months and years. Every hour she delayed diagnosis, an exponential swarm of lethal organisms was growing, consuming the victims in its path. Such organisms would soon be within feet of her, contained only by her space suit. She could match wits with the microscopic enemy, but she was not sure about how to handle the flesh-and-blood corollary about to arrive.

What if the patient was unstable? She struggled to remember a single scrap of first-aid knowledge. Could it be possible she truly knew nothing?

A mechanical hum whirred over her head. *Was that the elevator?* Eva wondered what the patient would look like. It would be easier if he was unconscious, she thought. She could collect samples and retreat into the lab, where she knew her role.

Steve had the easy job. Why had she agreed to wait in the lab?

Click. The door to the airlock opened. Eva counted as the outer door shut. Her eyes fixed on the inner door to the airlock. The door moved. What she saw completely unnerved her.

Four figures in yellow chemical hazard suits with gas masks carried a stretcher. On the stretcher, Eva could just make out layers of transparent plastic in the shape of a human figure. The plastic was tied down by two red straps around the chest and waist. A metallic voice spoke through a gas mask.

"Dr. Vanorden?"

"Welcome to Hamilton," she managed. Eva felt a chill from the artificial sound of her own brassy voice.

"Where shall we put her?"

Eva motioned to a bed in the corner of the room.

They carried the patient to the bed and laid their plastic package on top. One of the yellow men counted to three, and in one swift motion they slid the stretcher out from under the patient.

The yellow-suited man turned to Eva again. "This is Daru Shah. Dr. Nowers is on his way. Can we be of any further assistance?"

Eva wanted to keep the crew here, hoped she would not be left alone. "Is she stable?"

The man nodded. "For now."

"You go ahead. I'll wait with her."

The men walked briskly out of the room and shut the door to the airlock tightly.

Eva walked over to the patient. Frightened eyes looked up at Eva, watching her approach. Inside the plastic pod, two empty units of blood were connected to a line in her neck. Daru's long, thick hair was matted under the plastic. Eva could see, even through the plastic, that she was sweaty and pale, hyperventilating from a fear Eva sympathized with all too well.

Eva's hand trembled as she reached for the zipper lock on the pod. She slowly unzipped the plastic from around her patient. Dried blood caked the dressing over Daru's central line. Her gown was stained with blood around her legs.

If I feel scared, she must be terrified, Eva thought. She struggled to calm herself and forced a smile. "Hello, Daru. I'm Eva."

"Are you my doctor?" Daru's voice was tentative, weak.

"No. I'm one of the scientists in charge of finding out what you have."

"So we still don't know?"

"I'm sorry."

"Where am I?" She sniffled and rubbed her bloodshot eyes.

Eva thought about reaching out to Daru, but decided her gloved hand would be more frightening than comforting. "Montana, in a secured biosafety lab. We'll need you to stay here until we can figure out how to treat you. Your doctor is on the way."

"At least it's quiet here."

"Maybe too quiet—Do you want me to bring in some books or a TV?"

Daru shook her head. "Can I call my parents?"

"Of course. I'll bring in a phone next time I come in."

Daru sat up partially, putting her weight on her elbows. She winced with the movement.

"Are you in a lot of pain?"

Daru looked at her abdomen in response. "A little. They gave me some morphine on the flight." Daru sneezed.

"Where are you from?"

"California. Born and raised." Daru closed her eyes. "I hope I see it again."

"You will."

Eva shuffled on her feet, unsure how to proceed. "Daru, I know this isn't the right thing to say now, but we think it's important to find out what's causing your illness."

"Take whatever samples you want. I told them I'd help." Daru sighed.

An awkward silence ensued. Eva was at a total loss for what to say.

"Eva?"

"Yes."

"It's OK. You don't have to stay."

"I wish I had your courage."

"You know, I think you're right. It's too quiet in here.

Do you have any music? They wouldn't let me have any at the hospital."

"I can ask around. All I've got are some jazz CDs."

"You serious? Is it good jazz?"

"Some of it I recorded myself at some jam sessions when I went to a meeting in Chicago."

"Thanks." Daru lay back down, looking over Eva's head at the sterile walls. "I hope you'll stop in when you can. I know I'm going to go crazy here."

"I promise I'll let you know every development. We'll get you through this." Eva wondered if Daru sensed the doubt in her voice that she felt.

Daru looked away, pausing before she spoke. "I hear people talking. Nobody tells me anything. I heard somebody saying something about nanotechnology when they thought I was sleeping."

"That's just speculation."

"What does it mean?"

In a brief pause, Eva settled her inner debate in the favor of telling Daru more. "The ones who claimed responsibility for the outbreak used the word *nanovirus*. Nanotechnology is a new science that deals with making tiny machines and computers."

"Computers that cause disease?"

"Well, sometimes things that tiny can have lots of different properties. Proponents say that we could someday make tiny assemblers: machines that can pick up and drop an atom at a time, making virtually anything, including copies of themselves."

"Is that possible?" Daru wiped her nose on her sleeve.

Eva bit her lip in her space suit. She was talking too much. Certainly this information was more frightening than helpful.

"We don't know yet."

Eva turned around as she heard footsteps behind her in the lab. Another suited figure was walking briskly toward them.

A lower, tinny voice greeted them. "I'm James Nowers, the intensivist taking care of Ms. Shah. Dr. Goldberg asked me to manage her treatment while she's here."

Eva nodded, grateful for the backup.

"Daru, looks like you can't get rid of me so easy." He took her hand in his gloved hands.

"I hope you like jazz."

"We'll see about that." He connected monitoring equipment as he spoke, attaching ECG leads to her legs and arms. Soon her heartbeat sprang onto a terminal overhead with a rhythmic electronic *ping* for each beat. "That's the music I like to hear."

Daru grimaced.

Eva pulled Nowers aside. "We should get to work fast. Did you bring the cultures from the hospital?"

He pointed to a box on the floor behind them.

"Can you get a fresh set of cultures also? The works."

Eva looked one last time at Daru. Before tears could well up in her eyes, she waved good-bye.

Daru lifted a hand feebly in return. "I hope you come back, Eva."

She nodded and turned around to retrieve the specimen box, barely able to see through the fog on her faceplate.

NINETEEN

April 9

JIM Summers scrolled through lines of code on the right of his screen. It was exasperating to be using a single monitor. *How quaint,* he thought cynically. Although most of the program was constructed by a graphical interface with thin lines connecting pictorial icons, he preferred to look at the C-based source code when his programs wouldn't compile, and had to switch between interfaces frequently.

Programming was addictive. Whenever Jim had an idea, he routinely went thirty-six hours at a stretch, with only rare, short breaks to restock his junk food arsenal. After working most of the night, he still felt fresh and alert. The lure of fixing just one more bug was constant, and sleep a burden. As lines of code flew by, slowing periodically as he examined a segment more closely, Jim reexamined his argument.

How can it be so deadly, so fast? The idea disturbed

him conceptually. Most of his simulations in the past had always relied on one basic principle. Any bug that causes overwhelming infection takes time to reproduce. You can't have fast incubation and huge disease burden. Jim's simulations had borne out the principle time and again.

Yet clearly, the incubation period was a day or two at most, and the disease was fulminant within two days. What would this do to the spread? If people got infected faster, the disease was likely to be contained because fewer people could get exposed. People with deadly diseases get isolated quickly. These features were all built into his program already.

What bothered Jim was the E.R. spread. In a controlled environment like the E.R., three transmissions provided a gold mine of information. He could compare this to other diseases with a high level of confidence to get the key parameters for his simulations. The disturbing fact was that deadly diseases were almost universally difficult to transmit. Rapid transmission in a place like an E.R. where people generally washed their hands and limited their contact with the sick meant this disease might be uncomfortably more infectious than other diseases of the same virulence. It behaved more like influenza or a bad cold in terms of transmission than a hemorrhagic fever. It almost had to be airborne.

A nagging thought seemed just out of reach as he typed. There was something unusual about this pattern. In all the simulations he had run, he couldn't remember exploring this particular area of parameter space. It just had never seemed realistic to have something so contagious, so fast, so lethal.

How would that play out? Would the rapid transmission offset the incapacitating severity of the disease? *Will the disease hit the epidemic threshold?* That was the key question, and every time Jim's thoughts recycled to the question, he began working harder to get the simulation programmed in. He knew enough of the chaotic dynamics of disease transmission not to put too much effort into guessing what the behavior would be. With a phenomenon this complex, the only solution was to run the program in a virtual reality, with the emphasis on reality. Every available piece of data had to be included.

A window popped up stating that the program had compiled successfully. He typed a few phrases, rechecked his command line one last time for syntax, and pressed *Enter*. The calculations would take a few minutes for results, even on his Pentagon supercomputer. He could fine-tune his program later.

What time was it? Jim had no idea. He glanced at the corner of his computer screen. Nearly eight A.M. It would be seven in Los Angeles. Jim's computer gave correct time to a microsecond, thanks to periodic downloads from an atomic clock feed he obtained by satellite modem. He had always found this amusing, since he was probably the least punctual person of any he knew.

He wondered why Eva hadn't stopped in yet this morning. Surely she was up by now. A few clicks of his mouse later he had pulled up a window with the latest CNN video feed. His suddenly tired fingers reached for the volume control on the computer speakers. The headline BIOTERROR STRIKES L.A. was plastered across the bottom of the screen.

". . . That's right, Tom. As you can see, the crowd behind me continues to grow as reporters, police, and onlookers converge on UCLA Medical Center after reports that a series of unexplained deaths is occurring at Los Angeles hospitals. The deaths follow a threat posted by computer hackers on the Pentagon's Web site yesterday, warning of a plague to strike Los Angeles. Details are emerging slowly, and doctors treating these mysterious cases have thus far declined comment, but we will report any information as it is obtained in this breaking story.

"I have with me now Mark Lansdowner, president of the Drexler Society for Nanotechnology, to discuss the events thus far. Thank you, Mark, for agreeing to meet me on such short notice."

Oh, that's great, thought Jim. *Just what we need. A parade of quacks outside the hospital.*

"Thank you, Susan."

"Perhaps you could tell us about the Drexler Society and what it does."

"Absolutely. The Drexler Society is a nonprofit organization founded for greater understanding of nanotechnology, based on the visionary work of K. Eric Drexler. The society includes scientists, lobbyists, financiers, and enthusiasts of nanotechnology."

"And what does nanotechnology have to do with our situation here?"

"Well, most people think the message received yesterday on the Pentagon Web site makes a thinly veiled threat about some kind of nanotechnological weapon. Talk of nanomachines causing disease has long been feared by many of us in the Drexler Society."

"How so?"

"We've known for some time that self-replicating nanotechnology was on the horizon. The danger of such a technology has been suggested for decades. Bill Joy at Sun has been talking about this for almost twenty years. Now it's here, and they got to it first."

"Who's they?"

"That's a great question—someone with no love for America."

"What kind of technology are we talking about?"

"Computers—smaller than you've dreamed about in your worst nightmares. Computers where individual molecules are circuit elements; computers that can take apart blood vessels or cells an atom at a time. Computers that can reproduce, program each other, and manufacture whatever poisons their master wants. They can travel in our bloodstream, land at the programmed site, and carry out their instructions. They're small enough to float in the air, and there's no barrier they can't take apart with their miniature pincers."

Jim clicked off the window angrily. *So now every little old biddy in Los Angeles thinks her indigestion is really some microscopic submarine blasting away at her gizzard with a laser beam.* He'd better warn Goldberg to get control of the situation outside the hospital.

He maximized his program window. A table slowly appeared across his computer, one line at a time adding to the tally as computations were completed. A single glance told the story.

DATE	DEATHS (U.S.)
April 8	53
April 9	144
April 10	391
April 11	1084
April 12	3025
April 13	7241
April 14	15,624
April 15	34,828
April 16	75,983

Jim watched the numbers scroll up the screen with increasing speed as the epidemic took its virtual course. His brain began tracing the dots on an imaginary graph. The spread was exponential, likely with a broad base as it spread to multiple cities within days. This was bad. A few moments later, the screen displayed the result of Jim's simulation:

Total Estimated Deaths (U.S.):   31,475,861
Time Until 50% Deaths Reached: 61 Days

Jim raced through the numbers in his head: more than fifteen million people dead within two months in the United States alone. He sank back in his chair and rubbed his eyes. The numbers were unchanged.

He cursed in a low whisper to himself.

"Eva! Steve!" he shouted as he rose to his feet. "Eva! There's something you should see!" He jogged down the hall in search of his colleagues.

SIMON Westenfeld wandered through Emergency Operations headquarters as though he were looking for a lost puppy. He loitered by Janet Holbrook's desk and finally asked, "Any news yet?"

"No. You should get some sleep, Simon. We have to stagger our command or we'll all burn out long before this disease does."

"I can't understand what's taking Jack so long."

"You could call him."

"Not answering."

The Emergency Operations center had received a call the night before confirming the fears of a bioterror attack in Los Angeles and asking for emergency quarantine supplies stored at operations headquarters. Jack Harmer had gone to meet the federal response team, Biodefense, if Simon remembered the name right.

Simon continued walking in a wide arc past the media and security desks. As he returned toward his computer, the door opened and Jack stepped inside. He looked like he'd spent the night at the airport.

"Jack, where have you been?" Simon made a beeline toward Harmer. "You look terrible," he added.

"Five private hospitals in the east suburbs. Say, you don't look so fresh yourself. Is anyone here sleeping?"

"Simon's shift is over as of an hour ago," Janet spoke up from across the room.

"Something wrong with your phone?" Simon asked.

Jack's hand instinctively reached down to his side. He tapped a few keys, and replaced it. "Sorry. Must have been turned off."

"So what's going on? Is this for real?"

"Sure is. In fact, it's a lot worse than we were thinking. Each of the hospitals I visited had cases, each had at least one fatality. UCLA has had over a dozen."

"Hospitals under quarantine?"

"They are now. Some of them hadn't even taken the first steps. What a nightmare."

"Do you think the quarantine will work?"

"No way. The disease is being spread outside the hospital. We can't contain it if we can't find the source."

"So where do we look?"

Jack shook his head in frustration. "I don't know." He sounded angry. "Simon, this is never going to work. We need to consolidate our efforts, get the infected ones all in the same hospital. Can we get a concerted media campaign telling victims to head for UCLA?"

"Can they handle it?"

"No. Probably not, but it's better than having every instacare in the city spreading the disease. What we really need is a concentration camp."

"I'll pretend I didn't hear that."

"Simon, I'm not sure you understand how serious this is. It's not just a disease. I was there. It's hell. People are sick. It spreads fast. Kills young, healthy people in days. And nobody—" He leaned closer for emphasis until Simon could smell Jack's stale breath. "Nobody has a clue what it is."

"All right. I'll steer people to UCLA," Simon answered quietly.

TWENTY

April 9

SAM stared blankly at the beeping pager. His head throbbed to the rhythm of the noise. As his eyes adjusted to the light filtering in through the east window, he tried to focus on the digital clock. Eight-thirty. His sluggish mind went through the calculations. That meant he had almost three hours of sleep. He hadn't expected much.

The bed was still made. His shoes were jumbled at the foot of the bed, the only sign that he had wound up on the bed intentionally. *Where was the phone?* He found it on an end table, and dialed the number.

"You must first dial nine to . . ."

He dialed again. "Clinical pathology."

"This is Goldberg. I was paged."

"Just a minute, please."

Sam walked the cord around the bed and put on his shoes. He looked in the mirror and quickly looked away.

"Dr. Goldberg?"

"Yeah."

"Hi. This is Dr. Abramson, in pathology. I was given your number, and, well, there's something I think you should come see."

"Can you tell me over the phone?"

"I really think this is worth the trip. Are you in house?"

"Where are you?"

"In the basement. If you use the main elevator, you can just follow the signs."

"Ten minutes."

Goldberg hung up.

Walking over to the sink, he splashed some water in his face and nearly choked on a swallow of mouthwash.

Within two minutes, he walked out the front door of the Hilgard House Hotel onto Hilgard Avenue. With one longing look at the red brick building and the bed upstairs, he settled into a light jog until he stopped for the light at LeConte Avenue. He tried to remember what had happened throughout the night at the half dozen hospitals he had personally visited. It hadn't gone well.

Throngs of people were crowded outside the hospital. On the opposite side of the street, a makeshift booth displayed piles of blue biofilter masks. A sign read ANTITERROR MASKS—$10." The vendor was wearing two of the masks. "Ten bucks could save your life, mister!" Sam passed by with an angry glance. What he really wanted to do was give the vendor the finger.

Outside the hospital grounds, nearly a hundred people circled like sharks, most wearing masks similar to the vendor's. At least a dozen cameras on tripods were pointed toward the hospital, some bearing logos of major news networks. Sam pushed his way through the crowd toward the hospital entrance, hoping nobody would know who he was.

Demonstrators and onlookers were nearly as numerous as the reporters. A lone banner advertised NO MERCY. Two rough crowds of young men with flimsy surgical masks were kept at arm's length from each other by four police officers while four other officers stretched yellow perimeter tape around the hospital. A steady background of honking horns tore Sam's frayed nerves as drivers slowed while passing the hospital.

Breaking through the crowds of reporters, Sam saw the object of their attention. A large tent stood in front of the hospital entrance, in which half a dozen makeshift tables were set up. They had moved their triage outside, Sam realized. Hundreds of uncomfortable-looking people, some of them bent at the knees, pressed toward the tent. Others lay on the grass by the tent, apparently trying to keep their distance from the others while waiting for an opening at the tent. Sam saw a young woman, obviously pregnant, bolt from the line in front of the tent and bend over the bushes to throw up. Sam took the long way around the tent to the front entrance.

Reaching the front door, he was stopped by two masked officers. "Where are you going?" one asked brusquely.

"Pathology. I'm on staff."

"ID, please."

Sam pulled out the generic hospital ID he had received the day before.

"Sorry, people are trying to get in without going through check-in."

Sam nodded.

"Say, do you know what's really going on in there?" the guard asked. "I'm seeing a lot more people going in than coming out."

Sam shook his head and walked past the guards. The sight in front of him was utterly disappointing.

Hospital workers, visitors, and patients in gowns walked unescorted across the main hallway of the hospital. Two thin strips of red tape marked a corridor down the hallway. Sam was sure he was the only one of the fifty people in view who knew it was there. He took a deep breath and walked toward the bank of elevators beyond the lobby. *Had anything at all changed?*

Sam opened the door to a stairwell and descended one flight to emerge in a quieter, darker hallway. The hospital was less than a decade old, Sam knew, and the paint still looked sharp along the trim. As he rounded the nearby corner, he glanced down at the name badge of a passing orderly. "Vadim Mahmoud, Surgical Pathology."

"Which way to clinical path?" Sam asked.

The stranger turned slowly. He pointed down the hall. "Second hallway on the right, just past specimen receiving."

Sam nodded thanks, and picked up his pace through the winding corridors until he arrived at a glass wall with silver lettering: CLINICAL PATHOLOGY.

"Dr. Abramson?" He raised his voice rather than wait for help from the department secretary. *What had they found?* From the sound of the pathologist on the phone, it could be a significant finding. The sleeplessness had all but vanished at the anticipation of real news.

A high-pitched voice sounded several doors down. "Ah, Dr. Goldberg. Please come in. This is most interesting."

Sam walked toward the voice, and entered the room. In the center of the room, a white platform housed multiple layers of switches and controls. Two computer monitors rested on the desk. In the center of the assembly, a white cylinder rose up like a periscope. Seated at the station was a man in his sixties, with Indian features. Wisps of a white beard contrasted with his dark, round eyes.

Sam listened through the accent.

"Welcome. It is an honor to have the opportunity to work with you."

Sam nodded, his expression suggesting Abramson could cut to the chase.

"This is a transmission electron microscope. We have long been trying to secure funds from the hospital for a scanning tunneling microscope, but for now we have only this model."

Sam gestured with his hand to continue.

"We understand the importance of the cases this hospital has been receiving. And with over a hundred cases now at this hospital alone, we are struggling to keep up. My colleagues in the morgue have been working feverishly to find the organism responsible, but thus far have seen nothing abnormal. Last night, I had some slides from blood and stool samples prepared for electron microscopy. I was hopeful we might identify a virus by direct observation while cultures and assays were running."

"So what did you find?"

"Look for yourself." Abramson adjusted several of the controls on the microscope and an image appeared on the screen.

"OK. What am I looking at?"

"In the center of the screen is a red blood cell."

"It doesn't look like a red blood cell."

"Very good. It is a reticulocyte, really. Most of these patients can lose blood fairly quickly, and we see a high retic count almost on presentation. But that is not particularly interesting. Look underneath."

Sam looked carefully at the monitor. The game reminded him of his days in medical school, pimped by a long succession of mentors delighted with the opportunity to display whatever piece of arcane knowledge Sam and his fellow students never seemed to possess. He didn't mind in this case. The arcane knowledge here was too priceless.

"What's this here?" Sam pointed to a pair of tiny threads underneath the cell.

"Aha, very curious, no? What do you make of them?"

"Platelets on end?" Sam tried to imagine what shapes the objects might have in three dimensions.

"Much too small. I admit being puzzled at first, but in looking at the dimensions, I come up with only one answer."

"How big are they?"

"Only about a nanometer in width, and maybe ten microns in length. The strange thing is how smooth the edges are. This is unheard of in biology."

"I give up. What do you think they are?"

"No doubt about it. These are carbon nanotubes. Nothing else could be so perfectly formed."

"Carbon nanotubes?" Sam couldn't hide the surprise in his voice.

"Yes, I agree. I cannot explain how they would get there. But how could it be an artifact to see not only two of them, but hundreds, both in blood and stool? We have no such materials in our laboratory that could be a contaminant. And there is talk of a nanotechnological agent . . ."

"We assumed that was just hype."

"Perhaps not."

"Can you print me some photographs? No offense, but I need to get some other opinions on something this important."

"No offense taken, certainly not." Abramson appeared delighted at taking Sam through his discovery. He punched a few keys and the *whirr* of a printer sounded nearby.

"Have you told anyone about this?" Sam asked sternly.

"No, of course not." Abramson hesitated. "Only two of my colleagues, anyway." He smiled apologetically. "And the residents have seen it, of course. I needed to confirm my suspicions."

Sam stared at Abramson without blinking. "I want you to talk to every person you mentioned this to, and instruct them they are not to discuss this with anyone until I say. Is that clear?"

Abramson nodded glumly.

Sam wondered if it was wise to come down too hard. "And great work. This is a key finding. Please let me know if you discover anything new. Day or night."

"Yes, of course." The smile returned to the small man's face.

"How many patients have you found this on?"

"Only one so far. We are already making up slides for others."

"Keep looking. I don't know what this means. Carbon nanotubes have been talked about as an ideal substrate for mechanical arms in nanomachines. What we need to find is a more intact machine. These tubes can't cause disease; they're probably just shed."

"Yes, that makes sense. We will find them sooner or later."

"Sooner, I hope."

Sam snatched the photographs off the printer against the wall. He then turned to walk out of the pathology suite. He had to confirm this finding quickly. And Eva and Steve needed to know immediately. Besides that, it was time to make sure someone knew he was serious about the isolation precautions.

He picked up his cell phone, and then put it away as he passed the secretary's desk. "Where's your fax?"

TWENTY-ONE

April 9

"WESTERN." The voice grated from the speaker on the rusty ceiling of the train.

Amir checked his watch. It would be tight, but he would just make it. The train was packed, and each stop meant lengthy delays for the morning rush hour crowd. He held on to the ceiling grip with one hand and retraced the route once again on his palmtop map with the other, despite having already committed it to memory. He wished he could feel his Glock against his side, but knew there was no way to retrieve a weapon in time, and reasoned again it would be better without it. He knew that if he was discovered to be armed, the entire mission might be forfeited.

Amir lurched to the side as the train rounded a curve and plunged into a tunnel. The ratcheting of the rails sounded rhythmically in his ears. At least he had backup this time. From the plane he had prepared a detailed briefing, encrypted by his palmtop fax, and sent over the telephone in front of his seat. By now, agents would be descending on Al Rasheed in UCLA as well as on his destination, all waiting for his signal to move. The receiver in his pocket could transmit a radio signal that could be detected up to six blocks away under ideal conditions. His backup should be within one by the time he arrived.

"Damen."

He watched the impatient passengers on the train crowd together as a new bolus of commuters tried to squeeze through the doors. A voice from the back shouted, "All full. Just wait." The doors closed once and caught on a backpack, then jerked open again. After two more attempts, the doors settled closed as the student closest to the exit pushed himself up against the other passengers. "Next stop," an elderly woman announced from behind Khalil. No one seemed to be listening.

"Division."

As the train slid forward, the passengers swayed together with the motion. The key would be to find out if the trail stopped here. He suspected the network was tightly administered; no unnecessary intermediaries. Hopefully, he was going to meet a principal. If he could obtain another name, one more contact, that information would be priceless. Once any of the ring was apprehended, the entire network could disappear into hiding without notice. He didn't want to be the one who broke the chain before the leaders were identified.

"Chicago."

Amir leaned to one side as the lady behind him and a handful of others wiggled out of the train, only to be replaced by even more. The envelope was still in his pocket. He wondered if its contents had already seeped into his pocket, onto his hands, rubbed into his mouth or eyes unknowingly. Amir joined half of the other passengers in the train in staring inhospitably at one of the newly arrived passengers. The rap music from his earphones carried to the end of the car, punctuated by periodic bursts of profane rhymes from his own lips.

"Grand."

Al Rasheed had to be a courier. Amir doubted his only contact thus far had the expertise to engineer the whole attack. He daydreamed briefly about the praise he would receive, how he would be hailed as the one who saved thousands of lives. It made everything worthwhile. He had spent an entire decade in the FBI, painstakingly positioning himself as an expert in Islamic fundamentalist groups inside the United States.

As a child of eight, when his expatriate Saudi parents had immigrated to the United States as computer consultants, he found himself strangely torn between cultures. His acquaintances ranged from devoted Muslims to rabid materialists, and a sense of never belonging anywhere dominated his childhood. With few close friends, he took to reading. He loved espionage adventures where his imagination alternately fancied himself as a Saudi double agent or American spy. He attended college at Boston University, and gradually lost touch with his roots, at least until he found himself a semester from graduating and attending a State Department recruitment seminar on a whim.

Something reached him deeply, as the memories of stories he had spent his childhood with flooded back. Within a week, he had applied for a summer internship at the FBI, the CIA, and the State Department, was accepted at all three, and chose the FBI. His heritage had helped, and speaking fluent Arabic put him on a fast track within the bureau. At first it had been exhilarating, intense. He knew he would be the one to make the key breakthrough and crack open terrorist cells in the United States. Then came reality. Year after year he struggled to infiltrate local radical Islamic communities, visiting mosque after mosque and networking among the clerics. It was isolating, stifling work. How many times had he considered giving up field operations entirely? Until now . . .

"Lake."

The terse announcement jarred Amir back to his senses. He scrambled out of the train and onto the underground platform. He looked at his watch again. Five to nine. He followed a few other passengers and jogged up the stairs two at a time until the sunlight forced his eyes closed. Pedestrians passed by him briskly until he fell into step. He oriented himself with the green street signs. LaSalle and Lake. A few blocks to go.

The angst he had felt now intensified as he realized the waiting was over. At least he was moving now. The sound of his footsteps partially allayed his fears as he took in the atmosphere of the busy streets. The sidewalk terminated abruptly at a construction site, and he walked around with the crowd into the street, jutting back to the crosswalk at Wacker Drive. A final taxi squeezed through the stoplight before the advancing pedestrians arrived at the median. Amir started across the footpath over the Chicago River, glancing up at the lights on the Merchandise Mart on his left.

A short time later, Amir pulled out the envelope and confirmed the address. The apartment high-rise in front of him bore the same number. Amir walked into the foyer and found the buzzer. He looked over his shoulder as he waited.

"HE'S going in," Agent Rhodes announced over his encrypted radio to his partner. They had been in place for over an hour. It was part of the training on the NSAs elite counterterrorism operations detail to be anywhere in the city, any time of day or night within an hour of the page. Rhodes and Escovedo had both made it with time to spare on their first actual assignment.

The traditional foreign/domestic dividing line between the CIA and the FBI had been considerably blurred since the World Trade Center attacks. The NSA, which had long been "above the law" in regard to covert operations, had benefited from this immensely. One of the major functions of the CIA with respect to covert operations had been to take the blame for botched NSA operations, keeping the ultrasecret profile of the NSA operations/paramilitary division out of the public eye.

The counterterrorism unit was one of several in the NSA that operated heavily within the United States. Neither Rhodes nor Escovedo had ever been stationed abroad. Their role was strictly "training," which meant they were authorized to train local first responders in terrorism reconnaissance and countermeasures. Once that had been clarified to them, they had not undertaken a single training mission, and functioned as operatives with the authority of God should the proper situation arise. The NSA had provided a convenient umbrella for expanding counterterrorism operations inside the United States beyond the scope of the FBI. Although the NSA did not enjoy anywhere near the scope or breadth of operations personnel that the FBI had, they had a reputation for high-speed, low-drag efficiency that made them a natural choice as a force multiplier to either FBI or CIA missions. In this case, Rhodes' and Escovedo's involvement had been at the request of the FBI, which needed additional support for an agent who had made a crucial contact.

In truth, Rhodes had no way of knowing whether this

was a drill. Rhodes suspected it was. They had run at least a hundred drills on high-rise apartments in scenarios including everything from bomb threats to arson to surveillance. With training, the errors became fewer, and their confidence had increased. This case was only slightly different from the drills they ran at least once a week in that the information was a bit sketchier, and the target less well defined.

Yet the man walking into the apartment complex matched exactly the photograph downloaded to the car's central computer. So drill or not, Rhodes notified his colleague, who had been inside the complex for the better part of an hour, that the game was afoot.

"You coming in?" His partner's voice sounded on his radio.

"Not yet. We wait for a signal." Rhodes checked the batteries a third time on his receiver and waited for the green light from Agent Khalil.

AL Rasheed untied the cloth straps on his hood and pulled it from his head. He wandered over to the small refrigerator and helped himself to leftover Mongolian beef and crab wontons. *Probably from a drug rep last week,* he thought. It worked for him.

The vacant lounge had been a real find. Once the exit to the hospital was sealed, he decided he would have to take cover for the duration. What better hiding place could he find than within the flagship hospital during the epidemic? It was perfect, and he was safe anyway from the disease that raged outside. He had figured the hospital would be cleared of nonessential functions, and the outpatient dermatology clinic was a small ghost town within the hospital.

He checked in with his contacts in New York and

Chicago. Everything was on schedule. He picked up a pair of chopsticks from the cupboard and flipped on the television. He was good at waiting.

"YES." The voice was cold, businesslike.

"I have a delivery here for room six forty-one."

The door clicked and Amir pushed it open. Once he was inside the heated building, sweat began to collect on his back. He found the bank of elevators and stepped inside.

The sixth floor was dimly lit. The smells of curry overpowered the stale background scent of the worn beige carpet. Amir found the room and knocked on the door, breathing quickly.

He heard the latch on the door slide. The deadbolt snapped. He tried to slow his breathing. A sense of panic consumed him. Surely they would know he was a fraud, a mole. How could he hope to pull this off? He reached into his pocket and fingered the radio transmitter.

A coarse beard and dark eyes looked around the door. The eyes watched Amir for an uncomfortably long time.

"The package."

Amir reached into his other pocket and pulled out the envelope. A hand took it and closed the door. That was it? Surely he hadn't come this far for a dead end. Amir stood at the doorstep, unsure of what to do. He thought of turning around, of calling backup and forcing entrance, of knocking again.

The door opened again, this time wider. "Mr. Khalil, please come in."

Amir stepped inside. The room was furnished with two couches and an entertainment center. A single black floor lamp cast shadows across the furniture in the receiving room. His host made no effort to sit down. Amir followed suit, standing in the hallway after closing the door.

"The delivery was a test of the faithful."

Amir swallowed. What was the man saying? That he knew Khalil was an informant?

"I am grateful to be deemed worthy for the cause."

"As you should be." The man's eyes brightened, and he looked to Amir with fondness.

"What may I do for Allah?"

"America has brought death to itself. Now you must be the fist of Allah, crushing his enemies before his path."

"Praise to Allah."

The man motioned for Amir to stay, and he disappeared momentarily. He returned holding a water bottle, handing it to Amir.

"This is for you to be the lampbearer for Islam to New York. Unscrew the lid," he turned it a quarter turn, "and squeeze. A fine mist will spread the glorious cleanser onto the infidels. Aim for faces, hands, places that will be touched. They will not sense it. You are to take it to New York. This bottle is for the airport and flight. You will be met at the gate by the mullah, and he shall give you a replacement which you shall take throughout New York to begin the final battle."

"Will I die?" Amir asked.

"You will live forever."

"Praise be to Allah."

"Go, my son. A car is waiting to take you to the airport. Your flight is already booked." He handed Amir another envelope, and gave one final nod to his young accomplice.

Amir walked out the door and down the hallway. He handled the bottle cautiously, keeping the spout away from his face and hands.

He emerged from the building into the sunlight, and

made eye contact with the driver of a taxi in front of the building. The driver beckoned him to approach.

"From what room do you come?" the driver asked.

"Six forty-one."

"Please get in. It is an honor to meet you, my brother."

Amir slid into the backseat, sweat stinging his eyes as he looked at the container in his hand.

TWENTY-TWO

April 9

EVA leaned back in her chair. She closed her eyes and massaged her thumb. She was exhausted. It had been years since she had done so much bench lab work. She had spent the entire night in the hot lab, pipetting fresh samples from the UCLA lab as well as those Dr. Nowers had obtained from Daru into every culture medium she knew about. After the samples were incubating, she checked the cultures already brewing from UCLA.

She had been disappointed to find nothing growing. Actually, there were hundreds of colonies on the stool and nasal specimens, but almost at a glance, Eva recognized that none of these were dominant colonies. There was nothing but normal flora that grew in the mouth and the gut. She would have Susan call in staff to confirm that later. Her time was too valuable to be bent over the light microscope at this stage. After switching oxygen tanks, she had spent the next four hours preparing chips and fixing samples for electron microscopy.

"Susan, are those chips done yet?"

"Let me run check." Susan Patrick walked briskly out of the room.

Susan had been invaluable. Not only did she know every inch of the hot and cold lab space, as well as where all the machines were housed, but she could ferry samples back and forth to PCR or retrieve reagents while Eva worked. What helped Eva even more was having some company to take her mind off her conversation with Daru. She was more unnerved than she had expected by the confrontation, and images of Daru's bloodshot eyes and stained gown had made it difficult to concentrate on her work. Susan's presence in the hot lab had been reassuring on a fundamental level to her.

All the same, Eva could not have been more grateful to get out of the hot lab. Now she could work with the fixed specimens in a regular bench lab.

The door burst open. "Finally, there you are!" Jim was out of breath.

"What do you mean?"

"Why aren't you answering your cell phone?"

Eva remembered she had left her phone in the outer change room in the hot lab.

"Oops."

"Right, right. Anyway take a look at this, Eva." He handed her a printout.

Eva looked down to the bottom of the paper. "Is this some kind of joke, Jim?"

"I wish it were."

"Fifteen million people in two months?"

"This thing has the potential to rip through this country

like a brush fire, Eva. Global casualties could be catastrophic."

"I thought you said this could never happen?"

"That's just it. It can't. Nothing in the world is both this contagious and this lethal, with such a short incubation. It's like a bad cold that can kill in a couple days. There's no other organism remotely like this, Eva."

Eva rubbed her temples with her hands. She was too tired to think straight. "We have to shut down L.A. It's probably already too late."

"I already gave Alan a call. He's working on it."

"He better be."

The door opened again and Steve walked in. "Eva, where's your phone?"

She looked at Jim, "I said oops."

"Take a look at this." He handed another piece of paper to Eva. "Straight off the fax from Sam. Morning, Jim."

"Is that what they call it?" Jim yawned.

"What are those worms?"

"Good eye," Steve answered. "The guys at UCLA say they're carbon nanotubes. Nothing else fits. Sam confirmed it with the head of the materials science department there."

"Nanotubes? You mean . . ."

"Right, Jim. It's the real thing. Last I checked, we didn't make our own nanotubes in the bloodstream."

"Someone's made an infectious nanomachine?"

Steve nodded. His face was grim.

"And you haven't heard the worst of it yet. Show him your simulations, Jim," said Eva.

Jim handed Steve the results, and Steve studied the paper carefully.

"This is bad."

"What have you got so far, Eva?" Steve looked like he'd had a shower. Eva was jealous.

"Cultures are negative from L.A. I've got my own set growing on everything from chicken soup to blood agar. Then I prepped the electron slides and ran the viral chips."

"You did all that last night?" Steve sounded impressed.

"What were you up to?"

"Sleeping."

"Sleeping!"

"Hey, someone's got to be awake to take the next shift. You two look like hell."

"What are viral chips?" Jim asked.

Eva looked at her watch. "They should be done any minute. They're DNA chips. Microarrays."

"What do they do?"

"They don't do anything," Eva said irritably. "They're glass squares that have been prepared with DNA markers from thousands of test viruses frosted onto the glass with a robotic micropen. I took the RNA from patients' blood and nasal washings last night, and grew it out as cDNA with a fluorescent label. We just pour the cDNA over one of these glass squares. If the specimen cDNA sticks to one of the samples on the glass, it will light up when we read out the chip with a colored laser."

"Wow. I didn't know that was possible."

"People have been using chips like this for fifteen years. This chip's not commercially available yet. A friend of mine at Affymetrix gave me a bunch for testing a few months back. I never thought I'd get a chance to use them so quickly."

Susan returned to the lab. "All done, Eva, but not too exciting."

"What did we find?" Eva asked.

"Take a look. The array's online now." Susan punched a

few keys on a computer at the end of one of the lab benches.

Eva leaned toward the computer and began scrolling through the data. "So the controls all worked great. It looks like a good run."

Susan nodded.

Eva silently looked through the results, with Jim and Steve peering over her shoulder.

"What do you see?" asked Jim.

"It looks like a couple of the patients in L.A. are positive for Epstein-Barr, but certainly not all of them. That's not too surprising; people can shed mono virus for months after an infection. Looks like a couple more benign viruses show up sporadically. Wait, this is interesting."

Eva scrolled back and forth across pages of data. She became more excited. "We have a lead," she finally announced.

Susan, Steve, and Jim waited for her to explain.

"I only prepped samples so far from twenty patients, but every one has nasal washings positive for influenza A virus."

Steve frowned. "Lot of people harbor it, Eva. It could be just low-level contaminant. Remember, this is a very sensitive test. It doesn't mean they're all infected. We should check you for it as well."

Eva felt angry at the suggestion. "Steve, I'm not an undergraduate student. I'm more careful than that. Besides, I was in a space suit the whole time."

Steve seemed bothered by something. "I don't know, Eva. How do you explain the nanotubes? I think it's much more convincing we're dealing with a nonbiologic."

"How do I know? Maybe they engineered some influenza proteins into the virus. Influenza has some of the most clever tricks for getting into cells of any virus known."

"You should know," Steve admitted.

He was right. Eva had launched her career studying influenza virus. She suspected Steve thought she was overanxious to turn the search toward familiar topics.

Jim interrupted Eva and Steve. "Steve's got a point. We should focus on looking for the nanomachines. The nanotubes are probably just by-products. There's something more to find here."

Eva rubbed her eyes. "Then maybe you can see something I missed, because at least for Daru's samples, I didn't see anything suspicious."

"You already looked?" Jim acted surprised.

"The electron microscope is next door. Look for yourself. I was looking for viruses, but I'm sure I wouldn't have missed anything like the nanotubes on this photograph."

"Wait, I thought that stuff was supposed to stay in the hot lab." Jim looked angrily at Eva.

"Jim, I know what I'm doing. I decontaminated the slides before taking them out of the lab. Besides, everything is fixed so it's not infectious."

"Assuming this is your run-of-the-mill bacterium or virus," Steve agreed.

"All right. We'll have to be more cautious now that we're serious about the possibility of an actual nonbiologic agent. But I still think there's minimal risk." Jim's and Steve's expressions suggested they were not convinced. Susan shrugged.

"So let me get this straight. You used the same preparation that the guys at UCLA did, only you didn't see any of these nanotubes?" Jim asked rhetorically.

"Exactly."

"That's funny."

"Why don't you get some rest, Eva, and I'll check more of the samples for influenza. I can make some more electron preps as well and check for more of these nanotubes."

Eva had the sense Steve didn't trust her. Maybe she was just tired. A little sleep sounded like a good idea. But just a little.

TWENTY-THREE

April 9

PRESIDENT Sutherland took off his glasses and polished them with a white handkerchief from the pocket of his Italian suit. The other members in the room watched patiently until the president was finished.

"Let's just can the usual routine unless there's something that can't wait today, Richard."

Richard Stern, director of national intelligence, nodded.

Alan had spent most of the morning in a meeting with the secretaries of transportation and health and human services when the phone call came. It was Amanda. She said the morning intelligence briefing had contained some new developments, and that the president wanted Alan to attend a follow-up briefing at ten-thirty in the Situation Room. The call had come after ten o'clock.

After jogging through the corridors of the old Executive Office Building, where the three had commandeered a conference room to discuss quarantine plans, he worked his way through security checkpoints to the Situation Room. When he arrived, he found the others already there: President Sutherland, Vice President Atkins, Director of National Intelligence Richard Stern, Homeland Secretary Javier Rojas, Chairman of the Joint Chiefs of Staff Amanda Burgoyne, and Zack Collins. Shortly afterward, National Security Advisor Sandra Ewington was the last to arrive.

"Richard, why don't you start by bringing Javier and Alan up to speed."

Stern steepled his fingers, leaning back in his chair. "Absolutely. We have a human intelligence breakthrough in the case. It seems, Mr. Thorpe, that your suspicion of a U.S.-based cell may be correct. One of our field agents, Amir Khalil, reported last night that he had infiltrated a group in Los Angeles that appears to be responsible for the attack."

Alan pulled out a notepad as the intelligence official spoke.

"He made contact with a man named Ahmed Al Rasheed, on whom we have a huge file. He's a Ph.D. microbiologist, lives in Santa Monica, native of Saudi Arabia. He's been a U.S. citizen for more than fifteen years. Totally clean of any ties to known terrorist groups. This man, Al Rasheed, asked our agent to meet him at UCLA Medical Center last night, and gave him a package to deliver to a contact in Chicago. The package contained a tube with some clear liquid."

"Where's the sample?" Alan interrupted. He was angry that he was hearing about this only hours later.

"We're having it flown out to USAMRIID for analysis," the national intelligence director continued. "They should be off the ground by now."

"With all respect, sir, I think my team doing the analysis

on the patient samples in Montana is better equipped for the analysis."

Stern's face showed strained patience.

President Sutherland interceded. "I agree. Let's get that sample to Montana as soon as possible."

Stern nodded acquiescence. "Our agent was supposed to make contact with this next link about a half hour ago in Chicago. No report yet. We have a team standing by on his signal to storm the target in Chicago, and we are trying to locate Al Rasheed in Los Angeles."

"You think you have your man?" Rojas asked.

Stern paused a moment to think. "We're not sure. It looks promising, but the truth is that this Al Rasheed has basically been a business consultant for more than ten years. We don't think he has any active laboratory or research experience since he finished his degree. Plus, our agent has the sense that he's a middleman."

"So why hasn't he been interrogated yet?" Vice President Atkins asked.

Stern responded, "We'll find him. FBI's got a dozen agents on it in Los Angeles. We're waiting on this meeting in Chicago, though. Once we move on anyone in the network, the rest of them will scatter. We've seen it before. Best if we can nail them all at once."

"I'm prepared to give it a little time, but not much," President Sutherland stated.

"I'm sure I don't need to mention that any hint of our suspicions picked up by the media would have the same effect."

There was a knock at the door. Sandra Ewington opened the door to find a uniformed guard. "There's a telephone call for Director Stern."

"Yeah. Put it through." Stern said. He picked up the telephone and listened. After a moment he put his hand over the receiver and looked directly at the president. "Agent Khalil has met with his contact in Chicago, and is headed to New York where he expects another meeting. He's got a spray bottle with infectious particles. Looks like we've definitely infiltrated the ring."

"Let's grab everyone we can get, and have a team ready in New York to clean up," President Sutherland ordered.

"All right, let's pick up the guys in L.A. and Chicago. Have a team in New York in place to grab the contact when Khalil gets there. Get our interrogators in place." Stern replaced the receiver.

President Sutherland spoke again. "I trust your people understand the importance of the interrogation. Minor breaches in protocol may be acceptable."

Alan wondered what *minor breaches* included. He looked at Sutherland. "Mr. President . . ."

"We'll get that sample your way as soon as he lands in New York, Alan."

"Thanks, Mr. President."

"Richard, do you have any idea who these people are?"

Stern shook his head. "All we have on the guy in Chicago is a sketchy physical description. We'll find out who they're working for."

Sutherland turned to Alan. "What's going on in L.A.?"

Alan had no good news to give. "There have been more than a hundred deaths, perhaps more than a thousand people at area hospitals seeking treatment, three hundred at UCLA Medical Center alone. We still have no diagnosis, no effective treatment. We're predicting more than ten thousand cases by the end of the week."

"This is a disaster," Vice President Atkins cut in. "I really want to hurt whoever did this."

"There's more. Our epidemiologist has the best epidemic

model in existence, and he's predicting that some of the features of this disease make this potentially catastrophic. There's no easy way to say this. Possible casualties could run in the tens of millions within a few months if this thing takes hold. There's no precedent for this disease."

The president leaned back in his chair and took a deep breath.

"Just this morning, we've found in patient samples another alarming discovery. On a high-powered microscope, there are tiny threads that we've identified as carbon nanotubes."

"You'll have to spell that out for me," Sutherland said.

"Carbon nanotubes are one of the products of nanotechnology. They're used mostly for ultrafine wires in computer applications. They're also used as ultrasharp probe tips in our most powerful microscopes, and work sort of like the needles on an old-fashioned record player. It's undoubtedly an artificial material, and its presence in biological specimens can only mean that there is a high-tech artificial virus, presumably with the power to reproduce itself. It's hard to overstate the technological breakthrough this would represent."

"Alan, are you telling me that these terrorists have created something light-years ahead of our own best scientists?"

"Actually, Mr. President, I have to wonder if there is any chance this technology hasn't been stolen from our own research or from Japan or Russia or Europe. It's just too hard for me to swallow that anyone else could create something so advanced."

The president stood and paced with his hands clasped behind his head. "No way. I have never heard of anything like this at all. Sandra, find out for me if we have anyone working on anything like this, and have Tom ask around if anyone else has a program like this going on." He stopped and looked back at Alan. "Tens of millions? Forget what I said. earlier, Richard. Do whatever you need to wring the truth out of those bastards."

"I think it's time to quarantine Los Angeles, Mr. President."

"How are we going to do that?"

"I've been working out the details this morning. We put the National Guard on every road out of the city. Sea and air traffic has to be shut down in and out of L.A. In fact, that's not going to be enough. If we shut down the whole city this instant, there will probably be a handful of cases already spread to other cities. Lots of cities if they've targeted the airport. We need to shut down all nonmilitary air travel, period, probably for a week. Then we see where cases have popped up, and contain those cities."

"Los Angeles probably doesn't have a week's supply of food and fuel," Zack challenged.

"Clearly we'll have to allow supplies in under escort."

"Do it," the president ordered. "Zack, please let the appropriate people know that Los Angeles is under martial law."

IT had been forty-five minutes since Agent Rhodes had watched Khalil leave the building and board a taxi. The license plate number had been analyzed and the driver identified within five minutes. After that, Rhodes had done little else but sip his coffee and watch his receiver. He had watched the dozens of people entering and leaving the high-rise building. At this time of morning, traffic was high. As with most buildings of its type in Chicago, it housed tenants from a diverse pool of nationalities.

The light went off, and a quiet alarm sounded. A text

message stated simply, "Bring in target." Rhodes had the car door open and his radio to his ear instantly. If this was a drill, he knew he was being timed.

By the time he reached the door, his partner was in the lobby to let him in. "How are the doors?" Rhodes asked.

Escovedo was an expert lock picker, and Rhodes assumed he had used his time inside to practice on a few of the doors.

"No problem."

They took the stairs two at a time to the sixth floor. They could have gone twelve floors without getting winded.

Within a minute of the signal, they stood outside the door to room 641. Escovedo had the door open within seconds. Rhodes had expected a safety latch and braced to rip it out of the wall if needed. To his surprise, the door swung open freely. The room was dark.

Automatic pistols raised, the agents stormed the apartment. "Police. Don't move." The two worked quickly, clearing every room and closet in the small apartment. The whole operation took only fifteen seconds.

When they finally turned on a light, they had already confirmed that the apartment was empty. Around the corner from the entrance, a small photograph lay face down on a nightstand. It was a wedding picture from a young American couple. Rhodes went to the kitchen and found breakfast dishes in the sink, unwashed. The single bedroom displayed more pictures of the same couple, one at Navy Pier and the other at the Lincoln Park Zoo. The bed was unmade.

Rhodes relaxed his grip on his pistol. "Looks like another drill."

* * *

A knock came again at the door to the Situation Room. Alan opened it to find the same guard looking toward Director Stern. "Phone call, sir."

Stern picked up the telephone. "Stern."

A moment later he simply hung up.

"The Chicago target has vanished."

TWENTY-FOUR

April 9

"THERE'S no food, no blood. We're turning into a high-rise morgue." Lisa Holland's voice was muffled by the biofilter mask as she guided Sam toward the inpatient wards. "We don't even know what we're doing for these people. They're lining up outside, and we're full. Eight of my staff are sick. I don't know what to tell the others. Do you think they don't know?"

Sam closed his eyes. "We need more time." After wandering through the hospital, he decided the quarantine was completely ineffectual. He needed someone who could actually enforce it. The doctors had failed miserably. Even in a crisis, they were too distanced from the patients to keep order.

"OK. I'll do it. But I don't know how." Lisa removed a glove and dabbed at her eyes.

"Thanks," Sam answered. He had asked the seasoned

E.R. nurse to be the infection control officer for the hospital, enforcing the quarantine and keeping a semblance of order. "We need to have armed guards on every floor. This is serious business. No one leaves a hot zone without decontaminating their hands. There's no way to keep the hospital running if the staff can't count on being safe when they leave the bedside. Everyone in a hot zone needs a biofilter mask, and full chemical jumpsuit with disposable gowns at each patient room."

They turned the corner onto an inpatient ward.

Lisa pointed to an open door. "We already have two patients, sometimes more in every room. And these are sick patients. The nursing staff isn't able to put out fires with this kind of load."

Inside the room Sam saw two beds, with two very tired-looking Hispanic parents lying on top of one bed and two small children on another. The room smelled of disinfectant and human waste.

"People are scared, Dr. Goldberg. I'm scared . . ."

Sam turned his head as he heard a shuffling of feet farther down the corridor. "Sir, where are you going?" an authoritative voice spoke from the distance.

Sam focused on the source. A young man in a hospital gown picked up his pace, ignoring the question and walking toward Sam and Lisa.

"Sir, I need to you to come back to your room, please." A heavyset man in a blue jumpsuit and mask, stethoscope around his neck, fell into an awkward jog behind the patient.

The patient looked Jamaican, his dreadlocks swinging in front of his determined eyes as he walked. He paused briefly, putting one hand over his belly as though he felt cramping. He whirled around, still partially bent over, and outstretched one arm. "You stop right there. Dis place is a death trap. I'm outta here."

The nurse had almost overtaken the man, now just a few feet in front of Sam and Lisa. The patient straightened up and started into a dead sprint toward the stairs.

He was not three steps into his run when Lisa grabbed his arm and twisted it behind his back, pushing him into the wall. In one movement, she withdrew a syringe from her pocket, flicked the cap off onto the floor, and buried the needle in the patient's shoulder. An instant later, the needle was out and the other nurse arrived. He quickly took hold of the patient's arms and held him securely.

The patient began kicking his legs toward the nurse, who expertly dodged. "You can't do this to me! I have rights!" The patient looked like a rabid dog.

"It's not safe for you to leave right now, sir. I promise we'll do everything we can to help you," Lisa spoke softly. She turned to the other nurse and said. "He got two milligrams of Ativan. Put a posey on him when he's down." The heavyset nurse pressed the patient tightly against the wall in a wrestling hold, settling down for the wait.

Sam nodded approval. Restraints were OK, if necessary. Sending someone who was infected out of the hospital would not only speed up their own death, but perhaps cause several more infections as well. It had to be done quietly, though. If a mass panic broke out on the floor, Sam knew there was no way the staff could stop it. They continued walking.

"Lisa, where do we stand with blood?"

"We've used up all our O negative. The blood bank isn't keeping up trying to cross-match so many patients."

"I'll work on getting some shipments in. Let's stretch the crystalloid as far as we can and at least keep everyone hydrated. That's one thing we can do for them. I'll get food pouring into this hospital by nightfall. Good food. At least that will help morale."

She nodded.

"The experienced nurses. Tell them not to wait for an order to act. They need to be as autonomous as possible. Focus the docs on handling crises and giving supervision."

As they passed the nurses' station, a nurse was talking emphatically on the phone. "I know, but we can't squeeze anyone else in . . ."

Sam leaned over the desk and pointed to an open linen room. "You can put someone in there. What about utility rooms? Screw the fire code."

She threw up her hands. "Give us five minutes. Maybe we can take another five or six."

The secretary looked discouraged. She turned toward Sam and Lisa. "What does it matter? We can't fit them all."

"We can fit more. What we do now can make all the difference."

Sam raised his voice. "Could I have all the staff gather at the nurses' station, please."

The secretary repeated the page on the overhead speaker.

A dozen worn, angry figures assembled from patient rooms, removing gloves and rubbing their hands with gel as they approached. When all the nurses, doctors, and aides in view had clustered, Sam sat on a nearby counter and spoke.

"I know that nobody is telling you what's going on. That you've heard this is a bioterrorist attack. I know you're working sixteen hours a day, that you're overworked, overtired, scared. I am too. I want you to know that my friends are working just as hard on finding a cure for this disease, and they'll find it. The most important thing we can do now is keep a tight quarantine. I've asked Lisa Holland, who you know, to watch your backs and make sure when you leave patient rooms, you leave the disease there. I'll have some armed guards on the floor to help with enforcement.

Patients are not to leave under any circumstances. Protective gear is to be worn constantly. Fresh gloves and gowns must be used every time you enter a patient's room."

A few heads nodded understanding.

"We're not sure yet exactly what this is, or how it started. If it helps, try to remember that when this is all over, there will be a memorial right out there." Sam pointed out the window to the hospital grounds, where the triage tent was just visible below. "Each of your names will be on it for the service you provided to our country in a time of crisis. This is a new kind of warfare, and you are the soldiers now. This is where the battle will be fought, right on this floor. If we win, you will be the heroes of the battle. If we can stop this disease in its tracks here, there's no way to tell how many lives you will have saved. I'll give you more information as soon as I have some."

Sam stood on his feet. "Try to keep it up. Taking care of patients is often a thankless job. I promise you that if we can fight this back here, people will not forget this time."

The faces of the small crowd were softened. Sam sensed a palpable feeling of empathy among the group. One by one, they stood to return to work.

As Sam turned toward Lisa, his cell phone rang. He put it to his ear. "Goldberg."

It was Alan. "Any changes, Sam?"

"No good ones."

"We're going to quarantine Los Angeles in an hour. Can you head back to Hamilton?"

Sam stared out the window. "You know I can't, Alan. Things are too unsettled, and getting worse."

"We have a sample, and a suspect. One of our spies infiltrated the network."

"Thank goodness. We need a break about now."

"We'll talk later."

Sam closed the phone and replaced it.

"Lisa, I'm afraid there are dozens of other hospitals in the city that are in terrible shape. They're not getting the caseloads you are, but I better start making rounds."

Lisa touched Sam's forearm. "Thanks, Dr. Goldberg."

Sam's pager went off. He recognized the number instantly.

He picked up his phone and dialed. "Clinical pathology."

"This is Dr. Goldberg, someone paged."

"Just a minute, please." There was a short pause.

The voice of the Indian pathologist Sam had spoken with earlier that morning responded. "Hello, Dr. Goldberg. We have another development."

"Did you find an intact virus?"

"Not yet, but we are preparing more samples right now."

"So what did you find?"

"I say, this case is getting stranger and stranger. This makes no sense at all."

"What did you find?"

"It was quite by accident, really. A lucky stroke, I must admit. We had our toxicology lab screen some of the samples for known toxins. I thought, what could it hurt . . ."

"What did you find?"

"Ricin, Dr. Goldberg. The samples are loaded with it. Highly concentrated. We've tested three patients so far and they all confirm the presence of ricin."

"Where is it most concentrated?"

"The stool samples seem to light up most brightly, but we have found it in other places as well. Even in oral swabs."

"Ricin?" Sam thought aloud. The substance was one of the most potent toxins known to humanity. A few molecules were enough to kill a cell. Sam had seen cases before of accidental poisoning in South America, where ingestion of a few castor beans had contained enough of the poison to be life threatening. But how was it getting into patients here?

"Yes, that is what I said."

"Thanks. Let me know if you find anything else."

Sam closed up his phone.

"Ricin?" he repeated to himself. "What the hell is going on . . ."

He opened up his phone again and dialed another number.

"L.A. Emergency Operations."

"Get me Westenfeld."

"Mr. Westenfeld is currently unavailable. May I ask . . ."

"This is Sam Goldberg. I need him now."

There was a brief pause.

"Simon here."

"Mr. Westenfeld. This is Sam Goldberg. I have a few projects for you, if you don't mind."

"What do you need?"

"Blood. Lots of it."

"I'll see what I can do."

"We need it fast," Sam emphasized.

"Anything else?"

"How about some decent food. Impress whatever restaurants or caterers you can into service. There's a growing crowd outside, and before long I'm worried we need to feed the five thousand. We need portable restroom facilities. More personal protective gear. We're almost out of gowns."

"I'm on it. How is it going?"

"Don't ask."

TWENTY-FIVE

April 9

IT was a lousy nap anyway, Eva thought. After four hours of restless sleep with vivid, unpleasant dreams, Sam's phone call had been a welcome interruption. She downed a couple Tylenol from her suitcase with a generous swig of Diet Coke. A few minutes after Sam had told her of the ricin discovery, she got a call from Susan Patrick that a live sample had just arrived at the laboratory.

If thoughts of ricin were enough to keep her brain awake, she knew she sure as hell wasn't going to sleep knowing an actual sample of the bug was just around the corner.

She tried to fit the new pieces into a consistent framework. A nanomachine that can reproduce itself and churn out ricin? It seemed the best fit. That could easily explain the ulceration of the GI tract that patients had.

But how? How could a machine like that work? If it made a protein, it had to be essentially an artificial ribosome. That was complex enough. Who could design a nanomachine sophisticated enough to produce both proteins and nanocomponents? If anything, this new development made the story more unbelievable, more confusing.

She left her mug in her room reluctantly. Better to do without than to end up with a mug of nanojuice. It didn't belong in the lab. She grabbed her security pass off the nightstand and headed toward the elevator.

She thought again about the morning's work. The influenza had to be a red herring. There were too many pieces to the puzzle already, and that was just wishful thinking. She would know soon. Now that they had a pure specimen, it should be a snap to identify it.

Eva stepped inside the elevator and pushed the button for the fourth floor. She slid her security pass into the slot.

"Authorized biosafety level four, Eva Vanorden," the elevator announced.

Eva walked into the laboratory break room, where a lone secretary sat at the desk.

"You ever get bored in here?" Eva asked.

"Beats being in there. That's for sure." The secretary motioned with her head toward the hot lab.

"I guess so," said Eva.

"Dr. Adams has been inside for a couple hours. Dr. Nowers just left."

"Thanks."

Eva walked through the doors into the outer change room. The doors snapped shut.

A *whirr* of machinery hummed to life that Eva assumed was the filtration system coming from the airlock.

A voice came from nowhere. Each time it took Eva by surprise.

"Dr. Vanorden. Please remove all clothing and jewelry."

Eva hated undressing. She was certain she had spent

enough of her life thinking about the last five pounds she wanted off her tummy that the cumulative mental energy should long ago have burned them off.

The voice guided her as she assembled her suit, helmet, and oxygen tank. Ever since Jim had voiced the thought, she could never quite convince herself that, in fact, there were no cameras in the changing rooms. She looked every time she passed through. *Curse Jim for that.*

Once suited up, Eva started her oxygen tank, and rechecked the dial. *Four hours.* She pressed the button on the airlock and the door slid open, then closed behind her. Only then did the far door open into the shower room. She passed again through the airlock on the far end of the room, and found herself in the inner change room.

Eva walked immediately over to the autoclave and opened the door. Inside on the floor was a single metal box with biohazard warning labels. She took the box in her double-gloved hands.

She opened the box. Inside was a single microflask containing half a milliliter of clear fluid. She held it up to the light. Completely clear.

Setting the box down, she took the flask with her through the filtered hallway into the cabinet room. Steve was already there. She heard a faint hum from the room beyond, Daru's room. She recognized the faint sound by the beat as the music she had brought to Daru.

She wondered how Daru was doing. Should she go check? Not her job. She had work to do, and Daru depended on her just like everyone else. Eva knew that Dr. Nowers had access to Daru's vital signs on remote monitors twenty-four hours a day. And he had just left. In spite of herself, in spite of feeling as if she had only frightened Daru worse each time she had talked to her, she wanted to see her again. *Soon,* she decided.

"Hey, Eva, you're supposed to be sleeping." Steve's voice came through her earphone. "I'm perfectly capable of running these samples on my own."

Eva got right to the point. "We have a sample."

"What?"

"One of our spies has infiltrated the network. Some guy named Khalil. They say he got an assignment to deliver this to one of the principals in the terrorist ring in Chicago. He pulled off a small amount for us to analyze. They're trying to wrap up the whole ring."

"Thank God." Steve walked over to look at the tiny flask.

"Not much for analysis," Eva admitted. "Probably just a few drops."

"It'll be plenty."

"Guess what else, Steve. They found ricin in the patient samples."

Steve's face went blank as he processed the information.

"That's impossible, Eva. Just how many goofy leads are we going to get before this is solved?"

"Sam said they found it in a bunch of samples at UCLA. Concentrated in stool samples."

"It looks like we've finally got the answer." Steve pointed to the microflask. "What should we run first?"

"I think we should start with an electron microscope prep. We can do it quickly, and it won't take much of the sample. Then we know what we're looking for."

Steve thought that over. "What we're really wondering is what kind of beast this is, right? I mean, we've talked ricin, influenza, nanotubes. We have no idea."

"So why not look at it under the scope?"

"That will take us hours. Why don't we just run it through the mass spec. That will at least show us what it's made of."

As soon as Steve made the suggestion, Eva knew he was

right. A mass spectrometer could break the sample down into tiny ions, tell them what ions were contained and in what amounts. Viruses, bacteria, and certainly nonbiologic samples would have characteristic patterns.

She followed Steve into the corridor and back to the equipment room, where most of the heavy analytic machines were located. She handed the flask to Steve, who carefully unscrewed the lid and prepared the sample. Only a microliter of the sample would be needed. That was good, too.

After Steve closed the lid on the flask, he warmed up the machine and inserted the sample.

Eva watched Steve's composure as he handled the sample. *I'd have that poise too,* she thought, *if I'd had a real night's sleep.* Still, it was hard to feel jealous toward someone like Steve, because he never made her feel inadequate.

"You know, Eva, she's got a lot of guts."

"Who, Daru?"

Steve's helmet nodded.

"She sure does. I want to beat this thing just for her." Eva heard him sniffle in his microphone and she looked through his faceplate. There were tears in the corners of his eyes.

"No kidding." Her response seemed inadequate compared to the emotional force of Steve's comment. After all, Daru was *her* friend.

Eva looked up at the monitor over the spectrometer, where the readout was displayed. On the top of the screen was a ragged line running across the screen. There were no peaks rising from the baseline. Below the line were the words NO SAMPLE DETECTED.

"Run it again, Steve."

He repeated the process, even more meticulously. A few moments later, Eva saw the same display readout.

"Try one of the controls."

Steve was already reaching for a small vial with salt water. He drew up a sample and ran the machine again.

In a moment, characteristic sodium and chloride peaks rose above the jagged baseline. Below, the analysis window described the correct concentrations of the two ions.

Steve furrowed his eyes behind his faceplate. "Looks like whatever it is, it doesn't ionize."

"That's impossible," Eva said.

A moment later she reached the conclusion first. "Steve, there's nothing but water in there." She looked again at the monitor. "Why would they give him a tube of water . . . *Donder en blitzen!* They know he's a spy. We've got to tell Alan."

Eva broke into a run toward the outer change room.

TWENTY-SIX

April 9

ZACK steepled his fingers, leaning back in his chair. "We're never going to get another chance like this, Mandy. Your stalling could cost thousands of our troops. It'll happen anyway. Face it."

"No, Zack. I'm not the one putting lives at risk. You're trying to send them into Syria, not me," Amanda answered. Alan sensed she had planned this conversation to take place in her office, with Thorpe present as a witness. *Smart move.*

Defense secretary Jacob Feinberg pressed her further. "Zack's right, Amanda. I have orders waiting for the president's signature that will send in our special ops teams to nab the dozen terrorists we already know are active in Syria. We don't have to launch a full invasion. If we do it immediately, I guarantee you we'll get every one of them. You tell me which way you want it. We can do this without you, but if we had your support, it's a done deal and we can move in time."

Amanda held her ground. "And then what? Business as usual? What do we say? Do we just explain to a country we have full diplomatic relations with that we just kidnapped half their government and they just have to deal with it?"

"Damn right," Feinberg said. "And if they don't deal with it, we have a full strike ready that could pulverize their military, starting with their *illegal* chemical weapons program, within twenty-four hours." He leaned in further. "There's a new policy in play, Amanda. It's called screw the terrorists. It's no different than the Bush doctrine. Any country who harbors terrorists is in our scope. Only now, it should be clear we're not waiting around for the UN to finish picking its collective nose."

"We don't even know these guys in Syria were involved."

"Somebody was, and they're all in bed together."

"That's exactly the sort of sound bite that will unite the entire Islamic world against us."

"Bring it on. I say it's time. They want all-out war, let's give it to them. We can take the whole disorganized lot of them once and for all."

"Not on my conscience. I hold we find out exactly who did it, and make a measured response."

Alan ventured a stand. "If we don't focus on stopping this disease, it's entirely possible we could lose, whoever we fight." What he wanted to say was that targeting the whole Islamic world was suicide. Our attention span would never see it through. The easiest solution, Alan thought, was to overwhelm the Middle East with medical aid, television, and American culture. The best solution would be to organize the Islamic community within the United States and give it a prominent role in shaping Middle Eastern policy.

Alan's cell phone rang. He looked down at the caller ID and saw his own home phone number. *Could her timing be any worse?* Alan wrestled with whether to pick it up for another ring and finally excused himself to leave. He'd promised Anita that he would keep his phone close and answer if she called. It had been his one concession for taking a job that could be both unpredictable and dangerous. He stepped into the hallway and shut the door quietly to answer the phone.

"Dad?"

"Hi, Emily. Can I call you right back?"

"No, Dad! Do you know what those idiots are doing? They're putting the whole city of Los Angeles on quarantine. Can't you tell them what a bad idea that is?"

"Sweetheart, it's a very bad time to talk right now."

"But, Dad, everyone I know is in Los Angeles. That's where I go to school. All my friends are trapped there."

"This is a very serious problem, Emily. It could be important to stop this disease from spreading early."

"Yeah, it's serious. And we're making it worse. Do you know that there has already been a mass suicide pact in Los Angeles? It's all over the news. Twenty people died."

"I'm sorry, Emily, but I have to go. I can't tell you everything, but this quarantine has to stay for a while. I'll do everything I can to lift it when it's safe."

"Dad!"

Alan hung up his phone. As he put his hand on the doorknob, the phone rang again. He couldn't allow himself to be distracted any further. Emily would have to wait. He moved to shut off the phone, then noticed that the caller ID line had changed to DEPARTMENT OF HOMELAND SECURITY.

"Alan Thorpe."

"Hello, Javier Rojas. Listen, Alan. That spy is about to

be debriefed, and I thought it might be good for you to be there. In case there's something that could help your investigation. I ran it by Stern and he's cool with you sitting in."

"He's in Washington? What happened in New York?"

"Not a trace of his contact. We must have scared them off in Chicago."

"Sure. I'll come right over. Where are you?"

The homeland security secretary gave Alan the room number for the debriefing.

"And by the way, what about those samples?"

"One just arrived in Montana. The other one is already en route."

"Good, we should have an answer by tomorrow."

A half hour later, Alan walked into the room and thanked the officer who had escorted him up. He recognized National Intelligence Director Stern, Homeland Secretary Rojas, and National Security Advisor Ewington already in the room. Several other officials were spread around the room engaged in clerical duties. It appeared they were just getting ready to start. Alan walked directly toward the man on the other side of the table, seated alone.

"Alan Thorpe. You must be the man who provided the sample for my team to analyze."

"Amir Khalil. Pleasure to meet you, sir." He shook Alan's hand. Khalil turned his head and sneezed. He pulled out his handkerchief and wiped his face. "Sorry, springtime and allergies, you know."

Alan put his arm around the man. Tears welled up in Alan's eyes as he thanked Khalil for the sacrifice he had made to obtain the sample. Alan wiped his eyes with the back of his hand.

"It is my duty and privilege to have been able to serve

my country." Khalil was clearly moved by Alan's gesture of thanks.

Alan moved to take a seat at the table. On the table were voluminous files stacked nearly a foot high. Alan could discern that a few of the loose pages contained photographs and biographies. It was going to be a long debriefing, Alan suspected.

His phone rang again, and Alan assumed it would be Emily again. She never was able to stand it when she needed to talk. Alan had always been her main confidant, even in high school. He was surprised to find that the phone call came from Montana.

"Alan."

Eva's breathless voice answered. "We just got the sample."

"Do you have any result yet?"

"There's nothing there."

"What do you mean? They said they had a sample." Alan lowered his voice below earshot of the others at the table.

"No, there was a sample all right. But it was just water. Alan, what if they suspect him? He could be in real danger."

"He's fine, Eva. I'm in a room with him right now."

"They knew he was a spy and they let him go?"

"Eva, he told us the guy in Chicago said the first sample was just a test. It's the second sample we really want to look at carefully." Alan was practically whispering.

"Oh."

"Let me know when you get it."

"Sure, Alan."

"How are you holding up, Eva?"

"Barely."

"Hang in there, OK? We'll beat this."

"We better."

* * *

THE telephone rang in the back room of the Al Anwar restaurant in upper Manhattan. A thick hand with a tuft of dark hair on the back lifted the receiver on the first ring. "I've been waiting," the man answered in Arabic.

"I had to get to a safe house."

"So the recruit is a traitor."

"I have to assume so. When he delivered the test vial, some was missing."

"So what did you do?"

"Turned him into a guided missile. Sent him to New York in a taxi loaded with active agent."

"Both agents?"

"Yes, of course."

"He will not survive. Do they suspect you?"

"How could they? I left no prints. The meeting place was some yuppie's apartment that can't be traced to us."

"We needed the help. Our delivery boys are stretched very thin."

"I just heard from Al Rasheed. He has learned that everything is going as planned."

"Who is doing the analysis?"

"They're at Rocky Mountain Lab."

"Do we have anyone we can spare?"

"Do we have a choice?"

"Send him."

"Praise to Allah."

TWENTY-SEVEN

☣

April 10

"LOOK, Stew. All I know is that there are nanotubes in those samples, and more than fifteen hundred people are dead. Do the math." Jim had been awakened by a call from the security guard at the front gate. The guard had said there was a Dr. Rindler insisting that Jim had sent for him. After Jim had said he hadn't sent for anyone and didn't know what kind of prick would say such a thing at six in the morning, he had to call the guard back and say he actually did know a Dr. Rindler, and could he please send the man up. Jim and mornings did not mix, and he barely had time to put an elastic in his ponytail before his old college roommate began knocking on his door.

"Jim, you're such a stubborn cuss. That's exactly why I drove all night to get out here and knock some sense into you." Stewart Rindler smiled, and Jim returned the smile.

"Good to see you, Stew."

"You look awful, Jim. What, did you just wake up or something?"

"Don't start with me. Morning starts in about six hours."

Stewart Rindler made Jim look like a bodybuilder. He stood five foot eight, a hundred and thirty pounds, with none of it in his biceps. The frames on his glasses had been chosen at random from the local Wal-Mart, and random chance had not been kind to Rindler. His clothes had also been chosen at random from the pants drawer, the shirt drawer, and the sock drawer. At least the socks were almost the same color. Jim wondered if his fling with Sonia a few years back had worn off on him. Before that, Jim doubted he would have even noticed Rindler's attire.

Stew looked around the room, apparently searching for someone else. "What, did our whole scientific community die off and leave you in charge here?"

Jim picked up his phone and dialed a number, then another. "The others must be in the lab. I suppose you want to talk at them, too?"

Stewart nodded. "I thought that security guard downstairs was about to run me out of town."

"He's a marine. They sent real guards with us when we came out. Thanks for coming out. I just wanted to run a few questions by you—I didn't expect you to come all the way out here."

"Like I said, I didn't want you misrepresenting me."

Jim led his old friend toward the elevator and up to the hot lab. The elevator announced his security clearance and the two walked into the break room. It was empty.

Jim went to the desk and pushed the button for the intercom. "Eva, Steve? Come on out. I brought a physicist in for show and tell."

"Come in and get us," Eva answered back.

Two minutes later, she emerged from the doors to the inner change room.

Jim introduced her. "This is Stewart Rindler, Eva. He's a full professor working on nanotechnology at Caltech."

Rindler shook her hand. "I see you keep better company in women these days, Jim."

Eva looked over at Jim. "Jim's our mascot."

"Where's Steve?"

"Jim, we don't exactly go through the showers together."

"Oh, right."

A minute later Steve joined them. He looked tense as he looked over Jim's friend.

"This is Stewart Rindler. He's one of the country's best nanotechnologists. I thought we could use his help."

"Does he have a security clearance?"

"Screw the clearance, Steve. We need help."

Steve nodded. Jim wondered why Steve looked so much more tired than yesterday. It was the first time Jim remembered seeing Steve without his usual sense of poise.

"This isn't a nanovirus."

"What?" asked Eva.

"What I said. There's no such thing. Jim called me and brought me up to date. I held a closed-door seminar with the senior nanotech group yesterday afternoon at Caltech. Everyone agrees. I thought someone needed to hear this in person."

"Why are you so sure? Did you hear about the nanotubes?" Steve asked.

Rindler nodded. "They're a scam."

"A scam?"

"No other explanation. They're real, all right. That photograph was convincing, but it makes no sense. They're ten microns long. What good is something like that?"

"What do you mean?" asked Jim.

"Supposedly nanotubes are used as arms to assemble some kind of nanomaterial. But having arms that long would be like manufacturing widgets using wire manipulators fifty feet long. There's no way to maneuver them. It's ergonomically absurd."

"You would expect them to be shorter?"

"Definitely, by orders of magnitude if they're actually used for atomic manipulation."

Steve frowned. "What if they were used as some sort of scaffolding, or assembly design?"

Rindler shook his head. "You're talking about something five generations in the future. Something that complicated doesn't exist. The whole idea of the assembler is a pipe dream anyway."

"Why?" Jim asked.

"Nobody I know has even taken the possibility seriously. Suppose you want to design something that can move atoms around, assembling molecules. There's something called the sticky problem. Things on the nanoscale work differently. If you design pincers, say, to pick up an atom, they can't drop it easily. They're too sticky. And the pincers would have to be highly selective for one type of atom. They can't put a hydrogen atom down, then reload and pick up a carbon atom. Molecular manufacturing is not and never will be general purpose. Specific molecules require specific enzymes and catalysts to construct."

"Then what are those nanotubes doing in patient samples?"

"Have you replicated them?"

"No. Not yet."

"You won't. Somebody spiked the samples."

"How do you know?"

"We all agreed on this. There is no biological function for those tubes. They're big. They can't be missed. They have only one purpose, and that is to throw you off. It seems to be working, until now. That's why I came out."

Eva was deep in thought. "They have someone inside the hospital. We need to tell Sam."

"Why would somebody go to so much trouble?" Jim asked.

"Because it's treatable, and they know it. Why else would they take such a risk to throw us off?" Eva rubbed her eyes. "So what is this thing? They must know how virulent it is. If Jim's predictions are right, all they need is a few months for a huge outbreak."

"We've got to shift back to biologics. What if the influenza is not a contaminant, but the disease itself?" Steve's mood seemed to lighten up. "How hard would it be to engineer it to produce ricin?"

Jim shook his head. "I don't buy it, Steve. A modified influenza wouldn't be able to compete if it had to produce an extra protein in large quantities. It couldn't take hold so fast. And the incubation time is wrong. It would take at least a week to build up an infection this devastating."

"Jim's probably right," Eva said. "Influenza can't produce ricin. It's a virus and uses our own cells to produce its proteins. But ricin shuts down human protein synthesis. It acts on the ribosome. The instant it was produced, it would shut down the cell."

"Any better ideas?" Steve sounded deflated.

"Influenza is still our best lead. We need to sequence it."

"So let's get on it. Do we have the primers?"

Eva nodded. "If we shotgun it with all our sequencers, I bet we could have data coming in as early as tonight. I'll do it."

"Aren't you going to need an army of techs for that?" Jim asked.

Eva looked down her nose at Jim. "Jim, welcome to the

twenty-first century. I put the sample in and leave. There's a robotic empire down there."

"I'll keep working on the ricin angle," Steve added.

"Thanks for coming up, Stew." Jim said. "I guess I still need looking after now and then."

"I'll be saving your butt in your nursing home."

"Maybe by then you'll manage to match a pair of socks."

TWENTY-EIGHT

☣

April 10

"THE nanotubes are planted?" Sam rubbed his eyes again.

"That's what they said," Eva answered.

"And these are physicists?"

"The senior nanotechnology scientists at Caltech."

"Well, that's just great. Who am I supposed to believe?"

"I think they're right. I think the ricin is the real clue. Those tubes are a red herring."

"But Eva, the same guy discovered the ricin and the nanotubes. The ricin is probably fake too."

"I didn't think of that. Maybe all of this is meant to mislead and we should be chasing a prion or something else right under our noses. I don't know, just try every drug in the hospital and see if something works."

"This is too confusing. How could they get someone on the inside like this? There can't be many people with access to those samples. I'm sure as hell going to find out who did it."

"Be careful, Sam. We know they're willing to kill indiscriminately."

"So am I, if I don't get some sleep soon."

"Sam. That's what the police are for. Maybe you should come back. I worry about you being there."

"L.A. is locked down, Eva. I couldn't leave if I wanted to. Things are getting worse. People aren't even making it to the hospital anymore. We probably have thousands dead. No one's even sure. Call me when you know whether the ricin checks out." Sam hung up his cell phone.

He looked at the phone, wondering whether he should call his wife. She didn't even know he was in Los Angeles. What could he tell her, that he was trapped walking around in the epicenter of the deadliest disease in the history of the world? That would help. He put the phone down.

He started to get dressed, then thought better of it and flipped on the TV as he headed for the shower.

". . . Prayer services are being held at noon at the Santa Monica Baptist Church by Reverend . . ." Sam changed the channel as he turned on the sink and reached for his toothbrush.

". . . Demonstrations are becoming more heated since the recent quarantine of Los Angeles, with motorists at the city's edge joining the protesters. These pictures were shot several hours ago, before our helicopters were grounded. Miles of cars are stacked up on I-15 behind the security checkpoints . . ." He put the toothbrush down and clicked the remote again.

". . . Senator Embry has attacked the administration for failing to prepare the nation's bioterrorism defenses adequately. In a statement this morning, he said administration experts had downplayed for years the threat of a successful bioterror attack . . ." Again.

". . . Trading has been halted on both the New York Stock Exchange and NASDAQ as investors wonder how far the red ink will spill before this is over. After futures and options markets suffered the worst one-day loss in history, on the heels of the worst three-day loss in history, the Securities and Exchange Commission announced indefinite cessation of trading . . ." Again.

". . . For those just tuning in, city officials are urging anyone with symptoms of sudden abdominal pain or bloody diarrhea to report to UCLA Medical Center for treatment. This has been designated as the citywide response center for the nanodeath."

Sam cursed. *What moron came up with that idea? The place will be flooded.* He switched the channel.

". . . This is God that has chosen Los Angeles as an example. A message to you, sinners, and to me. Starting with that whorehouse of Hollywood, we are commanded to repent of our greed and unwillingness to *give,* give until it hurts and God will lift this curse . . ." Sam pushed a button on the remote and the TV went blank.

A half hour later, Sam squinted as he walked out onto Hilgard Avenue. He immediately sensed the change from the day before. Gone was the purposeful walk of pedestrians going to work, the usual sounds of horns honking and street vendors calling. The city felt dark, despite the sunlight streaming through the palm trees onto the asphalt.

The crowd outside the hospital was larger. Easily two thousand people, probably most of them sick, Sam judged. The entire plaza was filled. The order of the triage tent the day before was replaced by a handful of nurses in orange chemical decontamination suits, wandering amid the crowd and putting in IVs. A few hundred people held bags of fluids above their heads, dripping into their arms. A dozen people were retching over the bushes by the hospital wall. Many lay down, using each other or a shirt as a makeshift pillow. Others just looked as if they had passed out on the ground. The security detail had been increased, and now six armed soldiers stood at the hospital entrance, all wearing gas masks.

A chemical decontamination van had driven onto the lawn and had walled off a section for spraying workers coming into and out of the hospital. A pile of chemical de-con suits lay next to the van.

Sam paused at the outskirts of the crowd, surveying the hospital grounds that had become a virtual cemetery. He felt like crying. Not even in Africa had he felt so helpless. A short distance away, a Hispanic man in his midtwenties called out, "Hey! I need help over here now!"

Sam pushed his way through the crowd. He wondered about the wisdom of going into the crowd without a filter mask or suit, but the man looked panicked. He'd be careful.

"My girlfriend! I can't get her to wake up!"

Sam leaned down over the young woman, reaching for her neck. There was no pulse. Her pupils were dilated. Sam covered one of her eyes with his hand. The other pupil remained fixed. He watched her chest for a few seconds, but saw no movement. Slowly, he stood up and looked directly in the eyes of her terrified friend. "I'm sorry."

"No! No! Do something. This is a hospital! Take her inside! Shock her! Save her!"

"I'm sorry. Nothing can help now. She's passed on." Goldberg was almost whispering.

"No! No!" He was no longer addressing Sam in particular, and Sam started making his way through the crowd to the front entrance. "Hey! You come back here! I'm not through with you yet!" Sam ignored his command.

The man continued speaking, his voice louder, now speaking to anyone who would listen. "What's going on here! My friend just died a hundred feet from a hospital, and they wouldn't bring her inside! She wasn't sick enough! How about now? She sick enough now? What do you say?"

A number of heads turned toward the speaker, sympathetic expressions on their faces. Sam began walking more briskly toward the entrance. "I've had it! They've 'quarantined' Los Angeles." He held up two fingers as he said, "Quarantined?

"What does that mean? It means this country doesn't give a shit about Los Angeles! They're just putting us on the sacrificial altar and saying you can all die, but we're gonna be safe! You think any of us are going to survive out here? We're all infected! Every one of us! Well, I'm not going without putting up a fight!"

A few other voices shouted out encouragement. "This place is a morgue!" "I'm going inside!"

An explosion sounded deafeningly close by. Sam looked up and saw one of the soldiers poised with his weapon drawn. He had fired a shot into the air.

"They're trying to kill us!" someone shouted.

Sam was nearing the entrance. "*He's* going in. Let *him* take us!" He felt a hand on his shoulder. Sam broke the grip and took another step forward. At least a dozen people still stood between him and the gate. One of them was walking toward him. Sam glanced over his shoulder. Three more men were coming at him from behind. He was surrounded.

Sam heard a crash. He looked across to see that a hospital window was shattered. He used the surprise of the window breaking to bolt around, trying to outflank the man that stood between him and the door. He almost made it.

A hand grabbed his arm forcefully, pulling him backward to the ground. Sam's hip pounded against the pavement, his head twisting to see his attacker. A kick in his ribs took the wind out of him. *Not like this,* he thought. He had to get inside. He heard another gunshot. A fist pounded into his gut, and pain shot through his belly.

He swung an ineffectual blow toward one of the men pinning him down. A flood of obscenities washed over him.

Sam felt a tug on his wrist, yanking him up to his knees. Two of the soldiers stood over him, one of them brandishing a black club. His pursuers shrank back as Sam staggered behind the guards.

"We need backup, now. We have a full-scale riot here," a metallic voice shouted into the radio. The crowd was getting louder.

Sam made the last few steps toward the door, and one of the soldiers opened the door for him. The other guards stood in formation, their backs to the door. The noise died down as the door closed behind Sam. Through the glass door, Sam saw four men standing at the curb of the street beyond the plaza, hoisting a Volkswagen off the ground. The previously lethargic crowd had become a sea of activity.

He walked into the hospital, holding his left side where it hurt with each breath. Probably a broken rib. Time to find out who had spiked the samples with nanotubes. He headed straight for pathology.

TWENTY-NINE

April 10

PRESIDENT Sutherland looked out the window behind his couch. The ground fell away beneath them. "Look, all I'm saying is that it doesn't feel right for me to be hibernating. I want to be in the public, making speeches, having some kind of presence. That's all."

Alan sat on the opposite side of Air Force One. The inside of the jetliner looked more like a five-star hotel than an airplane. Most of the accessible areas of the airplane were on the middle floor, with the lower level mostly reserved for cargo, and the upper level for communications equipment. Alan was seated in a large conference room, containing a conference table and large sectional couch. The room doubled as a dining room. Doors to the galley and to a work room flanked by additional passenger space were fore and aft. The president's living quarters, office space for the president and his staff, and workout facilities were located forward.

His thoughts focused on the news from Eva that the second sample sent from Agent Khalil was inert. Was this some kind of additional test? Was it some kind of prank? No way. It was in much too poor taste for that. It had to be real. Then why didn't the New York contact show up? And why couldn't Eva find anything in the sample? It made no sense. If Khalil was suspected, why did they let him go with incriminating evidence? It made his head hurt. The conversation in front of him interrupted his train of thought.

Zack shook his head. "Mr. President. You are the commander in chief, and this is a war. As real a war as any other president has fought, and it was started on our own soil. Your place is at Northern Command. That's where the decisions are being made. That's where the *people* expect you to be."

Alan had been surprised how quickly the decision to relocate had come. While Alan had been troubleshooting problems with the Los Angeles quarantine, a war council had been held. Alan knew that Amanda's would have been the lone voice of restraint. When Alan returned to the White House, Amanda informed him to pack his bag and head straight for Air Force One. He had never unpacked. On arriving at the plane, he popped two Tylenol, swallowed them without water, and found a seat next to Amanda on the couch.

Alan had gleaned the relevant history of their destination from Amanda while they waited for takeoff. The Northern Command had been created in a major defense realignment in 2002, following the World Trade Center attack. The U.S. Space Command, NORAD, and several smaller defense task forces had been combined to form the tenth unified command center for directing combat missions of U.S. troops. Nestled in the Cheyenne Mountains near Colorado

Springs, the command had initially been intended for support of civilian response in homeland defense. It quickly outstripped its charter and became the heart of the U.S. command and control combat infrastructure.

The president, his chief generals, and advisors, including Alan, were to meet at Northern Command. Vice President Atkins flew simultaneously to Joint Forces Command in Norfolk, while the speaker of the house relocated to Strategic Command at Offutt Air Force Base, in the interest of diversifying command targets.

The president, apparently satisfied with Zack's answer, returned to the stack of papers on his lap. The half dozen other members of the president's war council were clustered together around the president, awaiting his impending decision.

"Let's go through these one at a time and get some final thoughts. Option one: Continue biocontainment efforts and hold military response until more clear intelligence is available as to the perpetrators. Does that sum it up fairly?"

Secretary Feinberg nodded.

"Discussion?"

Secretary of State Johnson spoke first. "It makes us look weak, Mr. President. The attack is unprecedented. If we sit on our duff, every tyrant in the world will think they can pull the same kind of stunt."

Feinberg interrupted, "More than that, we lose any opportunity for rapidly capturing the perpetrators who we might be able to squeeze for information that could help Mr. Thorpe's response team."

Amanda spoke next, "You know I favor this option, Mr. President. It's better to look cautious than potentially explain to the world in retrospect why we attacked an innocent party." Alan admired her courage to take the unpopular stand.

The president shuffled his folders and said, "Option two: We appeal to the United Nations, present our evidence against Syria, and build a coalition for a military response." He looked around the group. "I think we've all but ruled this one out. None of us want another Iraq fiasco. Given the circumstances, we can go solo on this and see who dares to give us grief about it."

"Option three: We send special operations forces to simultaneously capture these four targets in Syria presumed to be in league with the attackers, and respond as necessary based on information obtained from the suspects. Discussion?"

Feinberg answered, "I'm confident our elite troops could acquire all four targets within twenty-four hours. Risk of failure is low, and we strike hard, fast. An excellent option, Mr. President." He tipped his head casually with a look of uncertainty. "Although there will be those who say that isn't going far enough."

"Option four: We send troops to capture or neutralize fourteen targets in Pakistan, Syria, Indonesia, Lebanon, Palestine, and Iran. We, in essence, declare all-out war on known terrorists and completely disregard national boundaries in our pursuit of them. We move our carriers to the gulf, and prepare to move in four divisions of troops if a ground offensive becomes necessary." Sutherland looked to Feinberg.

"It's risky. We can't support a full engagement on that many fronts, but we can certainly get at least eighty percent of the targets on a first strike," the defense secretary summed up.

Zack spoke next. "Mr. President, you'll never get another chance like this. The circumstances justify it, even demand it. You would in effect castrate the entire worldwide terrorist ring in a way past presidents have only seen in their wet dreams. You could stop terrorism for the better part of a generation, here and now."

Amanda countered, "It's the worst precedent you could possibly set. It will vilify us throughout the Arab world for a generation. No way can you prove that all of these people were involved in the attack."

"Any other options?"

"None we consider viable, Mr. President."

Sutherland sighed deeply. He removed his glasses and polished them with his handkerchief. He slowly spun the glasses around in his fingers until he looked up from one advisor to the next. Quietly, he announced, "I choose option four. Please try to get our troops out safely."

Secretary Feinberg nodded, and punched a number into his cell phone. He waited for the encryption key to parse through. "Commence Operation Roundup." After hanging up, he muttered, "For all we know, our troops may be safer there."

"Mr. President?" Zack asked.

"Yes."

"I feel you should make it very clear up front in your next public statement that America's entire defenses stand at ready, including our nuclear arsenal, to respond to any attack on America. This is the situation the deterrent was built for."

Sutherland nodded. "Let's put missile command on full alert. Move Defcon to level two."

"You won't regret your decision, Mr. President," Secretary Feinberg said.

"I already regret my decision. I regret this whole damn mess. What kind of a legacy is this? A disease that could kill one out of ten Americans. A war fought in our own hospitals. Commandos sneaking around sniffing out enemies because we're not even sure who the hell our enemy is. I'll tell you what's happened. The tables are turned. When we fought the Brits, it was the enemy that was complaining about our not playing by the rules. We were sneaking around taking potshots at their formations from trees, and now look at us. The Brits are our only real ally in the world, and both of us are lined up with our flanks exposed passing resolutions in the UN while our enemy is shooting at us from the trees. Let's hope we learned something from history. I'm sick of playing by the rules. I say we go get those bastards, and pray God has mercy on us."

Secretary of State Johnson frowned. "I'll do what I can to smooth international reactions. It won't be easy."

"I know, Tom."

Amanda leaned over and whispered in Alan's ear. "This is going to get out of hand really fast. It would sure help if we could turn this around in Los Angeles."

"Tell me about it," Alan whispered back. His head was still throbbing. He fought back a sneeze for as long as he could, but ended up expelling a wad of phlegm onto his shirt sleeve.

"Mr. President." Sandra Ewington spoke. "I just got report of two confirmed cases in Chicago . . ."

The entire group stared at her as she paused.

". . . and five in Jerusalem," she finished.

THIRTY

April 11

JIM'S fingers pounded on his keyboard in spurts, taking in the results of each manipulation instantly. He rarely used the mouse, since he found he could use keyboard shortcuts and macros faster for almost everything he did.

He was comparing BLAST searches of the known influenza genome with the results trickling in from the sequencers. Eva had isolated the influenza particles in her sample by antibody-labeled chromatography. The viruses would stick to glass beads that were coated with antibodies against influenza coat protein. She ran samples from UCLA patients through the column of beads, and then washed the influenza off the beads and made quick work of isolating the DNA, amplifying it, and feeding it to the sequencers. The automated sequencers had been running all night, and had generated a sizable amount of data.

Jim worried about how flippantly Eva dismissed the risk

of taking the influenza DNA out of the hot lab to the sequencers, but ultimately trusted her judgment on the danger, given her experience working with viruses, and influenza in particular.

Once the sequencers had started running, Eva had gone to help Steve and Susan with the ricin assays. The first test Steve had done was a quick ELIZA screen showing that ricin was indeed present in the samples. Eva said Steve was going to start working with RNA next, and look for the mRNA that makes the toxin. Steve would inject fluorescent-labeled DNA probes into the samples that would bind to the mRNA molecules that coded for ricin. When viewed with a laser, the probes would light up and generate a photograph of which cells made the ricin. The process was labor intensive, and Eva hoped that with both of them working together they would have pictures sometime that morning.

Jim watched as the next chunk of data ran through his alignment algorithm. Since he had started at Biodefense, Jim had taken on genomics computing as a professional interest. He had been delighted to find that the mathematics involved in comparing large databases of DNA were fiendishly complex. It was as stimulating as anything he had worked on in population biology, and over the last three years Jim had become expert in designing algorithms to rapidly sequence and compare genomic samples.

This job was relatively simple. He compared the DNA Eva was sequencing with all of the known DNA in the influenza genome. Most of it matched, with tiny variations, the published sequence. What Jim was looking for were regions of DNA that didn't match, indicating something was added in. If no such DNA was found, either the influenza was simply a dead end, or they would have to find tiny mutations in the genome that produced big effects. That could take months.

Jim had found eleven sequences already that didn't match the published influenza genome. That was the meat of his work on the computer. Those sequences could represent DNA added into the influenza virus, or they could represent contaminants from cells not screened out by Eva's chromatography separation. Jim was searching the entire public-domain and Celera subscription databases for matches to these mystery sequences. He had identified five of them so far that matched human junk DNA—long segments of repeated patterns seen in the badlands of unused parts of human chromosomes. This was the sort of DNA used in criminal DNA fingerprinting. It was merely a contaminant to Jim.

As he waded through near misses for the sixth sequence, Eva walked in.

"Hey, Jim." She tossed a candy bar over to Jim, who grabbed it with one hand.

"Thanks. Why are you being so nice to me? Are you trying to make Steve jealous again?"

"For once, you're actually doing something practical. It's like Pavlov's dog. I want to reward you for good behavior."

Jim looked at the candy bar suspiciously.

"So how's it going?"

"Eleven unknown sequences. Five of them solved by yours truly."

"Anything good?"

"All contaminants. Nothing that codes for anything yet."

"Take a look?"

Eva walked over to the computer and Jim maximized a background window with pages of the letters *A*, *C*, *G*, and *T*. He offered the mouse to Eva. She scrolled through a few pages.

"This looks like junk, doesn't it?" she agreed.

"So how's Steve faring?"

"He's just doing the final prep work. We should have some photographs anytime. I sure hope he finds something."

"Doesn't he have to? You said he already proved there was ricin in the samples. Doesn't it have to show up somewhere?"

"Not really. Remember, he's not looking for ricin, he's looking for the golden goose that lays the ricin. There's no guarantee we'll find it."

"Oh."

"What's this here?" Eva scrolled up and down through one of the sequences. "It looks real."

"I haven't got to it yet. Want me to do that next?"

"There's something about it . . . sort of familiar, but I can't place it."

"Don't tell me you go around memorizing this stuff. How could you possibly know?"

"When you see it all the time, some of it sticks. Hard to describe."

She didn't have to. Jim had the same experience with lines of programming code. Often a one-second glance was enough to tell him whether he was looking at a recursive sorting algorithm or a linked-list data structure. Just the visual shape of the code often triggered recognition.

"Steve's barking up the wrong tree, Eva."

She grunted, staring at the sequence.

Jim continued. "It can't be a ricin-producing bacterium. There's no way something like that could successfully compete. We talked about all this before. I just don't see how a germ is going to survive when it has to produce all that dead weight that doesn't do jack for its survival. And the incubation period's all wrong. You already told us it can't be a virus, because the ricin would shut itself off. I'm telling you, it stinks."

"Hm?" Eva scrolled again through the data, pausing on one section.

Eva's cell phone rang. She continued looking through the sequence.

"You gonna pick that up?"

"Oh, sure." Eva answered on the fifth ring.

There was a long pause. "Are you sure? . . . That's bizarre, Steve. . . . Why don't I come over and have a look. . . . You're in the break room? . . . No, nothing yet." She hung up.

"So?" Jim asked.

"It's a bacterium."

"What?"

"There's a bacterium, some kind of coccus. Lights up like a Christmas tree. Steve's sure that's our bug. It's making ricin."

"No way. Like I was saying—it doesn't fit."

"Hm?" Eva was lost again, staring at the monitor.

She began scrolling more quickly, then stopped and took her hand off the mouse.

"Wait a minute . . . I know what this is." She froze, as though her brain had completely disconnected.

"Hello? Earth to Eva?"

She reached over and kissed Jim on the lips, giving him a big hug. He sat in shock, his arms limp at his sides.

Eva let out a whoop.

"I know I have that effect on women, but we've got work to do . . ."

"I have it!" Eva started jumping up and down.

"What's going on?"

"I know what this disease is. It's perfect. Hell, yes! I know what it is!"

"Eva?!"

"This is the sequence for *cre!*"

"Cre?"

"Yes! I've got to go tell Steve. I've got to tell the president!"

"Eva! Come back here!"

"No time, Jim!" She shouted over her shoulder as she ran out the door. "It's a Trojan horse!"

"Eva—what are you talking about?" Jim followed her out.

PART III
NANOWAR

I don't know what kind of weapons will be used in the third world war, but I can tell you what the fourth world war will be fought with—stone clubs.

—Albert Einstein

Molecular manufacturing raises the possibility of horrifically effective weapons. As an example, the smallest insect is about 200 microns; this creates a plausible size estimate for a nanotech-built antipersonnel weapon capable of seeking and injecting toxin into unprotected humans. The human lethal dose of botulism toxin is about 100 nanograms, or about 1/100 the volume of the weapon. As many as 50 billion toxin-carrying devices—theoretically enough to kill every human on earth—could be packed into a single suitcase. Guns of all sizes would be far more powerful, and their bullets could be self-guided. Aerospace hardware would be far lighter and higher performance; built with minimal or no metal, it would be much harder to spot on radar. Embedded computers would allow remote activation of any weapon, and more compact power handling would allow greatly improved robotics. These ideas barely scratch the surface of what's possible.

—Chris Phoenix, Director of Research, Center for Responsible Nanotechnology, 2004

THIRTY-ONE

April 11

ANWAR Mohammed opened his eyes, his prayer still echoing in his mind. He fed the gas nozzle into the tank.

He thought of the gas flowing into his truck, like blood that granted life to the rusty machine. It was a worthy vehicle, as humble as he was. He thought of his own blood, which someday would be spilled in all humility for the glory of God. In the trees he saw in the sticky green leaves a witness of rebirth and God's eternal mercy. In the clouds he saw the barriers that shielded the glorious truths of God from the faithless and foolish.

As a child, he had made a game of seeing the world come alive in symbols. Now it was nearly unconscious—enlightenment born of patience and years of perception. His eye was single, his soul at peace, his senses heightened with intensity and focus. He was one with the purposes of God, perhaps only moments from his reunion with the creator of the world, when he would fall to his knees as he was invited to paradise.

He replaced the nozzle and returned to his truck. He nodded to his companions, one in the passenger seat and two in the cabin behind the seats. One of the men behind withdrew a box from the back of the cabin and pulled it onto his lap in the passenger seat.

Only the pure in heart could carry out a mission with such patience and long-suffering. His companions were not the founders, but were true brothers. Anwar was proud to lead them into battle. Yet in the stories, Anwar would be the one that everyone remembered, he was sure. Who else could yet claim they were trained by the prophet in Afghanistan? Who else could have endured undetected until the Great War? He wished fleetingly that he would be able to witness the final victory, when the humble forces of God toppled the evil nation. But he would witness from on high.

The Indonesian man to Anwar's right opened the lid of the box, withdrew two immaculately clean automatic pistols, and began loading the grenades into his vest, passing the remainder to their companions. Finally, he removed a sniper rifle from the long box and leaned it against the seat. The remainder of the box was filled by bundles of plastique, wires protruding from the packages. He continued passing out the supplies to the men behind while Anwar started the engine. The man sitting directly behind Anwar would be the key. He held the detonator for the heavy explosives found under the hood of the truck.

He wondered if his truck would be remembered with him, painted in a corner on the mural of the Great War. As the Hamilton Amoco faded in his rearview mirror, he honestly didn't care. Such honors were not for him to decide.

* * *

SAM looked out the glass door to the hospital's front entrance. He motioned to get the attention of one of the armed guards keeping watch outside the door. The officer stepped inside.

"How did you get in already this morning? I've been here since five." The door closed behind him. It was the officer who had pulled him out of the rioting crowd the day before. He pulled off his gas mask to communicate more easily.

"Who says I ever left?"

"I thought *we* had rough shifts."

"Listen, can you fill me in on what happened yesterday? I was half expecting to see the hospital trampled under after you got me inside."

"Nearly was. We got a SWAT team here with riot gear about ten minutes after you went inside. Lucky the crowd was so disorganized. The SWAT team got in position and managed to defuse the crowd, get them talking. We were real close to losing control. It would have been ugly: tear gas, flashbangs, maybe even gunfire."

"How'd you calm them down?"

"We didn't, really. They just saw the SWAT team meant business and sort of called a truce. The crowd is twice the size today, and people aren't any happier. I've been trying to keep them occupied. We put a few portable bathrooms up; we've had some restaurants bring in food; we added a few more nurses to help start IVs and get some of the sickest inside. That's helped a little."

"So you think we're OK for a while?"

"Not really. This is getting a lot worse. We've had at least three dozen more deaths out here. People are so scared, they're getting desperate. Some of the crowd have guns. If I try to take them away, good chance I'll set the whole thing off. I have a real bad feeling about this."

"Let's get some more security here."

"I don't think we have any. I've been talking with Emergency Operations this morning and the National Guard, the police, the fire department—just about everyone is on border patrol. People are trying to escape the city in droves—little old ladies passing out hauling their shopping bags through the desert. It's a disaster. This isn't the only riot scene, either. We can't keep this up." He looked at Sam. "Neither can you. Get some sleep, doc."

Sam nodded and turned back inside. Maybe he was right. Sam had seen a couch down in the pathology lab. A few hours couldn't hurt.

AHMED Al Rasheed tightened his surgical cap and refastened his mask around his face. He spied a hospital employee wearing a white protective jumpsuit and pushing a cart with trays of food toward the main elevator. He jogged a few steps to catch up with the man.

"Headed to the floor?" Ahmed asked.

"Yeah. Six west. And this time I'm just droppin' the cart off. No way I'm going to sit around and breathe that stuff in."

"You've been up before?"

"Yesterday. And I'm not going back. I say, I've got a wife and kids, man." His eyes teared up. "I don't need this job."

"Tell you what: I'm headed to the floor. I'll run it up for you."

The man shifted on his feet silently. "If you want . . . thanks, man." He nearly pushed the cart into Al Rasheed and turned back down the hallway.

Al Rasheed pushed the cart into the elevator and rode to the sixth floor.

He drove the food cart to the nurses' station, where a woman said, "Just leave the cart. We'll take care of it." She wore full gown, mask, and goggles, a thin wisp of dark hair visible beneath a surgical cap. She didn't even look at Al Rasheed.

Ahmed answered, "It's all right. You need some help?"

She turned her head and stared at him. "That's the first time in days anyone's been willing."

"Not really. I was just transporting samples and some cafeteria worker begged me to take the cart up for him."

"Chicken shit."

Ahmed shrugged. "How's it going?"

Her voice was tired. "Terrible. It's like we're Nazis running experiments and nobody lives. They've just been trying antibiotics at random. One guy, though, over in seven, seems to actually be doing a little better. If so, he'll be the first."

"That's great. What'd he get?"

"Synercid."

"Never heard of it."

"It's still pretty new. We just use it for vancomycin-resistant bugs, mostly. Expensive stuff."

"Let's hope it pans out. We could use a break, huh?"

"We could use something."

"I better drop off a few samples, and I can come back and help deliver trays. Give me fifteen minutes. You folks look like you could use some help."

"Thanks. Everyone here has ten jobs. You're on. What's your name?"

"Vadim."

Ahmed turned around and removed the mask from his face. He took the stairs down one floor and headed straight for the supply room.

THIRTY-TWO

April 11

STAFF Sergeant Tucker Johnson kept one hand on the wheel as he pinched another wad of snuff with the other. "So where's our exit?"

Captain Mike Sherwood answered without thinking. "We have the two MH-60 choppers under cover forty miles from Damascus at the dropoff. That's our first exit. Second choice, we arrange a separate pickup from the 160th SOAR. Contingency plans require us to shoot our way out into Lebanon, where we've got a carrier to run rescue. If we don't get out quick, Tucker, we're screwed. That's all there is to it." As mission commander, he'd been through every minute of the operation in his head more times than he could count. He was pleased to see his team doing the same.

The air support had worked out surprisingly well, given

the extreme short notice of the mission. Fortunately, Syria was flat and altitude wasn't a problem for operating Black Hawks. One of the higher-altitude missions in Pakistan would have to use Chinook MH-47s to reach the target. Further, the Syrian air defense was concentrated in a ring around the border with Lebanon and Israel, leaving the wide approach from the east relatively unencumbered for two low-flying MH-60s. A minimum number of craft were stationed in Afghanistan for an upcoming joint special operations forces exercise. Sherwood shuddered to think what would have happened if they had needed to run the mission without air support.

As an officer in the First Special Forces Operational Detachment–Delta, Sherwood lived for a chance like this: a real mission with huge consequences. In one form or another, they had practiced such a mission cold. Sherwood was no stranger to combat, having spent three years as an officer in Delta Force. But this was bigger than anything he had ever been in on. It was bigger than anything the entire U.S. Special Operations Forces had ever been called to undertake. And it would practically have to be done cold.

Sherwood's unit had received notice three days earlier. No details, no warning. Just two hours' notice and the unit was airborne. They landed in Iraq, where they were paired with two officers from an OD-A operating near the Syrian border that would help with logistics and intelligence for the mission.

As commander, he was privy to some elements of the full operation. The entire U.S. Special Forces were simultaneously put in action. Delta Force would be operating in Syria, the most sensitive assignment. The Naval Special Warfare Development Group, formerly SEAL Team 6, was assigned Indonesia, operating off a carrier with marine support. Navy SEAL Team 1 would penetrate Pakistan from Afghanistan. A covert unit based in West Virginia, about which Sherwood knew little, had been assigned to Iran. The available craft from Army 160th Special Operations Aviation Regiment, Air Force 16th Special Operations Wing, and Air Force 352nd and 353rd Special Operations Groups would be providing air support as needed in each of these engagements. Operations in Palestine and Lebanon would be handled by Israel's Sayeret Matkal Unit 269, with U.S. Air Force cover. British SAS forces had been offered, but couldn't be integrated in time, according to Sherwood's sources.

Sherwood's assignment was not only unique in scope, it was completely unprecedented to perform extraction of suspected terrorist commanders from friendly nations in peacetime. It was sure to set off an overwhelming and unpredictable international reaction, and would require careful finesse on Sherwood's part to limit the collateral damage of the mission. His air cover was mostly limited to tactical support and would not be allowed to use significant firepower. The capture of targets chosen, fourteen in six nations, would be the single greatest blow to international terrorism since the war in Iraq and routing of Afghanistan bases, hopefully more so if helpful intelligence could be gathered.

"We coming up on the checkpoint?" Johnson asked.

Sherwood checked his vehicle's GPS reading. "Still ten miles before we scrap the NSTV and find ourselves some new wheels." Sherwood was still thinking about their flight in. No amount of training would prevent his surprise and admiration at the skill of the 160th chopper pilots. The approach was totally silent, with a perfect landing on the lee of a hill with barely enough room for the chopper to rest.

Sherwood's men had made quick work of assembling the nonstandard tactical vehicle and making toward their next objective. Separate teams would coordinate fourteen separate extractions in multiple countries, hopefully at exactly the same time. Sherwood's was the most difficult, as it involved a senior member of Syria's government, housed on a military base, where collateral casualties were most likely to set off hostilities. And where security would be tightest, Sherwood suspected.

"What do you think the fallout will be?" Johnson had asked the same question on the flight to Iraq.

"Tucker, the only way I see this is we are our first salvo in World War III. There's no way Syria is going to take this lying down, and there's no way in hell Pakistan or Iran will. What we're doing is uniting the entire Middle East into a new kind of war that will last for a generation. We're going to see what Israel's been living with for half a century."

"You think we're doing the right thing?"

"We're doing our job, Tucker. And we're going to do it perfectly. The consolation is we're the ones who get to put our hands on these animals. We didn't start this, but we're damn well going to finish it."

PAUL Vallos stared at the first page of the dossier. The logo of the Homeland Security's Information Analysis and Infrastructure Protection division was printed in blue at the top.

"We got 'em, Paul. Black and white."

Paul looked up at Ross Dunford, one of his top NET Guard agents. Ross had been personally recruited by Paul more than three years ago, and was one of Vallos's favorite co-workers. Paul had found him after he received a call from Microsoft claiming they had figured out who it was that engineered a simultaneous e-mail to the entire Microsoft workforce containing a doctored picture of Bill Gates outside Wal-Mart with a box of Depends. Paul had agreed to track down the twenty-three-year-old hacker. When he found Ross, he offered him a job on the spot.

"You're going to have to take me through this one step at a time," Paul admitted.

Ross pulled his chair around Paul's desk, so both were able to read, and flipped through a few pages. "So this is the object code used to hack the name servers that displayed the initial threat. The original code was probably written in plain old vanilla C with a text editor—no tags from any commercial compilers. The worm infiltrated the name servers by piggybacking on a name resolution using some of the new SNMP features."

"Got you so far, I think."

"The next step was reverse engineering the code. When we do that, we come up with this source code, right here." Ross flipped a few pages to show the start of the C program.

"Right. We already went through this. It's patterned after Jackal. Uses a known security breach in the operating system to get a foothold. But it's generic. Anybody could write this. Jackal source code is available on the Internet, and the operating system patch hasn't been installed in the servers that were affected."

"OK. So what about this?" Ross moved forward four pages of small print in the source code and pointed to a single line.

```
(*ex_ptr)(31A6);
```

Ross sat back in his chair with a smug face.

"Ross, this means nothing to me."

"It's a pointer to a function, boy."

"Okay . . ."

"All right. Pointers to functions are pretty routine. There are three in this source code alone. But this one is different. It shows up in the middle of nowhere. It doesn't make sense with the flow of the subroutine. And the function doesn't exist." Ross tapped the page as though he had just nailed the coffin shut.

"What do you mean it doesn't exist?"

"Exactly that. This function isn't created anywhere in the source code or object code. The pointer address is defined here, three pages back in a different subroutine." Ross thumbed through the code again. "And all we have is a single hard-wired address with this cryptic argument 31A6. What kind of goofy programming is that? The function call requires only two lines, they're widely separated, and they're completely cryptic, as though they were designed to avoid detection. Clever, actually. Anyone looking at this code would think the purpose is to put in an Easter egg to redirect the name server when someone tries to look up the Pentagon's IP address. Except for this line, that's all it does."

"So what does this line do?"

"Hey, throw me a bone here. This is pretty impressive detective work, eh? Who else would have even caught this?"

"OK, Ross, you da man."

"That's better. So old Ross went poking around in one of the affected core name servers, and guess what? The address activates a resident stealth function in the server that has probably been lying there waiting for a trigger for who knows how long. In other words, this program activated a second virus already dormant in the computers, real sneaky-like."

"How did that second virus get there?"

"Once we knew it was there, it was pretty simple. It sneaked in with a maintenance utility program used to monitor memory allocation in the servers. All of the affected servers, and some of the ones that weren't affected, use it. It's been used for more than three years, in fact. *Three years,* Paul."

"You saying someone has been planning for three years to hack the Pentagon?"

"Or more."

"Wow. That's interesting."

"Although, it's not three years of planning to reroute the Pentagon's Web site. It's been years of planning to crash the entire network backbone of the United States."

"What?"

"This little function call activates a ticking time bomb. What I've pieced together of it so far gives it the capacity to utterly crash the server, destroying most of the BIOS along with it."

"You're kidding."

"I wish. This is the most impressive virus I've seen in my career. When it triggers, it sends a self-mutating worm out with packets requested by end users. Millions of private users could be infected within a few hours. Since this thing has been hiding out for years, all of the tape backups we have for the servers will be infected as well, and they would crash immediately on restoring. There's no telling how many private computers and servers are infected with the same program already."

"What are we talking about here?"

"Unbelievable. The Internet could be totally disabled. Communications would be paralyzed. Power grids could go offline. Remember all that hype from Y2K that never materialized? This is exactly the scenario that makes a good bit of it come true."

"What about government communication, banks? You saying this thing could bring them down?"

"Naw, most of them use private WANs or private networks, so they probably won't get hit. But don't underestimate the ripple effect from disrupting even private e-mail. We've never seen anything that could be so globally disruptive to the economy. And we're vulnerable as hell right now. The economy's already strained to the breaking point."

"You guys figured all this out in the two days I've been gone?"

"Most of it last night. That function call cracked everything wide open. This is big news, Paul. Rumor mill on the Internet's dark side has claimed for years that there was a bunch of trapdoors on root domain servers. They say around twenty percent of Tier 1 servers. Maybe they were right all along."

"OK, who makes this maintenance program?"

"A startup company, run by a computer science professor at NYU. Name's *Faud Khan*. He's a Saudi national, been a citizen for fifteen years."

"Ross, YOU DA MAN. Bring him in."

"That's your call to make, boy. This is FBI territory."

"After what they pulled? They took my report, butchered it, and used it to justify their damn war. I'll give this Faud guy to CIA or NSA, then, but we're running the show here this time. Someone attacks the Net and it's our turf. So when is this thing set to go off?"

"That's what I'm still working on. There are so many layers of code, and the code is like a maze. I'm not sure yet."

"Try to find out before it goes off or you gonna be da punk. This could be as devastating on our economy as the biological attack. Together, they could wipe us out."

Ross looked hurt. "I'll find it, boy."

Paul wondered just how old he would have to be before a kid who still had acne would stop calling him "boy." Right now, he didn't care.

THIRTY-THREE

April 11

EVA burst into the lounge with Jim struggling to keep up. Her eyes darted around the room.

"Where's Steve? He said he'd be here."

Jim was still out of breath from the jog to the elevator.

Eva walked next door into the security station. No one was in yet, but a bank of television monitors was running. Eva found the displays for the hot lab and looked through each room. She found what she was looking for in the medical suite: Steve and Dr. Nowers were bent over Daru. Eva couldn't tell what they were doing.

"So are you finally going to tell me what's going on?" Jim asked.

"May as well wait in the lounge," Eva decided out loud. She led Jim back through the door to the vacant break room.

Jim leaned against the table.

Eva's enthusiasm was still considerable, but she was thinking too fast to show much emotion. She retraced her mental steps to play back to Jim. "That DNA you showed me: It came from the influenza, right?"

"Or contaminant."

"Not contaminant."

"How are you so sure?" Jim challenged.

"Because that is the gene for cre. It's not in the influenza genome, but it's not human either." Eva replied.

"What's cre?"

"It's an enzyme, derived from an obscure microorganism. More important, it's one of the most widely used systems for genetic engineering."

"How so?"

"It works like this: Cre is an enzyme that binds to a specific sequence of DNA called loxP and causes it to rearrange in a specific way. The way it's usually used is to make a gene with a whole bunch of garbage in the middle. The garbage is tagged with loxP. When you sprinkle cre on the DNA, it cuts out the garbage and leaves a functional gene."

"So it's a genetic switch, lets you turn genes on and off?"

"Exactly."

"I still don't understand what you see in this that I don't."

The door slid open, and Steve and Dr. Nowers walked out. They barely acknowledged Eva and Jim. Steve sat on a chair and held his head in his palms. Dr. Nowers nodded absently and walked out of the room.

"What's the matter, Steve?"

There was a long pause before he answered. "It's Daru. She's a lot worse, almost comatose. Dr. Nowers doesn't think she's going to last much longer. He went to call her family."

Eva sank into a chair herself at the news, feeling completely deflated. "But Steve, we're so close. I think I just got the solution. Do you think there could still be time?"

Steve looked up. "You what?"

"It was Jim who found the key evidence. It's the influenza sequence. It contains DNA that codes for cre."

Steve zoned out of the conversation.

Jim asked again. "All right, so you were about to tell me just what that means."

Steve made eye contact again. "It's a stealth virus?"

"Right."

"Right what?"

Eva turned toward Jim. "The cre means that the influenza is genetically modified to serve as a switch. It produces probably low amounts of this cre gene that triggers another infection already inside the host. With what Steve has found, we have the whole picture. You said bacteria, right?"

Steve nodded.

Eva continued, "Here's how it works. Sometime in the past, perhaps days, perhaps years, all of the victims were infected with a harmless gut bacterium. Maybe *E. coli* or lactobacillus or any of a hundred other normal bacteria that hang out in our intestines."

"It's enterococcus, on my mother's grave."

Eva raised an eyebrow at Steve. How could he tell from just a photograph? Identifying bacteria based on the most arcane characteristics had always been Steve's most impressive skill.

"Anyway, these harmless gut bacteria aren't so harmless, because they've been engineered to contain a deadly gene that produces ricin, one of the most poisonous toxins known to humanity. The ricin gene is silent, because in the middle of the gene is a garbage DNA sequence with loxP on either end. That's the Trojan horse."

"OK."

"So now your terrorist comes along with a modified influenza virus making trace amounts of the trigger, cre. Once the gut bacteria get a whiff of this cre, it starts an autodestruct sequence that turns these gut bacteria into massive ricin factories. It fits the clinical symptoms perfectly. It spreads so fast because it's airborne, following influenza transmission patterns. It becomes fulminant so rapidly because the infection doesn't have to build and fight the body's immune system to take hold. It's a full-blown case as soon as a few molecules of the trigger float down and switch on a few of the gut bacteria. They're already there in sizable numbers."

Jim whistled. "Wow." He paused for a moment. "What if you're wrong?"

"She's right." Steve left no room for argument.

"That explains a lot," Jim thought out loud. "The influenza doesn't get crippled by having to produce this cre, because it only makes it in tiny amounts. Won't require much energy to make. Plus, you can use a relatively harmless strain of influenza that won't provoke a big immune response. That would be easy to spread. On the other side, the gut bacteria are immune to our body's defenses, since they normally live there and are just like every other innocent lactobacillus until the switch is tripped. They're probably modified as well to be antibiotic resistant to give them a survival advantage. That way they would be selected from among the normal gut flora and passed from person to person."

"I think he's got it, Steve," Eva's mood was again improving.

Jim was becoming more animated as well. "So these guys knew exactly what they were doing, and I bet they did it carefully after putting so much thought into this. They've probably been silently preinfecting the entire U.S. population over five or ten years with this modified ricin bomb. Amazing."

Steve agreed. "I wouldn't be a bit surprised if they've been at it at least that long. Ten years of walking through supermarkets squirting a puff or two of bacteria on the lettuce, walking around airports coating the railing or doorknob with bacteria, a trace of enterococcus soup in the local buffet. There would be no way to stop them, and once enough people get infected, it gets propagated on its own from person to person."

"So how do we stop it?" Jim asked.

"That's the question. An influenza vaccine would take months to develop and fabricate. They probably designed the trigger as a weak virus strain that isn't in our current vaccines," Eva answered.

"If there's one thing I'm convinced of now, it's that my simulations are dead on. This is no fluke. If it takes months, we'll have millions of casualties. No wonder they tried so hard to throw us off with this nanocrap. This thing acts fast, and a few days may make the difference whether it reaches epidemic threshold or not." Jim's face was as serious as Eva had ever seen it.

"So we knock out the enterococcus. Our immune system may not kill it, but antibiotics sure will. We just have to look and see what antibiotic resistance genes are engineered in, or rather, which ones aren't. We choose whatever will kill it, and we've cured the disease. All we need is a culture of the bacteria. We plate it out, sprinkle different antibiotics on it, and see which one kills it. And we already have the cultures. They've been sitting under our noses this whole time and we didn't even realize it."

"So what are we waiting for? Daru's life, not to mention millions more, may depend on our choosing the right antibiotics." Steve stood up.

"Wait a minute. Does all this mean we may harbor this stealth bacteria as well?" Jim asked.

Nobody answered.

"Then we're a breath of influenza away from catching this ourselves. Just so everyone is clear on that up front. I don't want that stuff tracked in on somebody's shoe."

Eva squirmed at the thought that she had taken samples of the influenza out of the lab. Probably minimal risk, she thought, but not zero. Certainly not zero.

"And another thing," Jim said. "How sure are you we're going to find an antibiotic that kills this thing? It's been bred for resistance."

"We're sure going to try," Eva answered.

Steve frowned. "We should call Sam and Alan, too. And I wonder what's taking Dr. Nowers so long. He said he'd just be a minute to make the call. Daru needs him. And we have to warn him about what the risks are in the hot lab. If he's going to be spending that much time in there, he should know exactly what he's dealing with."

Eva nodded. Her thoughts were disrupted by a rumble shaking the floor. "What was that?" she asked nervously.

"What the . . ." Jim looked around confused.

"The hot lab is encased in steel. Something is going on."

Eva moved toward the bank of security cameras.

Steve and Jim followed her into the security room, and they began scanning the television monitors.

Eva looked through row after row of monitors. Nobody

was visible. It was still early enough in the morning that even the skeleton crew that had been working in the lab during the last week hadn't arrived yet.

She saw Jim instantly stiffen next to her. He looked frozen in place. "What did you find, Jim?"

When she followed Jim's eyes, her throat began to close from the shock of what she saw.

THIRTY-FOUR

SAM never made it to the couch. He made it as far as the pathology office, when he saw a new face behind one of the desks. After a complete failure the night before to identify anyone new among the staff or technologists, he thought he might as well try another round of questioning. After introducing himself, Sam asked her to step into one of the consultation rooms and closed the door.

Sam wasn't about to show his hand to anyone yet, not without some idea of who might have infiltrated the lab. He stated only that he was compiling a comprehensive list of who had access to specimens collected in the first three days of the outbreak.

"Is something wrong?" the administrative assistant asked. "I was here two of those days."

"We're not sure yet. We just know so little about this disease that we're keeping close tabs on exposures. Helps us track under what circumstances someone exposed to the disease can contract it. You can imagine how worried people are—not just in your hospital but all over the city—that doing laboratory studies on this thing may make them the next victims."

"I'm glad I'm not the only one terrified about it. How are we supposed to even do our jobs with that thing coming in and out of here?"

Sam reviewed again names of all of the pathology staff, residents, and technicians with unlimited access to the samples. He got basically the same list of names, all of whom had been in the hospital for at least a year or more.

"What about other people coming in or out of the lab when you were here? Anyone ask to borrow slides? Anyone else that could have been exposed?"

"It's been so hectic. I'm sorry. I just can't remember names. There's always people dropping off samples or clinicians coming in to review slides, especially lately. I never remember any of them. Faces I sometimes recognize . . ."

This was going nowhere. A flash of insight crossed Sam's mind. "I got directions a few days back from someone with a pathology nametag." He searched his memory in vain. Maybe if he had slept a bit more his memory might be up to the task. "Can't come up with his name." Sam did his best with a description.

The woman shrugged. "Honestly, these messengers I just don't have enough contact with to remember."

Sam's cell phone rang, and he thanked the woman and excused himself. It was Alan, telling Sam of the relocation to Northern Command in Colorado. Sam got an earful about the problems with the quarantine as well. The guard had been right. It was like trying to stop Moses from crossing the Red Sea. Thousands of people were trying to escape from Los Angeles in every direction, and it had already come to gunfire in two cases. There were five deaths from the quarantine alone.

Next was a crisis on the floor. An already critical nursing shortage got even worse when three more of the day shift nurses failed to show this morning. Sam had no magic solutions for that, and punted the problem to the hospital administrator. He couldn't do everything.

His biological rhythm was starting to kick in and the extreme fatigue he had felt a few hours earlier was now just a headache. He decided against trying to sleep for now and went to the O.R. to get a shower. He'd learned a few lessons about sleep during his days of inpatient medicine. A shower counted for two hours of sleep, and if you could make it until nine in the morning, you were OK until evening.

He dressed in scrubs, and before he could even find a disposable toothbrush, his pager went off. It was a text page from the front desk. It read 911—FRONT ENTRANCE. Sam ran all the way to the front door. What he saw was so disheartening, he felt like running away. If only there were somewhere to run.

The guards at the front gate stood in defensive posture, their backs to the door and their weapons drawn. The crowd visible through the glass door was even more numerous than an hour or two before, drawing reinforcements with daybreak. And the relative peace was gone. Those healthy enough were circling the guards at the front entrance. Alan could see that one of them carried a rifle. The standoff looked like a deadly game of chicken.

Sam's phone rang as he stood inside the door.

"Hello, Dr. Goldberg?"

"Yes."

"This is Lisa Holland. Do you have a second to talk?"

"No. I'll call you . . ."

"Well just thought you could use some good news. One of the patients is doing better."

"Better?"

"Definitely. He's eating again, pain is down."

"What'd he get?"

"Synercid."

"You're sure?"

"Started him on it yesterday."

"Talk later." Sam snapped off the phone. He took a deep breath and opened the door.

The guard who had seen him earlier spoke without turning his head. "Dr. Goldberg! Stay inside. We'll handle this. Just wanted you to be ready in case this gets out of hand."

"Ready for what? If this gets out of hand there's no getting ready for anything." He walked up to one of the other guards and unfastened the megaphone from his side, taking two steps in front of the line of guards. He raised his hands in the air and took a few more steps toward the crowd. He glanced briefly at the chemical decontamination van, his eyes fixing enviably on a gas mask lying by the van.

"It's that doctor again!"

"He's one of the ones keeping us out!"

Sam stopped abruptly as he heard a gunshot explode from farther into the crowd. A window shattered on one of the upper floors of the hospital. Goldberg scanned the faces of the crowd, waiting for a bullet to come ripping through his chest.

ANWAR Mohammed drove his truck to the shoulder of the road near the sign that read ROCKY MOUNTAIN LABORATORY—NEXT RIGHT. The passenger door opened, and two men in dark clothes exited before the door closed again. No words were spoken. They were not needed.

Anwar waited patiently beside the quiet road. A few cars and trucks sparsely populated the road lined with evergreens and wildflowers leading past the laboratory. Traffic was never heavy in Montana, least of all here.

Five minutes later, Anwar pulled up to the heavy metal gate leading to the parking lot. A military jeep labeled U.S. MARINE CORPS was parked outside the gate, and two uniformed soldiers stood guard. Anwar pulled up to the guard station.

"State your business," a gruff voice announced. The soldier held his sidearm at ready, disciplined eyes searching through the truck.

Anwar held out a brown paper bag, slowly, letting the guard inspect the contents.

"Ve are bringing order. Ah, Monsoon Spring. For a Mr. Summers," Anwar's companion offered helpfully. The bag smelled of curry.

"Nobody told me anything was expected. I'll have to check it out." He walked back to his companion at the guard station.

Just as the soldier began to converse with his associate, his body fell limp as a sniper's bullet found its way into his head. His companion had barely understood what had happened before he too fell to the ground dead.

Anwar's passenger leaped from the truck with surprising agility and pulled back the gate, allowing the truck passage. Within seconds, two dark figures followed him through the gate.

Anwar sped into the parking lot, picking up speed as he traveled. The noise had alerted the company of four marines standing watch at the front door. Anwar could hear shouting from the truck. He held his course.

Bullets began raining down on the metal of the truck, pinging into the metal side as Anwar accelerated toward the roundabout in front of the entrance. He ducked low as bullets smashed into the front windshield. *Almost there*.

A tire exploded and the truck careened to one side. Anwar gripped the wheel tightly as he crouched below the windshield, his foot firmly on the gas pedal. The truck began to swerve from side to side. Anwar felt the lurching of bullets slamming into the radiator. The noise was deafening.

The engine sputtered as he neared the front entrance. Soldiers scrambled for safety as they realized the truck wasn't stopping.

They were too late. One of Anwar's accomplices pushed a switch, and the truck exploded into brilliant orange flames, blasting a hole through the wall near the front entrance and dismembering the guards who stood at the spot of Anwar's fiery entrance to eternal glory.

SAM raised the loudspeaker to his mouth and switched it on. *This had better work*.

"I have some news to report. Some good news for all of us, finally."

The crowd fell silent.

"We have our first patient feeling better. We tried a new antibiotic, and it seems to be working. It's too early to know how effective this will be, but we're prepared to try it immediately on everyone. It's a safe drug, one that we have a fair amount of experience with."

Sam let the words linger over the crowd, making every move slowly and deliberately.

"What does *immediately* mean?" someone shouted.

Sam breathed deeply. "Within a few hours. Starting with the sickest ones first. Our pharmacists are already mixing up the drug. It needs to be given intravenously, so those of you without an IV will need to have one placed."

One of the young men assuming a point position in a small crowd nearest the door yelled out, "This better not be a trick, or you'll pay for it!"

Sam swallowed hard. He tried to be as honest as possible under the circumstances. The more he played up expectations, the greater likelihood the riots would be back. "I can't tell you if this will work or not, but it's our best lead yet. It's all I have to offer you."

The group in the front of the crowd conversed among themselves, then sat down in unison. The rest of the crowd slowly followed suit.

Sam wiped the sweat off his forehead. He needed another shower. He held the megaphone up again and said. "I'll be back before noon with the first batch of the medication. We're ordering more in, and we'll get to everyone as soon as we can."

He turned to walk back in the front door, tossing the megaphone to one of the guards on his way. "Thanks," the guard said softly.

Once inside the door, he picked up his phone and dialed the pharmacy. "This is Dr. Goldberg. Could I have one of your pharmacists?"

A voice answered after a brief pause.

"Hi. Sam Goldberg. I want five thousand doses of Synercid, 500 mg, in two hours."

"Five thousand! I'll be lucky to get you fifty. This stuff doesn't grow on trees. We only use it on a couple of patients a month. There's no way."

"There's a fair chance that this might actually kill whatever's causing this disease."

"I don't know what to tell you, Dr. Goldberg, except there's not that much of the drug in the whole state, let alone Los Angeles. I'll give you all we've got, but it's nowhere near five thousand."

"Then water down the dose and stretch it as far as you can. We're sitting on the Titanic, filling lifeboats, and I can't be picky. When you run out, start sending bags of saline and write Synercid on it in red crayon. That's a direct order. The crowd's rioting, and I have to have something to stall them with. Just make sure I know which doses are real so I can tell if it's working."

"That's totally against our code of ethics."

"Then you can explain that to them when they cut through security and point their guns at your heads."

"Five thousand, coming right up. And I'll start rounding up every dose in the country."

AHMED brought the trays into room 7 and set them on the patients' tray tables. The nearest bed housed a woman in her thirties, stroking the head of a sleeping child on her lap. In the far bed was a portly man in his fifties reading a newspaper.

"Your dinner, sir."

The man smiled. "I never thought I'd be so grateful to see food again. I tell you, I thought I was going to die."

"I'm so glad to see you feeling better."

"I hope the others are getting better as well. I heard it's been a nasty disease. Sure gave me a ride these last two days."

Ahmed smiled. "Anything I can get for you?"

"Get me out of here. I'm feeling like I could go home. From the talk I hear, there's others who need this bed more."

"I'll bring it up to your nurse, but I bet they'll want to make sure you're OK before you go. Why don't you get some sleep while you can?"

"Breakfast and a nap works with me. I didn't sleep most of the night. Thanks for the food."

Ahmed nodded, looking at the man's IV and fingering the syringe in his pocket. Nothing he could do right now. He would come back.

THIRTY-FIVE

April 11

EVA couldn't take her eyes off the monitor. The front entrance was completely obliterated, leaving dust still hanging in the air over metal, masonry, and plaster debris strewn across the path. A few body parts of the marines who had stood guard at the door were identifiable. A gaping hole marked the path through the entrance to where the largest piece of the pickup truck was still visible.

"Someone's after us," Eva whispered. "And they're in the building."

Eva, Steve, and Jim stood momentarily transfixed at the bloody scene outside the front door.

"We have to get out of here," Eva whispered first.

Steve shook his head. "We can't go back down. It's too risky. We might end up right in his lap. Their lap. We don't even know how many there are."

Jim whispered back, "So we just wait here to get shot?

Not me. How hard do you think it's going to be to find this place? All the orange biohazard signs are a road map to our door. They're probably already on their way."

"You have a better idea?" Eva hoped that he did.

"Any weapons here?" Jim asked. He started fishing around, opening cabinets and drawers.

"There's no time to look," Steve hissed.

"Can we seal off the elevator?" Jim started looking over the numerous buttons and controls on the main security desk.

"They're fire-shield doors, but Nowers is out there with his ID; Susan's out there with hers. I have no way of overriding . . ." Eva left her thought dangling as her brain sped forward.

"There has to be a computer here. Maybe I can break in."

"There's no time! Are you two coming?" Eva raised her voice above a whisper this time.

"Where are you going?" Jim followed her out. "Oh, no. I'm not going in there. Talk about sitting ducks."

Eva continued toward the hot lab.

"Your choice." Eva kept walking. Steve ran to the control desk, pushed a button, then caught up with her.

"What are you going to do, just wait in there for a visit?" Jim asked.

"There's an exit to the roof through the lab. It's where we brought Daru in."

"That sounds better, wait on the roof where we go from one exit to none." Jim's sarcasm scarcely covered the fear in his voice.

"Eva's right," Steve said. "There's got to be a fire escape. We should be able to get down and make a break for it."

Jim shook his head. "I have a bad feeling about this."

"Come on!" Eva insisted.

The three went through the double doors into the outer

change room. Eva walked straight to the clothing rack.

"Are there enough suits?" Jim asked.

Eva began unbuttoning her blouse, wondering if she would ever hear the end of stripping in front of Jim.

"No time to suit up. Come on, move." Steve pushed the panel to open the airlock to the shower room.

"You're going in without any protection?" Eva asked.

"The corridors are filtered. Minimal exposure. It's a lot safer than hanging around waiting for company. Just hold your breath in Daru's room."

Daru. Eva had completely forgotten. "We've got to get her out too, Steve."

All three walked into the shower room.

Steve shook his head again. "What are we going to do? Carry her on our shoulders? She can't even walk right now, let alone climb the fire escape."

"I can't leave her here, Steve." Eva began to feel her eyes tear up. "Not after what she's been through."

"Eva, we don't have any choice!"

Jim bit his lip. "Steve's right, Eva. There are lots more lives at stake if we don't get out of here and find a cure for this thing. We're too close. Plus, how do we avoid exposure . . ." He gave Eva a pained look.

Steve had already opened the next airlock door out of the shower room. All three went inside. They waited for the door to close, then Steve pushed the panel opening the door into the inner change room.

Once inside they could hear the labored breathing from Daru's room straight ahead. Dr. Nowers had left the door open going into the medical suite.

Steve and Jim were practically running toward her room and the airlock at the far side. Jim held his sleeve over his mouth and nose.

"Steve, wait!" Eva called out.

Steve and Jim stopped and looked back.

"The cultures! We have to go back for them. We could lose days waiting for new ones."

"It's too dangerous, Eva. They'll be safe here. We can come back."

"What if he destroys the samples—blows the place up?"

Jim started walking toward Eva. "We can't wait two days, Steve. We could hit epidemic threshold by then and may not be able to turn this around."

Eva motioned back to Jim. "I know which ones to get. Go with Steve. Scope out our exit. See if they're waiting outside. I'll meet you on the roof." Steve stood indecisively looking at Eva. He didn't move until Eva practically shouted, "Go!"

Eva darted back into the cabinet room, fingering through the cabinets clumsily. She dropped a beaker on the floor, where it shattered. She cursed under her breath and kept searching.

She tried another cabinet. Her eyes searched the table-top under the hood. *There!* She grabbed a stack of petri dishes and tucked them into her pocket. Then she froze. She heard the overhead speaker announce, "Biosafety level four authorization, Susan Patrick." Someone was coming out of the elevator. *Was it Susan? Or not?* She heard the *whirr* of one of the airlocks closing. The sound came from behind her, from the change rooms. She cursed again. She didn't have time to make it to the airlock. She jumped out of the room and ran down the corridor to the animal containment rooms.

She had to find a place to hide, but there was nowhere. She heard the sound of the next airlock. The chatter of the mice and the screeches of monkeys now filled her ears.

As quickly as she could, she began opening cages of the mice, reaching in and throwing them out onto the floor. Then she darted into the chimpanzee room, leaving doors open in her path. She unlocked each cage in turn, then dived out of the room into the centrifuge room across the hallway. She stood behind the door frame, scarcely able to control her rapid breathing. She scanned the rows of tables and equipment, looking for a hiding place.

The sound of another airlock came, followed by rapid footsteps. She heard the clatter of cages as the chimpanzees banged against their cages, then scampered out into the hallway. The footsteps came, louder.

She heard a gunshot.

Definitely not Susan. Instantly the chimps began screaming at the sound, erupting into chaos. Footsteps came closer, only a few feet away. She could hear the intruder moving behind her into the chimp room.

Eva peeked around the corner. The intruder's back was to her as he surveyed the open cages. She slipped around the corner and jogged on tiptoe toward Daru's room. She dived inside.

As soon as she was in the room, she scanned the room for the airlock. At the same time she heard a loud ringing sound coming from her waist. *Her cell phone!* Footsteps pounded rapidly down the hall. *No time to reach the airlock.* Eva jumped behind Daru's bed against the far wall and crouched behind the blankets, pulling them out from where they were tucked to shield her from view behind the bed. She tossed the cell phone, still ringing, up on top of Daru's body. She fought her fear to synchronize her breathing with Daru's. Daru didn't even move, her eyes closed. The phone rang again, not a loud ring, but deafening to Eva.

A few seconds later the footsteps bounded into Daru's room, then stopped. The only sounds Eva could hear between rings on the phone were her own and Daru's breathing and the scattered screeches of the chimps. She felt something. She shook her leg reflexively. *Did he hear her move?*

On one of Eva's feet, a mouse was crawling. The mouse looked up at Eva, then walked slowly onto her foot, peeking up her pant leg. *Flink!* she thought. *Stay strong.* A moment later, it scurried away under the bed. Eva bit her lip trying not to move.

Then Eva's ears exploded with the sound of gunfire.

THIRTY-SIX

April 11

PRESIDENT Sutherland walked into the room. Alan couldn't help but think he looked lost, confused, more like a candidate who had just lost the election than a president who had just led his country to war. Sutherland stopped by the table and picked up a bagel, poking a knife into a container of cream cheese, and then leaving the knife there while he took a bite.

Alan felt sick to his stomach. *Bagels?* How could he eat? How could any of them eat after just launching an attack on half a dozen countries, *at the same time.* Alan couldn't shake the thought that it was his fault, his team's fault. If they had been able to stop this disease, maybe his own country wouldn't be starting the most ill-conceived conflict of the century, certainly the deadliest. Now, tunneled under the mountains in Colorado at Northern Command's War Room, Alan felt anything but safe.

Alan hadn't slept all night, and he felt it. Between popping over-the-counter cold remedies, he traced meticulously where this new decision would take them. Pakistan and Syria would only be the beginning. What would Iran do? What would Jordan do? What would the two dozen militant organizations do that transcended boundaries in the Middle East? These countries were packed with Americans. There would be hostages, reprisal attacks. Europe would be confused; Russia would be venomous. With the West in disarray, how far would the united anger of a billion Muslim citizens go against the United States?

Sutherland sat down and looked around the faces of his War Council in turn. His eyes lingered on Alan. *What does he want from me?* Alan wondered. The president spoke.

"Why don't you bring us up to speed, Amanda. It's going to be a long day."

Amanda picked up her notes. Alan sensed a twinge of resentment in Amanda as she looked at Sutherland, who had obviously slept better than she had.

"Operation Roundup has begun. Our forces are moving into place, and should be ready to move in a few hours." She looked to the chairman of the joint chiefs for reassurance, and moved on.

"Domestically, the toll this is taking is enormous. The exchanges are still closed at your order. Secretary Benton estimates we're losing more than a billion dollars a day in lost productivity and financial panic. The Bank of Los Angeles has failed on paper, and the treasury is working on trying to cover it up until we can shore it up.

"Public transportation in New York, Chicago, Dallas, Boston, and Seattle, just for starters, are completely shut down. Every state in the country has a curfew imposed. There are riots in half a dozen cities, worst in Los Angeles, where the National Guard is shuttling from one riot to the next.

"The disease is no longer confined to Los Angeles. We have confirmed cases as of last night in Chicago, New York, San Francisco, and Atlanta. Idaho's governor has just sealed off the state's border, refusing to let any vehicle in without Idaho plates. That's the kind of fear that we're dealing with. Emergency rooms are overflowing with false alarms. For every case that has been seen outside Los Angeles, there are probably a hundred people who think they have it.

"Los Angeles is completely overwhelmed, and every hospital in the city is overrun with casualties, literally camped outside the hospital, dying. There was a riot outside UCLA yesterday that almost penetrated the hospital. And yesterday evening, as you know, there was an explosion in a grocery store in Los Angeles. We still don't have much information on what happened—police just don't have the resources to handle it—but it looks like a suicide bomber. Twelve people were killed; I still don't have information on where the injured were taken."

The president stared off away from Amanda. She waited. Sutherland spoke softly, "I feel like I've woken up to find myself in Tel Aviv." His eyes teared up. "It's a nightmare. We're so helpless. A suicide bombing right in our own country, and all I can think of is that it's the least of our worries." He sighed. "Any new leads from intelligence?" He searched for the intelligence director's face. "Where's Richard?"

"Director Stern is not feeling well this morning, and asked that I take his place for the briefing . . ." Amanda sounded apologetic.

"Who the hell is feeling well? I'm sorry." The president's expression softened, Alan noticed. Probably because everyone in the room was exhausted, and the president knew it. "Please continue."

"Yes, Mr. President. As you know, we debriefed Agent Khalil yesterday, and have focused our efforts on finding his contacts in Los Angeles and Chicago. Our stakeout outside Ahmed Al Rasheed's home in Los Angeles has yielded nothing."

"What do you mean nothing?"

"His wife and children are home, but when one of our agents talked to his wife, she said he hadn't come home for two days. Doesn't know where he is. She was worried, said that occasionally he would spend the night away without telling her but not for this long. Most likely he already knows we're on to him and has bolted. Perhaps we can find some useful leads there."

"You're asking me? Do it. For heaven's sake. Do it."

Alan stared directly at the president. *He doesn't know what to do,* Alan thought. He felt a powerful sense of empathy for the president.

Alan looked down. Maybe a bagel wasn't such a bad idea. His stomach was on fire. He hadn't had heartburn for years, not since he'd started the medication. Then again, he hadn't had this kind of stress in years. He wished he had stopped by the restroom on his way to the briefing.

Sutherland thought for a moment as all the faces in the room watched silently. "So where do we start? Thorpe. What's our containment strategy now that we've spread out of Los Angeles?"

Zack commented from the far side of the room. "The quarantine isn't working. I say we pull it. The only thing it's done is scare the daylights out of everyone."

Alan wondered if he looked pale. He tried to compensate by speaking deliberately. "We have to keep at containment. I'm working on a strategy for adding quarantines in every new city as cases are discovered."

"What are we going to do—quarantine the whole

country? How do we move supplies?" Zack threw his hands in the air.

"I know we can't continue this indefinitely, but it might buy us enough time to find a cure. I can't emphasize enough how important early containment can be in controlling casualties."

The president nodded. "Go ahead . . . for now."

The telephone rang. Zack moved to answer it as the president stood, walked around the table, and picked up the phone himself. "Yes." He flipped the telephone on speaker.

"Mr. President? This is Paul Vallos. I wanted to inform you immediately about an attack on our computer infrastructure that we've just discovered. There's a virus waiting to go off that could bring down the entire Internet backbone of the country and I want to activate our national cyber alert network."

Alan felt it again. *Not now!* He stood and walked slowly out of the room, attracting stares from everyone in the room as he left. He had to get to a bathroom. He hadn't felt such a wave of indigestion since he had been in high school. He used to get the runs before big tests, and was so incapacitated during his campaign for student body president that he barely made it onto the podium during the awards assembly. That was so many years ago. He thought his digestive tract was tougher after twenty years of stressful jobs.

Internet attack? Suicide bombing? What was going on? Was there more than just the disease being levied by the same group? How could such a coordinated series of attacks escape detection? He couldn't think about it now. Once out of the War Room, he broke into a jog. The soldiers standing guard outside the room exchanged smiles and pointed toward the restroom.

Alan threw open the door and stepped inside, half bent

over. He loosened his belt and took his cell phone from its holster, where it felt as if it were digging into his abdomen. Setting the phone on the counter, he headed for the nearest stall.

The cramping was getting worse. He tried to focus on his breathing, settling into a rhythmic pattern of deeper breaths. He tightened his mouth and winced in pain.

It will pass, he reassured himself. It always did when he was stressed. He just had to focus his thoughts.

Then something caught his eye. The toilet bowl was stained bright red.

THIRTY-SEVEN

April 11

STEVE and Jim hurried out of the elevator onto the roof. The helipad was empty, and the sun came directly into their eyes from the eastern horizon. Steve put up a hand to shield the sunlight, and Jim looked away.

"You check over there," Steve ordered, and began searching the near wall for a fire escape. He went to the railing that circled the roof and began walking along it. The railing continued unbroken all the way around the roof.

Jim jogged over to the other side and searched rapidly for a way down. He cleared one corner of the building, then looked over the railing along the next side of the building. His eyes met Steve as he looked over the side of the final wall. There was no fire escape. The only way down was through one of the two elevators back into the building.

"Where's Eva?" Steve called out as they jogged back toward the elevator. "She should be here by now!"

Jim's eyes were fixed on the elevators. "Can we jump them?"

"Depends how many there are."

"I'm worried about Eva. We need to go back."

Steve nodded. They went back down the elevator and opened the outer door to the airlock.

Jim reached up to open the inner door when he heard the sound of a gunshot. The sound paralyzed his hand.

Steve motioned to wait. They both leaned into the door to listen more carefully.

A moment later they heard footsteps moving away, then silence.

Jim looked sick. His breathing accelerated, coming in short gasps. Steve grabbed him by the shoulders and whispered harshly, "Don't think about it, Jim."

Steve tightened his grip until Jim's breathing slowed down a notch. "Now listen, in the control room is a panel that allows you to switch off the airlock to the outside, the one we're in right now. I don't know what else is there, but Susan showed it to Eva and me the first day here. If we can get him out on the roof, I can shut it off and trap him out here. That should give us a head start."

Jim nodded, regaining control of his breathing. "How do we get him out?"

"The airlock door stays open for about ten seconds. I'll go out and make for the security room. When I give the signal, open the door and duck down behind Daru's bed. He's got to see the open door and think we've gone to the roof. As soon as he's in the airlock, I'll see it on video and seal the airlock."

"Hide behind her bed? Why not give her mouth to mouth as well?"

"Jim, I'd do it but I can't explain where the controls are

for the airlock. Keep your mouth covered as best you can, and the risk is pretty small. It's our only chance."

Jim fingered his ponytail. "All right, let's go."

Steve opened the inner airlock door. They both stood against the side of the door, out of direct line of sight from the room, both knowing that if an intruder was in the room, there was no way the door would close fast enough to save them.

The room was empty. Daru's breathing had been silenced, and blood was spattered against the wall behind her. Jim started to gag. Steve mouthed the words, "Maybe Eva got out."

Steve took only a short glance, then crept toward the corridor leading to the cabinet room. He looked around the corner, then jumped through the short hallway into the room beyond. Jim stared at the open doorway into the corridor, watching for a sign of motion. He hit the button on the airlock door to reset it, then made clumsy stomping sounds with his feet to simulate the sound of running. Next he crept over as fast as he could go toward Daru's bed, his eyes glued on the doorway. Just before he reached the bed, he saw a chimpanzee emerge into the doorway and stumbled from surprise, banging into the side of the bed with a loud metallic clang. The chimp screeched in delight.

Jim's arm stung. In one movement, he dived behind the bed as the sound of running footsteps came from the hallway. He could no longer see Steve in the room beyond. He tucked himself in behind the bed, then adjusted the covers in the dim light of the room to shield himself from view.

He looked to his side and nearly leaped off the ground to see Eva's bloodstained face lying beside him. Everything inside him made him want to stand up and run as fast as he could. Then the footsteps came into the room.

Eva shook her head with a confused expression, as though she didn't recognize Jim. She was still alive. He scanned her face and torso in the dark, looking for a bullet wound. All he saw was blood splashed over her face and clothes.

He felt sick again.

The footsteps stopped. Jim could just make out the sound of the airlock door closing. The footsteps came again, this time heading toward the airlock. He stuck his head out a few inches to see around the bed. The intruder was alone, his gun pointed at the airlock door. He reached up to reactivate the airlock.

Nothing happened for a second. A flash of panic ran through Jim's mind. *What if Steve shut off the wrong airlock?* What if he trapped Eva and Jim inside with the intruder? What if he did it on purpose?

Jim shook off the thought. The airlock door slid open again. The intruder whirled around suddenly, as though he had heard something. Jim looked directly into his face. He could make out the gunman's eyes. He slowly withdrew his head, an inch at a time. *Don't let him see motion.*

A second later, the gunman turned around and walked into the airlock. Jim heard the sound of the airlock door closing. He took a deep breath, then he remembered where he was and blew out the breath as hard as he could, covering his mouth and nose with his sleeve.

With his other hand, he reached over and shook Eva. Nothing. He shook her again.

Her eyes blinked, and her arm moved.

"Eva," Jim hissed.

She opened her eyes and blinked.

"Eva! Are you hurt? Pull yourself together!"

Eva looked catatonic. *Paralyzed with fear,* Jim thought. Jim put a finger to his lips.

"Where is he?" she whispered.

He pointed his head toward the airlock.

"Steve's trying to lock him out. Can you walk?"

She thought for a moment, then nodded. They both stood, crouching as they walked for no practical reason. When they hit the main corridor, both of them broke into a full run. A chimp stood at the entrance to the corridor to the inner change room. Jim and Eva slid around him, and hit the button for the airlock door. The chimp followed them into the airlock.

When the door shut, the chimp gave a menacing screech, and Jim and Eva backed submissively against the outer door. Jim hit the panel with the back of his hand and they jumped out into the inner change room.

"Come on, hurry!" Eva led the way.

They dashed across the shower room into the next airlock and waited impatiently for the door to shut and the next door to open. In a dead sprint, they ran out into the lounge and into the security room. Steve was waiting by the controls.

"Did it work?" Jim whispered intensely.

Steve nodded. "I think so. He's still outside. But not for long, he's got the south elevator to get back into the building."

"Have you called the police?" Eva asked.

Steve pointed to the control panel where a flashing light marked ALARM was blinking silently.

"Let's get out of here, now."

They ran toward the elevator, but stopped abruptly when they saw the bloody body of Susan Patrick lying on the floor by the elevator.

Jim clenched his fists, and stepped over the body.

"Those bastards!" Eva whispered as she followed Steve toward the elevator.

THIRTY-EIGHT

April 11

SAM refastened his biofilter mask and stepped out of the elevator onto the patient ward. He could still feel his heart racing from his encounter on the hospital grounds. Dr. Andrews met him as he stepped out.

"Wanted to see this firsthand. You really think he's better?" Sam asked.

"Definitely. And he's the first one that's come down with this that's shown any sign of improvement. Every single other case has gone straight downhill." Andrews fell into step behind Goldberg.

"When was he dosed?"

"First dose was actually yesterday afternoon. He's about due for another dose."

"Synercid . . . This is really strange, Rob. What does that tell us?"

"We only keep a small amount on hand. It's used so

rarely. Really the only known application is for vancomycin-resistant enterococcus. Sometimes it's used for vancomycin allergies to staph or strep, I guess. It basically has no activity against gram-negatives."

"So let's run with this for a second. I already told you we think this nano thing is completely bogus. Let's say this disease is caused by some kind of gram-positive organism. Have we tried vancomycin?"

"At least a dozen patients. Didn't even touch the disease."

"So what if we're dealing with some kind of modified vancomycin-resistant staph aureus or enterococcus?"

"Sam, that fits clinically. But why bacteria? They're clumsy; they're treatable. It's just hard for me to believe that's what's going on. They just aren't contagious enough. And the incubation period should be longer. Why wouldn't a terrorist use a virus?"

Sam fingered his beard under his mask. He was so tired he was having trouble focusing on the conversation. "Maybe not so treatable. What kills vancomycin-resistant enterococcus?"

"VRE? Well nothing, really. Synercid can keep it at bay. Linezolid works pretty well. Those are the only two I know of. It tends to colonize the elderly and chronically ill rather than causing an overwhelming infection—usually it's just not such a big deal. We don't even try to eradicate it because it's so hard. It's just a nuisance bug—it doesn't kill very often."

Sam snapped his fingers. "It does now. Maybe it's not such a dumb choice after all. It's nearly impossible to eradicate, but Synercid might be enough to treat the disease. Probably take months of treatment to wipe it out. And linezolid! Why didn't I think of that? If we're suspecting Synercid works, why not try that too? If this is staph, maybe we could try an older drug like chloramphenicol. That might work."

"Sam, linezolid is even harder to come by than Synercid. With those two drugs combined, our entire national stores would be lucky to treat our own patients, let alone all of Los Angeles."

"But it doubles our choices. Go get pharmacy on it right now. Tell them to get every molecule of linezolid in the country headed this way now."

Andrews shrugged. "I'll try."

Al Rasheed slipped into room 7 and moved directly toward the far bed, nodding at the woman in the bed by the door. The tray table was nearly empty, a carton of milk opened and tipped on its side. Only a trace of syrup remained on the plate.

The patient's eyes were closed. Al Rasheed listened to the man's breathing as he silently walked toward the bedside. The breathing was heavy, slow. *Probably asleep,* he thought. *Good.*

Ahmed looked over his shoulder at the door out to the nurses' station. It was still ajar, but he saw nobody through the opening. He reached slowly into his jumpsuit pocket and withdrew an empty syringe. Carefully, quietly, he pulled out an eighteen-gauge needle and fastened it to the tip of the syringe.

He bent down, softly fingering the tubing running from the IV into a central line in the patient's neck. Al Rasheed drew back the plunger on the syringe, drawing up sixty cc's of air. Softly inserting the needle tip into the plastic tubing just an inch from the patient's skin, Ahmed pushed the air into the tube in one long movement. He withdrew the syringe, refilled it with air, and repeated the act. Two more times in rapid succession, he filled the syringe with air, buried the needle in the tube, and released the air into the patient's bloodstream.

He made to refill the syringe, then startled as he heard footsteps. The door was opening. "Mr. Nelson?" a voice sounded from the doorway.

Al Rasheed whipped the syringe out and back into his pocket, the needle still on the tip. He slid over toward the tray and began gathering silverware onto the tray, making a movement to leave. Sam Goldberg entered the room and began walking toward the patient.

"Mr. Nelson? I'm Dr. Goldberg, and . . ."

Ahmed put a finger to his lips, and said quietly, "He is asleep, doctor. And it looks like he had a big breakfast."

Goldberg walked over next to Ahmed, standing between him and the doorway. He watched Goldberg read his nametag. Ahmed felt a moment of panic. Could the traitor have remembered his name? He forced a smile.

"Why is someone from pathology cleaning up breakfast dishes?"

"Just trying to help out, sir. One of the nurses asked if I had a minute to give her a hand . . ."

Goldberg's stare was icy, calculating, peering right through him. It wasn't working.

"I'd better go, sir. They're expecting me back."

Goldberg's eyes were transfixed on Ahmed.

The trance was broken when an alarm went off. On the overhead monitor, the number 85 blinked in red, indicating the patient's oxygen saturation was dropping. The beeping was the loudest sound in the room.

Ahmed moved toward the door.

"You stay right there," Goldberg commanded Al Rasheed. "Security!" he shouted.

Al Rasheed sized up Goldberg. He scrambled back to

the bedside, pulling out his syringe as he moved, then thrusting the tip into the patient's central line. In one movement, he drew up blood into the syringe from the infected patient.

Holding the syringe up, thumb on the plunger, Al Rasheed circled around toward Sam in a defensive posture.

The alarm became more shrill, raising in pitch as the number on the monitor dropped to 75. A new alarm sounded as the ECG winding across the screen showed a large, erratic waveform. The patient's breathing was now rapid, labored as the air blocked off the blood flow in capillaries in his lungs.

Sam fell back a few steps on seeing the syringe. The woman in the bed closest to the door screamed, picking up the child on her lap and jumping out of bed, knocking over an IV pole that crashed to the floor in front of Sam. She ran behind Sam out of the room, blood dripping from where her IV had been ripped from her arm.

Ahmed watched her escape, then immediately focused his attention on Sam. *There was no way out.* Ahmed had seen the troops patrolling the hospital front entrance. Maybe if he could get to one of the side entrances he could slip out into the crowd. But then where? Surely the traitor had identified him, and his home would be watched. At that moment, he realized that he would never see his family again.

He lunged toward Sam, then feinted and broke for the open door. Sam grabbed the wrist containing the syringe as he passed, and spun him around. Ahmed shook his wrist violently, trying in vain to break Sam's grip. He quickly swung his other hand around and grasped the syringe with his left hand. He put his finger on the plunger and swung to bury the needle in Sam's arm.

At the last second Sam gave Ahmed a shove that sent him backward onto the floor, narrowly missing the needle as Ahmed's arm swung by, glancing off Sam's wrist and knocking his cell phone from its holster.

Ahmed jumped to his feet, but Sam was already out the door, and Ahmed arrived just as Sam slammed the door in front of them. Ahmed continued running, lunging against the door. Nothing gave. He swore.

Trying the door handle, he wrestled against Sam's strength, holding the knob firm on the other side. He was trapped.

The patient monitor above the far wall was ablaze with blinking red lights, sirens sounding. The ECG strip was completely erratic. Ahmed looked once more at the patient who threatened the entire plan. The one who survived.

He picked up the cell phone on the floor, looked at it briefly, then threw it on the floor, smashing it in pieces. He kicked the wall in fury.

He looked out the window onto the distant grounds below. Then with both hands he picked up the fallen IV pole and yanked it off the floor, sending it crashing through the window.

Ahmed Al Rasheed smashed the remaining shards of glass along the window's edge. Stepping on the patient's bed, he looked back once more at the door. It was still closed. He removed a vial from his pocket and hurled the vial out the window as far as he could throw it. The stolen sample of nanotubes would never be found. Only now, when everything was clear, did he face the question he had thought through so many times over so many years. What if he was captured? He knew everything. Could they pry the information from him? Would he stand up to torture or betray Allah? Ahmed fell to his knees and said a prayer. Resolve temporarily calming the terror in his thoughts, he stood and dived out the window headfirst onto the pavement six stories below.

The patient in the room heaved a final breath, and the cardiac tracer on the screen above burst with artifact before settling into a thin line across the screen while sirens blared through the otherwise still room.

THIRTY-NINE

April 11

STEVE pushed the button for the first floor and waved for Eva to come inside.

Eva stared at Susan's body a moment longer. She was still shaken from the hot lab. Looking inside the open elevator, she saw her reflection on the glass back wall and realized she had been splashed with Daru's blood from the gunshot. The sight of her own bloodstained face paralyzed her, and Jim had to pull her inside as the door began to close.

"Nothing you can do about it now, Eva."

Daru's blood. Eva felt the blood mixed with sweat on her lips, could taste it in her mouth. Time stopped as she remembered every graph, every slide she had made showing how influenza virus could attack human cells, especially around the eyes, in the mouth, and in the lungs. And Daru by now would be a virus factory, spilling it freely into her blood. Eva closed her eyes. In a matter of hours, she could be infectious. In a matter of days . . .

"Eva!" Steve put a hand on her shoulder. "Jim's right. Look, we'll have plenty of time. We'll find something that treats this. Focus, OK?"

Eva nodded absently.

She watched out the back of the glass elevator along the central scaffolding and sculpture that ran between the paired elevators in the heart of the building. The first time she saw it, she thought it breathtaking. Now it felt like a fig leaf, covering the group from the eyes that could see her in the elevator from so many different directions.

She tensed and pointed breathlessly. Across the atrium, beyond the glass DNA sculpture, the elevator cables started moving. Whoever they had trapped on the roof was coming down.

She inched closer to the back wall, looking up and down to locate the elevator car. She saw it above, then jumped to the back of the car as the echo of gunfire reverberated through the atrium. Eva pressed against the side wall as shattered glass clinked downward, cascading into an avalanche of broken fragments, crashing into the fountain below.

The back wall of the elevator shattered from a direct hit, and a gaping hole opened out over the remaining three stories below. With the glass removed, the sound of each new shot was deafening.

The carnage of the explosion by the front entrance was now clearly visible. Blood, metal, and chunks of wallboard lay around the hole in the wall near the front door.

The elevator lurched with momentum, the cables creaking as the open platform they rode swung gently from its pendulum. Eva tightened her knuckles around the bar behind her. She looked down, then quickly looked back.

Another gunshot, this time ricocheting off the scaffolding to the side of the elevator car. It came from below. Eva saw a single figure standing in the atrium, gun raised toward the elevator. He began walking toward the elevator shaft.

The orange light at the top of the elevator door changed from 3 to 2. Eva whipped her hand out toward the control panel, smacking the button for the second floor with her fist. There was no response from the elevator. Had she missed it?

She watched in horror for the longest second of her life, until she felt the elevator lurch and begin to slow down. The car came to a stop as another bullet pelted the metal of the elevator shaft. The orange light still read 2.

As soon as the door was halfway open, Steve sprinted out of the entrance, followed by Jim and Eva. None of them had been in this part of the building. She had no idea if the killers above and below them knew the building.

Eva ran to keep up with Steve, careening around the first corner. The gunman in the elevator would be sure to get off on the second floor, and could see them in the balcony around the atrium. They instinctively ran into the nearest corridor radiating from the central opening into banks of offices.

We should hide, Eva thought. *But where?* The police had to be on the way. They needed more time.

As she thought, Steve skidded to a halt, with Jim nearly crashing into him from behind. On the floor in front of them was the body of James Nowers, blood still oozing from open gunshot wounds in his chest. His eyes turned outward and his tongue protruded in a sickening postmortem pose. Eva held her hand over her mouth.

Down a side corridor, a red lighted EXIT sign was posted above a doorway. They ran toward the door.

Steve immediately turned upward and climbed the steps two at a time.

"Where are you going?" Eva hissed.

"They'll expect us to go down. We'll never make it out this way. We'll double back and go out from the south. Now keep it quiet."

He softly opened the door to the third-floor corridor and held the door until it slid closed. Steve led the group back toward the atrium balcony, walking briskly on his toes, and Jim and Eva followed.

When he got to the balcony, Steve searched ahead into the atrium, listening for sounds of footsteps. It was totally silent. He led the group onto the balcony, leaning against the far wall as they walked.

Halfway across the balcony, Eva saw one of the gunmen on the first floor. He was bent over the elevator shaft. What was he doing? Then she looked closer. A small package lay at the base of the shaft. *Explosives. That has to be a main structural support for the building.* "They're going to blow this place up!" she whispered as quietly as she could.

Steve motioned that he had heard and continued walking toward the far side. The man below stood up and looked up to the ceiling. *Could he see them?* Eva froze for a second. The man looked away again. *Only a few feet from the end of the balcony now.*

As they crept into the corridor radiating south from the atrium, they heard the faint sounds of sirens coming from outside.

Steve led them into a corridor that was a mirror image of the one on the north side. He opened the door and they quietly descended to the first floor. Steve put his ear to the door. He shrugged, then opened the door a crack. Peering out, he emerged into the hallway.

Eva followed him back toward the atrium, when Steve

flattened against the wall. Not twenty feet away, the gunman stood bent over near the elevator shaft on the north
side, again setting a package in place. His back was facing
them.

Steve quickly crept on his toes around the back of the
elevator shaft, toward the door.

The man stood and ran toward the south side, then disappeared from view.

At that moment the door burst open and four officers
with SWAT gear jumped into the atrium.

"FREEZE!" one shouted.

Eva heard an exchange of gunfire coming from the
second-floor balcony, answered quickly by shots from the
officers. They saw the gunman on the second floor sprint
away from the atrium.

Taking advantage of the cover, the three ran toward
the officers. Steve put one hand up in submission as they
approached.

Eva panted as they reached the hole by the front door,
expecting a gunshot in the back any second.

Steve whispered intensely, "They've got a bomb! We've
got to get out!"

All seven funneled out the chasm when they heard two
earsplitting explosions from inside. The front windows shattered from the force. The seven ran at a dead sprint as
tongues of flame and smoke seared out the windows behind them.

The building trembled, and within seconds began to
collapse in on itself with growing speed.

Eva continued running past the SWAT vehicles, motioning to the backup crew to get clear.

The smoke from the crumbling building billowed outward, and Eva choked as she ran into the trees flanking the
lab. She gasped for breath.

Jim was panting next to her. He threw himself on the ground, and Eva heard his stridorous breathing. She sat down next to him and held her chin in her hands. Steve walked around them in circles, watching the building crumble.

She reached into her pocket. The petri dishes were still there. "We made it!" She held up the stack of cultures to Steve.

He started laughing, then pulled her up with one arm into an embrace. "Damn, we're good!"

Jim crawled up and rested on his elbows, still breathing deeply. "Gotta love this job."

FORTY

April 11

FAUD Khan acknowledged the NYU department secretary as he walked back from an early lunch to his office. He took a sip from his espresso and set the cup on his desk. His fingers rattled on his keyboard, and the pair of flat-screen monitors blinked to life as he typed in the password.

He would miss the espresso. Small loss, in all, but he would miss it when the United States finally toppled after so many years of domination and oppression. In truth, he would miss many things after living in America for twenty years. But mostly the espresso.

The plan was beautiful. Faud was rightfully emotional on the day when the computers would fail, the disease would spread, and the unfaithful would decline into chaos and barbarism. He reflected on the chance meeting with Gopal Khabir, fifteen years ago. What had started with a mutual interest in fund raising for Al Qaeda became a face-to-face meeting, and the beginning of the plan to change the world.

They shared a common surreptitious bond that seethed under the surface for each of them. Faud was raised in the United States from age ten, and was teased mercilessly in the small suburb of Des Moines where he grew up. The children at school labeled him "Chico," and his accent, his small stature, and the faint smell of garlic and coriander on his clothes were enough to set him at odds with a relentless bully who made elementary and middle school a living hell. His parents, working two jobs each to keep the family off the streets, ignored the fact that he came home with ripped or muddy clothes. Faud internalized his struggle at school as a battle with "the others." He sought ways of setting himself apart from those to whom he could never relate, and by age fourteen surprised his parents with the avidity he took to Islam. He befriended a local cleric who told him stories after school of the martyrs of Palestine, and promised that some day Allah would bless his sufferings with praise and glory.

Khabir was a visionary Indonesian biologist, schooled in molecular biology at Yale, yet faithful to his childhood dream of destroying America with a plague worthy of its iniquity. Khabir was raised in Indonesia and came to America on a student visa to study biology at Yale, already wild with anger at the outrages of an evil nation. He hid his ambition carefully, and feigned interest in finding the next generation of antibiotics for drug-resistant organisms. A postdoc at Cold Spring Harbor followed, on an H1 visa, and he eventually landed a tenure-track position at Northwestern, allowing him to gradually set up a home laboratory where he devoted his life to developing the ultimate weapon.

On their first meeting, Khabir had laid out the possibilities, and Faud had begun the process of assembling a network to deliver the silent epidemic to the infidels. The process was painstaking, as they had to avoid contact with any known operatives. A few recruits they met in mosque over the years, but most had been recruited from abroad. A single meeting on a visit to Indonesia many years prior had been the only contact that Faud had chanced. He had found a member of Jemaah Islamiah and left instructions to have any new recruits who successfully immigrated to the United States contact him on arrival. By the time Khabir had completed his assembly of the bacteria and the virus trigger, the network to distribute the bacteria was in place. For eight years, Khabir produced as much of the bacteria as his home laboratory would allow, and his followers faithfully spread the preinfection throughout the country.

It had succeeded beyond their wildest dreams, with easy penetration of livestock yards, airports, supermarkets, and nursing homes with the harmless bacteria. Al Rasheed had been a marvelous find, complete with his own ready network of willing soldiers to take the germs from city to city, slowly infiltrating the country. And now he felt giddy with the report of each new outbreak, each mounting casualty report. Khabir's latest results estimated a third of the population would harbor the latent infection.

With Khabir's microscopic warriors, three men would succeed where tens of thousands had failed. There had always been those willing to fight for Allah. Now in Khabir and himself, Allah had found warriors with wisdom to match their zeal. And if this infection was inadequate, Khabir had nearly completed the DNA for the next.

Now Faud waited the final hours in his office before his special contribution to the jihad took force. Apart from organizing and funding the effort, his planned dismantling of network and communications infrastructure was a particularly satisfying project. *Synergistic attacks* was how he described them to Khabir. It was the aesthetics that pleased him most about his creation—also a latent virus that symbolized the biological attack. A stealth biological virus was symbolized and celebrated by his stealth computer virus. That was another thing that separated him and Khabir from those who had perished in the era of Usama bin Laden. Attacks were not just about deaths and psychological impact—style mattered.

Now that the first computer virus attack was imminent, Faud began the process of destroying the final piece of evidence that would link him with the attacks, the source code on his office computer. He pulled out his screwdriver and disassembled the hard drive. Tonight he would incinerate the drive and dispose of it. Permanently.

RICHARD Stern checked again to make sure the room was empty. He'd asked to borrow office space in General Cornelis's section after finding out that there was no dedicated intelligence office space in the Northern Command headquarters. It always helped to have the chairman of the joint chiefs looking over your shoulder when you asked.

He dialed the number. "Hi, Luann. This is Richard. Could you get me a secure line to John, please?" He gave his secretary the security codes to patch his line through to John Randolph, CIA director.

"Richard?"

"Yeah, John. Hey, I was actually wanting to check in with you because . . ."

"Wonderful news, eh?"

"What news?"

"You haven't heard?"

"Hell if I know. We're starting a war. There's a thousand different issues we're following. What is so important?" Stern had always been irritated by the CIA director's habit of assuming people would follow him when he abruptly switched topics.

"About the NYU professor, Khan?"

"Better fill me in, John."

"I got a call from Paul Vallos in Homeland Security. Says they solved the break-in to the Pentagon Web site and tracked it to this guy Khan. He's a Saudi native, works as a computer science professor at NYU."

"That little weasel just called here. Didn't say a word about this, just that there was some computer virus."

"A big virus—Vallos thinks it could totally crash the Internet."

"So we have a suspect. What have you turned up?"

"We've only been on this an hour, but so far Vallos's stuff checks out. He owns a software company, sells some maintenance application for large mainframes, run on a lot of servers. Catch this, though. We cross-checked his cell phone log and found half a dozen calls in the last week to a Chicago number. One of the calls was made within minutes of when Khalil met with the contact there."

"Who'd he call?"

"Guy named Gopal Khabir. Guess what he does."

"Please tell me he's a biologist."

"Damn good one. Trained at Yale. Has a bunch of 'Free Palestine' B.S. on his Web site. He's a full professor at Northwestern, teaching molecular biology. Studies bacterial drug resistance."

"Put his ass on a stick for me. Then find out what he knows."

"We've got some NSA guys moving in on both of them, as well as the taxi driver that drove Khalil to the airport."

"NSA?"

"You didn't think I was going to let the bureau have all

the glory, did you? But they're reliable. You go ahead and tell 'em we've got the bastards."

"Actually, that's why I'm calling, John. I've gotta duck out. I can barely stand up."

"What?"

"Get out here. You've got to fill in for me. I've been up with the runs half the night, and now someone's got my guts in a vise grip. I look weak. It's not good for intelligence. I know we haven't always seen eye to eye, but honestly, I'm a little concerned about the motives of Defense and Justice, and I'd rather you represent intelligence."

John paused for a moment, then asked delicately, "You were there at Khalil's briefing, right?"

"Don't tell me he's sick."

"Just checked in to Bethesda Naval Hospital. And so have half a dozen other staffers that were at the briefing. If you're sick, that could mean the entire war command is . . ."

"Infected," Richard finished. "The president. The entire war council has been exposed. *Dammit,* John. How could I let this happen?"

There was a pause on the other end.

"It's not your fault. You couldn't have known. No one else looks sick, right?"

"No. I don't know. It's too early for them to be symptomatic. But by tomorrow . . ." Richard closed his eyes, the nightmare he refused to consider now playing across his mind. "Just come out, John. The ship's yours." He switched off the phone and buried his face in his hands.

AGENT Escovedo's fingers expertly manipulated the small metal lockpick until the deadbolt clicked and he turned the knob on the two-story Logan Square brownstone apartment.

The door immediately caught on a latch at the top of the

door. Escovedo exchanged a glance with Rhodes. "Looks like someone's home," he commented softly.

Rhodes looked behind him onto the street. From the Schubert Avenue apartment in northern Chicago, he could make out the traffic on Logan Boulevard next to the el stop, but there were no cars coming down Schubert. He took a breath and slammed into the door with his shoulder, splintering the lock from the door frame. The door crashed into the wall and bounced back.

Escovedo had his gun already raised when he jumped into the apartment. Rhodes followed close behind, fixing his pistol up the stairs, looking for a target. Escovedo motioned toward the open door into the downstairs unit. The door was unlocked, and he stepped inside.

Rhodes followed behind, looking over the main room: a beige leather couch, a TV, sparse furniture, and a small kitchen. Everything was immaculate, and the walls were bare. Escovedo moved quickly through a door across the room into a corridor. In a few seconds, they had found a bedroom, bathroom, and a study. A back door was deadbolted shut. No one was inside. *We'll come back to the study,* Rhodes thought.

Rhodes turned quickly and led Escovedo back to the entrance. They climbed the stairs quickly and tried the door at the top of the stairs. It was locked. Escovedo stared at the lock, then shook his head. "It's not a key lock. Some kind of magnetic system. I can't break it," he whispered.

Rhodes motioned for him to step aside, raised his pistol, and fired three rounds into the lock. The frayed wooden door frame offered little resistance as Rhodes lunged against it.

When Escovedo stepped inside behind Rhodes, they both slowly lowered their weapons and stared in disbelief.

The main room had been transformed into a laboratory. Glass cabinets filled with reagents lined the walls. Benches with gas outlets, burners, centrifuges, and tubing filled the wooden tables in the room. A fan was blowing in a hood along the wall where a fireplace had once been. The smell of yeast wafted through the room. This one was not a drill.

FORTY-ONE

April 11

EVA watched as the marquee for St. Patrick Hospital drew closer. The police on the scene had been stunned by the collapse of the laboratory. It took a half hour before Steve could get the attention of one of the rednecks-turned-officers long enough to explain that the scientists needed to move quickly. "Don't bother me, son. We have a major incident here. You folks are lucky to be alive," the officer had said. Steve finally had to call the governor's office to get the sergeant's ear. After a tongue-lashing from the lieutenant governor, the officer personally drove the three into Missoula.

She had been quiet the entire trip from Hamilton, her face never once turned from the side where she looked out the window. There was nothing to say. She just hoped not to infect Alan or Steve, wondered whether the cultures in her pocket would be vulnerable to any known antibiotics.

They had decided quickly to try the closest major hospital, abandoning level four precautions. It was too late now, anyway, and it would take a full day to find another hot lab.

"Sam's still not answering his phone either." Steve switched off his phone as the three got out of the police car they had commandeered to drive them to Missoula.

"Weird. Not like Sam, and Alan's way too anal to forget his phone." Jim walked in front with Steve.

Eva followed Steve and Jim into the hospital, following the signs to the microbiology lab. The officer walked behind them, already winded by the brisk pace.

"We have to talk to your chief of pathology *now*," Steve announced at the specimen receiving window.

Eva could see from the look on the clerk's face that he was uncomfortable with the idea. She imagined how they must look. Her face was still caked with dried blood, and all three of them were tired and disheveled. Jim, wearing cut-off shorts and a tie-dye shirt, got an extra look. The cop behind them threw his belly toward the front counter. He pointed to Jim's ponytail and said, "It's his Indian heritage, son. Now you go do what these folks say." That seemed to work.

"Gotta know how they think," the officer said smugly to Steve, ignoring Jim completely.

Two minutes later a balding man in his fifties opened the door and looked over the four. "I'm Dr. Wilson. What can I do for you?"

Steve answered, "I'm Dr. Adams. This is Dr. Vanorden and Dr. Summers. We're the lead scientists studying the outbreak in Los Angeles. Rocky Mountain Lab was just destroyed in a terrorist attack, and we need lab space immediately to follow up some leads until we can relocate."

"Is this some kind of joke?"

The police sergeant responded, "No joke."

The pathologist struggled to find words. "I . . . you're studying the nanodeath?"

Eva held up her stack of petri dishes and smiled.

"Listen, I sure respect what you're doing, but we can't let that stuff in here. We're not equipped for those kind of pathogens. You'd probably have better luck in Great Falls. Maybe Central Montana Surgical . . ."

Eva stepped closer to the pathologist. "It's not going to look good on CNN when you explain to people why the cure was delayed because you didn't think you could lend us a few pipettes."

"I guess we could clear off our hood."

Steve nodded. "And we need samples of vancomycin, Synercid, linezolid, chloramphenicol, every beta-lactam, quinolone, and macrolide you've got. Anything that could possibly treat a gram-positive bug."

"I'll see what I can do." The three stepped into the lab area past the pathologist, who stepped aside with his back pressed against the wall.

"I'LL send you the coordinates."

Rhodes waited while the GPS relay on his car downloaded the information. The NSA operations command clicked off the channel.

After discovering the laboratory, they had immediately verified no one was home and called in the biotech division to evaluate the site. Within an hour, the apartment would be cordoned off, with agents swarming over it to collect samples. Rapid-detection ultrafiltration machines would detect trace amounts of anthrax spores, nerve gases, or commonly implicated agents such as smallpox. Rhodes was happy to leave that analysis to the experts. In the meantime, he and Escovedo had another mission:

Find the key to the laboratory, the one who created it.

The cell phone was crucial. Once Khabir's cell number was identified, the NSA had checked to see if the phone was registering anywhere in Chicago. Cell phones now operated by registration-based paging, Rhodes knew from basic operations training. In a city as densely populated with cell antennas as Chicago, the routine registration signals sent out by any cell phone that was switched on could track its location to within a few city blocks.

"We got him pegged, ay," Escovedo said as he studied the coordinates and map on the dashboard display.

"Well, him and five thousand other people. We'll get him." Rhodes pulled onto Western Avenue and headed north. Escovedo paged through photographs of Khabir until they pulled onto Foster Avenue, aligning themselves with the coordinates shown on the map.

The street was thick with pedestrians, most of Indian or Pakistani descent. Cars pressed bumper to bumper along shopfronts with lettering in Urdu and English advertising their wares. Rhodes' eyes scanned across windows featuring mannequins wearing saris, men with dark eyes and beards playing cards in front of Pakistani bakeries, and antiques shops plastered with small statuettes and icons of Hindu deities. Aromas of a hundred small restaurants coalesced into a nondescript smell of shisha pipes permeating the street. Rhodes backed into a parking spot along the curb, and the two agents stepped out.

They exchanged a weary glance and walked toward the nearest shop.

"GIVE me one reason I shouldn't blow your head off right now and save the taxpayers the money." Agent Stoddard buried his revolver deeper into Khan's neck.

Faud's head was pressed against his keyboard, his arms stretched tightly behind him in the grip of the NSA agent's partner. The computer beeped incessantly as the depressed keys fired simultaneously. Faud maintained a dignified silence.

"Then let me give you one. There's something I want from you, something that might persuade me to turn you over to the police instead of cutting off your leg an inch at a time." He pulled the gun from Faud's head while his partner held the man down and knelt by Faud's face.

"I'm an American citizen."

"I don't care. You see, I don't work for the justice department. I turn your bloody carcass over to the coroner and I get a promotion. The only thing the rest of the world will know is that you attacked a federal agent, and got shot down like a rabid terrorist dog the way you deserved. Someone going to feel sorry for you?"

Faud said nothing.

Stoddard leaned in an inch from Faud's face. He whispered, "As we speak, Internet name servers are being shut down one at a time to clean off your pathetic virus. Every major corporation in this country knows about your Easter egg. You are nothing." His voice was barely audible over the maddening beeping of the computer.

Tucking the revolver into its holster, the agent reached into his pocket, pulled out a small object, and put it behind Faud's head. The object snapped with the sound of a switchblade opening. He gave a signal and his partner raised Faud's head by his hair. The beeping stopped.

Stoddard showed Faud the object, a cell phone. "It's your friend we want. Gopal Khabir. I'm going to dial his number, and I want you to find out exactly where he is. Right now."

Faud nodded.

* * *

GOPAL Khabir closed his phone and looked at it quizzically. *What an odd conversation.* Why was Faud speaking English? And why would Faud call just to make sure he was OK and had found a safe location? Something was wrong. Why wouldn't he be safe? Unless . . .

Khabir stood quickly and began gathering his belongings into his backpack. He was compromised, and so was Faud. He had to move quickly. How was it possible? He had no weapons. His heart began pounding. How much time did he have?

He quickly opened the door and flew down the stairs into the Pakistani restaurant below. He nodded to the cooks and looked carefully over the counter toward the seating area. He saw two men jogging toward the door, carrying guns, and ducked out of sight behind a wall. *Where was the back door?*

Khabir looked to each side and grabbed a spray bottle sitting on the counter. He made a beeline toward the back alley. He opened the door and stepped out onto the stone steps. The alley behind the buildings was desolate.

"Stop right there!"

Khabir slammed the door shut and took off at a dead run.

Only seconds later he heard a gunshot and the sound of footsteps. *He could never outrun them.*

He spun around, holding the spray bottle in two hands toward the attackers. "Stop or you die."

They stopped.

Khabir slowly backed up. He could barely breathe from the terror that choked him from inside. His feet stumbled as he walked backward, and he held the bottle with one hand to the side.

He watched helplessly as Rhodes lifted a revolver and fired a bullet into his wrist. The bottle fell to the cement as Khabir screamed in pain and dropped to his knees.

FORTY-TWO

April 11

ALAN turned over on his bunk in the base infirmary. It felt good to have the pressure against his stomach, like rubbing a paper cut with his fingers. A few moments later he decided it was worse, and rolled back onto his side.

It was hard to think of a place he wouldn't rather be. He was all but shut out of the loop, quarantined by his own order from the people making the decisions Alan felt so passionate about. Away from his family, unable to talk to them for fear they would rush out and get infected as well, he walled himself off as the fear and anticipation grew with each cramp in his side. First the bleeding, then the wrenching pain as the infection liquefied his intestines, eating its way inside until his heart gave out.

He should at least tell the rest of the team. He reached for his phone, but felt nothing. Where did he leave it? In the War Room? He wasn't sure. It was difficult to focus since he had realized that he was infected. *Who else have I infected?* he wondered.

It had to have been Agent Khalil. Alan cringed at the thought of so many senior figures thinking they had outsmarted the enemy, only to breathe in with each arrogant question the enemy's army. *Like a modern-day Trojan horse.*

Not that it mattered any more. Alan's battle was fought, and he was a casualty.

MIKE Sherwood craved a cigarette, but sat at alert and kept his mind focused with the discipline of a Delta Force soldier. His legs ached from hours of sitting. His entire platoon was crouched behind in the bed of the Syrian military supply truck. He alone sat in the driver's seat, waiting for a signal. His night vision goggles rested on his lap.

At three in the morning, only an occasional sentry drifted by the parking lot on patrol. Sherwood had been watching them for two hours, timing his cigarettes to their beat. The approach would be easy enough. The base security was atrocious, and he could move his men unseen to the commanders' barracks within three minutes. It was the escape that dominated his mind these last hours.

The officers' quarters were sparsely populated, and their target and his family would be the only ones sleeping in that building. If someone managed to sound an alarm, though, all bets were off. Then he would see if he was ready to perform the full scope of his mission: Capture the target, if possible. If not, eliminate him.

He looked at his watch. Sometime after three A.M., the orders said, he would get the signal to advance. No one was to proceed or be discovered before the signal. Otherwise, an alarm could quickly spread to multiple targets in several countries, endangering the lives of the bulk of the

U.S. Special Operations Forces. Sherwood liked the part about "not being discovered"; not much he could do about that now.

Not a sound came from the back of the truck. They were good soldiers, every one of them. He promised himself again that nobody would be lost, not on his mission.

"THE signal, Mr. President?"

The words from the chairman of the joint chiefs were intended as a gentle reminder, but they fell on the president like an ultimatum. His face didn't flinch, a combination of horror, anger, resolve, and doubt fought so far beneath the surface for control of his mind that no emotion could get out.

The tension in the room mounted unrelentingly until the digital screen showed 5:00. That meant 3:00 in Pakistan, 5:00 in Jakarta, midnight in Beirut. In every location, teams were in place now, waiting. They waited for his signal, one that would change American foreign policy forever, a signal that would begin the most tactically complicated, dangerous engagement in the history of the United States military. All planned in three days. More than a dozen missions, simultaneously triggered, would succeed or fail within the next two hours. How could it ever work—even for the best trained of American troops?

Defense Secretary Feinberg broke his concentration. "It's a good plan, Mr. President. They're good men. It will work. One operation, and with surprise on our side we take out the upper tier of every major terrorist sponsor in the world."

The president nodded.

"Mr. President, I have to ask you to reconsider one last time." Amanda drew glares from the defense secretary and the chairman of the joint chiefs.

Sutherland took a deep breath. "Go ahead, Mandy. This is the time to say it."

"It's possible things may work out just as Secretary Feinberg says. I grant that, but I have severe reservations about a joint operation of this magnitude with Israel. Let me outline another scenario I think is at least as likely. Within hours of the attacks, leaders of Pakistan, Syria, Iran, and Lebanon piece together that there is an invasion by a common enemy. If there is a hint of Israel's involvement, which there is sure to be, we could see Iranian long-range missiles raining down on Israel the same day. We'd have no choice but to respond by coordinated air strikes against their missile batteries.

"Under direct attack, Iran and Pakistan both meet to consider the use of nuclear weapons against Israel. Either one may do it. If they don't, diplomatic efforts to unify the Middle East that we've kept balkanized for decades may find the voice to do in two weeks what has eluded them for centuries. We could face a unified Islamic army that could move against Turkey within weeks as a show of defiance. NATO has to respond in open war. Iran uses its supplies of VX nerve gas on NATO forces, with heavy collateral casualties in Turkey.

"North Korea takes advantage of the chaos to move into the demilitarized zone. Another nuclear power enters the conflict. At that point you have the worst nightmare the world has faced since Hitler invaded Poland. Only this time the stakes are a thousand times higher, with our country disorganized and frightened, our people under attack by a whole new kind of nanotechnological weapon, our computerized communications structure jeopardized by a time bomb that could go off any minute. Are you sure that's the war you want to fight, Mr. President?"

Secretary Feinberg responded venomously. "Nobody

wants a war with the United States, Mr. President. There will be sympathy for us because of the nanodeath attack. The worst you'll get is a tongue-lashing in the UN."

Amanda shot back, "To start this war has been the primary terrorist objective for decades, and frankly, I like their odds."

President Sutherland held up his hand. "I appreciate your candor, Mandy, but if there's something one of these people can tell us that could help us stop this disease, I have to take the chance." He turned to the chairman of the joint chiefs. "Give the order, general."

"Aye, Mr. President." He picked up the telephone.

There was a knock on the door. A soldier opened the door with a crisp salute. "Director of central intelligence, Mr. President," he announced.

John Randolph strode into the room. He was jubilant. "WE HAVE THEM, Mr. President! We have them!"

"What are you talking about?"

"We have the bastard who created this disease. We have his laboratory. We have the programmer of the computer virus. We have the whole damn cell."

The president called to the chairman of the joint chiefs. "General, abort the mission."

"Mr. President," he protested. "We have one chance at this!"

"Abort!"

FORTY-THREE

April 12

ALAN leaned over the toilet, dry heaving. Which was worse: the pain, or the nausea from the pain medication? *What kind of a choice was that?* He wandered slowly back to his bunk. What time was it? How long had he slept this last time, an hour? The room was still dark. He turned on the bedside lamp and pulled out the clipboard, his dry eyes reddened as he reread the words now committed to memory.

Dear Anita and Emily:
There's no way to describe the way I'm feeling right now, but I'll do my best. I'm sorry I couldn't see you again in these last few days. I wanted to send for you a dozen times, but the thought of my illness spreading to either of you stopped me each time from telling you I am dying. I hope my case will be one of the last, but wish I had more faith that were true. . . .

It went on for ten pages. He told them how much he loved them, how much he wished they were still back flailing on the river, that none of this had happened. He remembered on paper old vacations, favorite memories, promises made at his wedding. As the substance of his life passed through his pen, the pages became stained with tears and in one case blood. He thanked them, blessed them, and promised to wait for them if his eyes ever opened again. He wrote like a soldier on the front line watching the sunrise and listening for the first gunshot.

He folded the letter and put it under his pillow. His head was throbbing, his mouth dry from acid and dehydration. The blood trickling into his veins could scarcely keep up with the exodus of blood from his intestines.

He had waited long enough. It was time to tell the rest of the team. They deserved to know. He pressed the nurse call light. When a voice answered, he asked if a telephone could be brought in.

Maybe it's best this way. If a ship captain fails in a battle, he doesn't expect another chance. Why should he?

There was a knock on the door.

"Just leave it outside the door. I'll pick it up." Alan knew that none of the nursing staff were eager to get anywhere near him.

The door opened. "I'd rather deliver it in person."

Alan stared at the open doorway as his eyes confirmed what he had heard. President Sutherland walked into the room.

"Mr. President, you shouldn't . . ."

"The hell I shouldn't. Here's your phone back, Alan." He held out the phone Alan had left in the restroom.

Alan didn't move from his bunk. This was crazy.

The president stepped closer. "Since when was a commander not allowed to ride with his men into battle?" He winked. "Besides, I've been treated." He lifted his sleeve to show Alan the IV in his arm.

"What?"

"Come on in, Dr. Goldberg."

Sam walked into the room and stood next to the president.

"Sam? How . . . the quarantine?"

"Lifted last night," Sam said. "You're a little out of the loop, Alan."

"What are you saying?"

"The disease is cured, Alan. At least we have a treatment."

"Sam, how? A nanovirus. What could possibly?"

"Nanovirus my ass, Alan. It's a game. A bluff. We're treating it with Synercid."

"Synercid . . ." Alan's thoughts were spinning. "We don't stockpile it. There's not enough . . ."

"There's enough for you, Alan," the president interrupted.

"I don't believe it." Alan broke into sobs, covering his face with his hands as he cried openly.

Sam stepped forward, putting his hand on Alan's shoulder before hanging the bag on the IV pole and connecting the tubing into Alan's arm.

"It's over, Alan. Now get some sleep. Doctor's orders."

Alan stood up slowly and buried himself in Sam's arms. The few tears he had left fell onto Sam's back.

"Thank you," Alan whispered.

EPILOGUE

May 14

IN MEMORIAM

21,564 victims of the "Nanodeath"
Names posted on Memorial Obelisk
Ronald Reagan UCLA Medical Center

INVOCATION:	Reverend Michael Orland Chaplain, UCLA Medical Center
TRIBUTE TO VICTIMS	Arnold Schwarzenegger Governor of California
PRESENTATION OF MEMORIAL OBELISK AND MEDALS OF FREEDOM	Anthony M. Sutherland President of the United States

PRESIDENTIAL MEDAL OF FREEDOM RECIPIENTS:
Alan H. Thorpe, James R. Summers, Samuel L. Goldberg,
Eva Vanorden, Stephen J. Adams, Susan Patrick*, James Nowers*

*Posthumous

Excerpt of remarks made by President Anthony Sutherland at May 14 Memorial Service:

It is with great humility I address a gathering with so many heroes. Many of your names are inscribed upon the memorial behind me as those who have shown such distinguished courage in the face of the greatest terrorist attack of our country's history. Names of many of your friends and associates lie above on the obelisk, victims of the attack who were not as fortunate, but no less brave. America is saddened for their loss, but thanks to you I can stand here today and announce that America is victorious.

The reality first glimpsed on September 11, 2001, has now become a panorama of modern history. We live in a new world. It is a world where one man can declare war and a nation of three hundred million may rightfully tremble. It is a world where our common birthright is a vulnerability to weapons ever more diabolical and clever, weapons that can kill millions, yet fit on the head of a pin. It is a world where an army that would dominate the world of our forebears may be utterly helpless.

The events of the last five weeks forced us to reconsider our defense against enemies who hide in shadows and work alone or with lunatics, tyrants, and villains on the other side of the globe. This time, we have overcome.

The attack was started more than ten years before the first casualty, when a handful of fanatics obtained a weapon that could infiltrate the rank and file of our society. It was a weapon that could be spread by hand, city by city, spread further by every handshake and kiss over a decade of American history. More than a hundred million people were infected before the first symptoms were noticed. Then, like a brush fire, the infection that triggered the beast within was unleashed on innocent people.

It is a diabolical scheme involving germ warfare the likes of which the world has never known, clothed with the threat of a new and unknown type of weapon meant to terrorize us and mislead our response. It has now spread to fourteen nations, and the names on the memorial above are only the first wave of a disease that will be with us indefinitely. The terrorists chose one of the most resilient organisms known to humanity as their starting point, a bacterium that has acquired resistance to every drug in our arsenal, save two. These two drugs, as you by now know, can fight the infection back, but rarely eradicate it.

I commend again the pharmaceutical houses that have stepped up production of these drugs. They have shared their materials and manufacturing methods with government-funded laboratories to provide these drugs to affected cities on mass scales. I share in the grief that many of our citizens early in the epidemic did not have access to these lifesaving drugs. I assure you this will not be a problem with these drugs in the future.

The suppression of this disease now takes its place as a part of our routine healthcare and that of the entire world. Our vulnerability waxes and wanes with the detection and treatment of a bug that will not die, and must not gain resistance against our evolving defenses. Our nation's scientists, including those who have received the presidential medal of freedom today, have by ingenuity and tireless effort stopped the disease in its tracks within a few days of its emergence. The five heroes up here with me today withstood personal attacks and risked their lives to save ours. Two of them were infected in the course of duty, and thankfully recovered. Two of their colleagues was not so fortunate, killed during a brutal, evil attack on their laboratory. Were it not for the work of these seven scientists, this attack might have shaken the foundation of our nation and the free world.

Now I call on our scientists to unite in a much more difficult project. We must find a vaccine to the strain of influenza that can trigger the infection that has become our new Achilles heel. We must discover and deploy redundant defenses that can treat the bacteria we harbor and the toxin they produce. When our treatments fail, we must have new ones prepared. Ultimately I call on you to rid the world of this evil that has been unleashed upon us. I have faith in the power of American innovation to destroy this enemy as it has others in the past.

I promise today that we will share every scrap of knowledge we gain with the world in this pursuit. I expect our friends in the world to do likewise, forming a strategic partnership against a threat to all civilization.

I commend our intelligence, military, and homeland defense community on bringing to justice the perpetrators of this act. They will indeed be held accountable for every one of the lives they have destroyed. I know that justice will do little to heal the void in your lives for the loved ones you have lost. But justice will be done.

And I propose to take that justice one step further, stopping the villains of the future before their dreams ever come to fruition. I announce today broad new funding for a comprehensive counterterrorist offensive. I call on Congress to establish a new branch of the armed forces, equal in stature and funding to the existing branches. A biodefense league of scientists, inventors, engineers, and first responders will fight the wars of the next century, waged by cowardly villains who lack any respect for life or civilization.

I announce new and broader funding for our NET Guard, to protect our computer infrastructure against future attacks. We have become increasingly dependent on our technology to sustain a complex and beautiful culture, and we will not allow it to be vulnerable to attack in the future. I commend the actions of the NET Guard in preventing a catastrophic economic and psychological blow to our nation at a time when she could least afford it. Let's make sure they have the resources to do their work in an even more dangerous world.

Finally, I warn those who yet hide and plan to attack our nation. You will fail, and you will be brought to justice. The sun will not set on our efforts to root you out of your caves, your laboratories, your homes. There is no place on earth a terrorist may be safe from the reaches of this nation's and the free world's searching eyes.

Today, we mourn for our brothers and sisters, fallen soldiers in a war in which they never enlisted. Tomorrow, we will double our efforts to protect our children from a similar fate. Thank you, and may God bless our nation.

References

Alivisatos, A. Paul. Less is more in medicine. *Scientific American*. September 2001: 67–73.

Ashley, Steven. Nanobot construction crews. *Scientific American*. September 2001: 84–85.

Cello, Jeronimo, Aniko V. Paul, and Eckard Wimmer. Chemical synthesis of poliovirus cDNA: Generation of infectious virus in the absence of natural template. *Science*. August 9, 2002: 1016–1018.

Collins, Graham P. Shamans of small. *Scientific American*. September 2001: 86–91.

Drell, Sidney D., Abraham D. Sofaer, and George D. Wilson, eds. *The New Terror: Facing the Threat of Biological and Chemical Weapons*. Stanford, Calif.: Hoover Institution Press, 1999.

Drexler, K. Eric. Machine-phase nanotechnology. *Scientific American*. September 2001: 74–75.

Lieber, Charles M. The incredible shrinking circuit. *Scientific American*. September 2001: 59–64.

Prokop, Ales. Bioartificial organs in the twenty-first century: Nanobiological devices. *Annals of the New York Academy of Science*. November 2001: 472–490.

Roukes, Michael. Plenty of room indeed. *Scientific American*. September 2001: 48–58.

Sipper, Moshe, and James A. Reggia. Go forth and replicate. *Scientific American*. August 2001: 35–43.

Smalley, Richard E. Of chemistry, love, and nanobots. *Scientific American*. September 2001: 76–77.

Stix, Gary. Little big science. *Scientific American*. September 2001: 32–37.

Whitesides, George M. The once and future nanomachine. *Scientific American*. September 2001: 78–83.

Whitesides, George M., and J. Christopher Love. The art of building small. *Scientific American*. September 2001: 39–47.

Whitesides, G. M., J. P. Mathias, and C. T. Seto. Molecular self-assembly and nanochemistry: A chemical strategy for the synthesis of nanosystems. *Science*. November 29, 1991: 1312–1319.